Margaret Keeping taugh
time before working in proba

She took a Masters in Englisl
her interest in Edward Thon

She has had poetry published but this is her first work of fiction,
begun when she took the University of Oxford's two-year
Creative Writing Diploma.

A Conscious Englishman

Margaret Keeping

StreetBooks

StreetBooks

First published in 2013 by StreetBooks

ISBN 978-0-9564242-3-5

StreetBooks,
3 Windsor Cottages,
Broad Street,
Bampton.
OX18 2LU

www.streetbooks.co.uk

Cover image by Marc Thompson: Dawn, May Hill

Cover photograph by Marie O'Hara Photography
www.marieohara.co.uk

Cover designed by Andrew Chapman
mail@preparetopublish.com

In memory of my mother, Phyllis Pettit, and her blackbirds

'I am slowly growing into a conscious Englishman.'

EDWARD THOMAS, September 1914

Author's note

Most of what occurs in this novel is based on fact. All the characters were real people and their settings are real places. Extracts from their letters, books and articles are in their own words, italicised if exactly quoted, but also freely threaded throughout the text. I have imagined many episodes and conversations as well as the thoughts of the protagonists, and so this is a novel, a fiction which is grounded in fact.

Prologue

February 1917

At dawn the thaw began. Snow slid from the holly hedge, at first in a sprinkling shower, then in heavy tumbling lumps. Clear ice blades that lined the ash twigs fell suddenly, chiming as they struck each other in the silence, then melting into the greying snow.

An hour later a thrush sensed the change and began to sing, but as there was no answering challenge he stopped and the silence returned for a time.

Half-frozen grasses and dead campion umbels showed a drab grey against the lighter snow. A man passed through them, below them, as he walked the trenches, and the scrape and rustle against his tin helmet taught him to keep his head down.

He was walking to the British line looking for possible observation points. Stark poles jutted out of the dingy snow, barbed wire strung between. Through his field glasses he watched intently, anticipating a sight of the enemy. He saw no one, only posts, wire, dead trees and ruined houses. Yet from the enemy lines, every few minutes, shells came, screaming through the air and over his head. As they passed, he felt a sickening sensation in his ears – not so much sound as pressure. The shelling is the enemy, for both our sides, he thought.

Every evening he wrote in his notebook: about trees, splintered, snapped and dead, about filling sand bags to shore up the trenches. About how he'd enjoyed the digging, as he always did in the garden at Steep, the scent of chalky earth as his spade cut through dead leaves and bracken reminding him of home.

He dared not think too much about home. He held on to the natural world, its continuation, its immunity to what was happening. Larks still soared and sang, though it became more and more difficult to hear them over the noise of shelling. They carry on their business in the midst of it all, as I do, he thought.

From his observation post he watched the Engineers swarming over No Man's Land, making a board road between the shell-holes to bring out the wounded, shell-holes full of blood-stained water and beer bottles among the barbed wire. But larks, partridges, hedge sparrows and magpies were busy with their young around his post.

How to describe the effect of the continuous shelling on air? The word 'flap' was the nearest he could get: *'The air was flapping all night as with great sails in strong gusty wind,'* he wrote. But appallingly the air also somehow sagged – *a sag and flap of air.* Was that it? He scribbled two lines that were in his mind:

Where any turn may lead to Heaven,
Or any corner may hide hell.

Every evening he wrote letters too.

'I should like to be a poet, just as I should like to live,' Edward wrote to Robert Frost. *'But I know as much about my chances in either case.'*

Book One

One

August 1914

Robert passed the day preparing for a siege. When he heard the news of war from Edward he took action. He strode the four miles to Ledbury and in the grocer's bought every packet of wheat cereal he could find, then tins of cookies, and soap for Elinor. He arranged to have the goods delivered later that day and set off for home, for Little Iddens.

He looked a true countryman. His thick hair was a dark sun-bleached blond tinged with grey, and he had striking jade-blue eyes. With his tanned face, open-necked shirt and cord trousers anyone would take him for a farmer, just as he would wish.

He was worried; should he not be thinking of taking his family back to America, right away from this war? But he'd pinned his hopes for recognition on this English venture. Forty years old, nothing at all published until he came to England and that bringing in no money and barely noticed. If it weren't for his grandpa's shares they'd be sunk.

When the carter arrived at the house Robert stacked the goods against the pink-washed walls of the sitting room. There was no space in the kitchen, and it was too damp. He knew Elinor wouldn't mind; she was so unconcerned about the appearance of the place – she'd been a teacher and the top graduate of her college so it was not to be expected. And a good housekeeper was not what he wanted in a wife.

The cottage had a hall running from front to back, with the sitting room to one side and a shed of a room, hardly habitable, to the other. The tiny earth-floored kitchen with an old iron range was at the rear. Water came from a pump in the yard. Upstairs were two bedrooms and an alcove for sleeping.

Elinor watched listlessly as Robert piled shredded wheat

boxes against the walls.

'You know Helen and her girls are arriving today,' he said. 'It will be late, Edward says, so they won't any of them be up to much. It's pretty sure we won't see them till tomorrow.'

Elinor shrugged.

'Why you know, Elinor, it will be good for you to have some company.'

'These Englishmen's wives don't take to me, nor I to them. Oh Rob, all these visitors! It is as bad here as in Beaconsfield. It wears me out, so many new people. It's too much, when we've always lived so much alone back home. The kids are the same, we've always only looked to each other.'

'Ah, but you were too much alone on the hill farm, far too much. It's not right.'

'You know I prefer it that way.'

'Ellie, you listen. Thomas has been good to me and he can help us on. As a reviewer he's mighty influential. I know what's likely bothering you – the new book. Waiting for some better reviews. But I tell you, these friends of mine you find so wearing are making sure that reviews get written and that they're good. And besides, I never met anyone whose company I like so well as Edward's. So different from those literary characters in London. That fellow Pound.'

'I like Edward too, but he steals you away every day on those long walks.'

His broad frame towered over Elinor; he laid a hand on her shoulder and turned her pale face towards his.

'He's only here for a while. So help me out here, girl. Bear up, won't you? Alright?'

Then Robert was out of the door, heading across the fields towards a stand of elm trees. He would stay in that place of shadowy quiet for a time.

Elinor picked up her book. It was PG Wodehouse's *Mike* and soon she was laughing quietly to herself. When Marjorie asked her why, Elinor read to her. Irma, who was playing with the water pump in the yard, stamping her feet one at a time under the water flow, came in and listened too. By late afternoon,

Elinor thought she would have to do something about a meal. Sighing, she filled a pan with water from the pump and threw in some rice. Lesley was bringing in tomatoes from the garden when her father came home.

Edward crossed the fields to call on Robert. He had something for him – proof copies of his three reviews of *North of Boston*, each intended for different journals.

'Do you want to see them now?' he asked. 'Or take them and read them overnight?'

'You're joking, aren't you? For God's sake, now, right now. Ed, put me out of my misery.'

'All right – look, let's go to the oak tree in our field and sit there, then you can read them. And I'll smoke my pipe patiently and be quiet.'

They shifted their backs into comfort against the ridged bark and Edward handed Robert the typewritten pages, explaining which was for each journal. Robert was pale and sweating as he read. His hand, holding the pages, was shaking. But his colour soon came back and he started to grin.

'*A calm eagerness of emotion* – yes.' He read on, sometimes shaking his head as if he could hardly believe what he was reading. Once he frowned for a moment. Then he sped on through. When he'd finished he stayed silent and when Edward looked at him he saw that his eyes were full of tears.

'Thank you, my dear friend. That'll do. That'll about do. You understand. *You* don't think simplicity is born of simple-mindedness!'

'Well, you see I haven't stinted my praise. These poems are revolutionary, Robert. As I said, they remind me of Wordsworth's experiment with the *Lyrical Ballads,* but with a difference.'

'I'd expect it to be to my disadvantage knowing how you feel about Wordsworth and his set.'

'No, it's not a question of advantage or otherwise. It's that you show more of other people's feelings than Wordsworth did and less of your own. And you know the lives you're writing about, rather as Dorothy Wordsworth did. Where Wordsworth contemplated people, you sympathise with them.'

'I guess. I truly appreciate what you've written about Death of the Hired Man and Home Burial – *masterpieces of deep and mysterious tenderness.*'

'I hoped you like that phrase – because I believe it to be true.'

Robert flushed and seemed near to tears again. Edward suggested they walk over to the stile that led to Dymock lane; they were more used to walking as they talked. Clouds of pink dust flew up from the baked red ground and they created a flutter of butterflies from the cornflowers.

'Such a pleasure for me to have something of quality to review, Robert. I can't tell you how much of the rubbishy poetry that's printed comes to me. Review copies just bury us at home; I have to give them to the school for paper-chases or to make kite-tails. Or if we're desperate enough I go to stay with friends and *accidentally* leave a whole suitcase-full of them behind.'

'I do recall when we met in London last year you were trying to sell some off.'

'Very likely. Heaven knows, we're well into this new century – we need new poetry, but good poetry, not rubbish. We need a poet with a voice of his own, but not an egotistical voice. That's what I like in yours.'

Edward's long legs carried him fast as he talked; he paused to lean on the style, watching the great golden disc of the setting sun. Robert, a little shorter and four years older, caught him up. When he did, Robert started reading his reviews again.

'You know Ed, truly I need to get home and show these to Elinor – she's been worrying herself crazy. It matters so much, you know, how I'm recognised here – that's what counts in the States. They don't give a damn for you till you've been published in England. And I've come to realise how much *your* opinion counts. So again, Ed, thank you.'

They climbed over and turned for home along the stony lane.

'But what about you?' Robert asked. 'Those rubbishy poets not worth the trouble – I'll lay you've got more poetry in your little finger than they have in their whole body. Good poetry's the only worthwhile thing, poetry, and writing about poetry maybe.'

'No, not me – I started out too young, Robert. I got in the habit of imitating other men's fine phrases. It's spoiled me, Pater and the like. Those words – well, they haven't really lived in the world. I've been trying to strangle that kind of thing and write simply. It's hard for me, like strangling a flock of gaggling geese, but it must be done. And if I can manage that in my prose, and the subject interests me, I can be quite content.'

'You're right, words start in the mouth, not in books. But I'm going to convince you that you should try poetry. Tell me, if you were to, what would your subjects be?'

'You won't convince me, I know that. As for subjects I suppose, as now – England, Wales, the country life.' He thought for a while. 'But they're not enough on their own. The Romantics almost had it right – for them it's nature and Man, the life of Man in nature. For me, I see Man as one small part of nature and by no means the best part. It's as much the life of everything other than Man that interests me. With you it's the relationship amongst people in the face of nature that matters. I'm much more of a solitary. And of course I must keep my writer's melancholy!'

'Oh I know you'll do that, my friend. No one can equal you for black talk, but I reckon you could spare some of your melancholy for those who are deficient in it!'

Edward laughed. They parted at the Little Iddens orchard gate.

He was not going to lose these talks when Helen came. They were too important to him. The freshness of Robert's writing had energised him in some way. He had been so jaded, almost broken the year before, by the grinding out of words to earn a living whether the subject was of his choosing or not.

But words were all-important to him, and his walking, the places and the thoughts they brought to him, and the half-thoughts. Then that striving to express, as far as it was possible, what he saw and felt. Talking to Robert about his writing kept alive a hope that he might have the freedom to write what he chose, without constraints, and to love the making of a work, for its own sake.

Robert was wrong of course. How could he be a poet? He could never write a poem that, with his critical mind, he could believe in.

Two

From *Half a kiss, half a tear*

And now, hark at the rain,
Windless and light,
Half a kiss, half a tear,
Saying good-night.

So it had happened at last. War was declared. I saw a newspaper hoarding as I lifted our luggage down onto the Oxford platform. Bronwen held tightly onto my skirt with one hand and to Myfanwy with the other and I was glad of her, because the station was chaotic. There were soldiers everywhere, grumbling about being recalled from leave, but slapping each other on the back and laughing. Small, worn-looking men most of them, with red-rimmed eyes, drawing on cigarettes. Their bulging kit-bags, as big as themselves, were heaped up at the far end of the platform.

I'd had no idea as I set off with the girls on holiday that we were at war. At Petersfield station everything was just as usual. The porter, with all the time in the world, trundled our luggage along the platform and helped me load it into the netting racks. 'There you are, Mrs Thomas. You have a good journey now.'

Rags, our old terrier, curled up on the carriage floor and went to sleep. Myfanwy was excited.

'I want to see out of the window,' she said, kneeling up on the coarse blue plush. 'What's that lady got in that basket?'

'Hens, look, you can see their beaks.'

'Why are they going on the train?'

'Perhaps someone has bought them.'

'How much would a hen cost?'

The endless questions of three-year-olds! Bronwen was a seasoned traveller and was already reading a girls' magazine that a school-friend had passed on to her.

As the stopping train made its progress across Hampshire, Berkshire and Oxfordshire I could see something strange was happening. The stations were crowded, people's .faces exhilarated and urgent. There were families returning from their holidays, some children sullen, some caught up in the adult excitement. Some men were in their everyday clothes but carrying army kit-bags, and as we pulled into Oxford station, dreadfully late, I saw troops of soldiers in uniform on the platform. A guard came to our carriage.

'You have to leave this train.'

'But why? What's happening? We're going on to Malvern.'

'Because of the war, Madam. The Army needs this train. That's it and all about it.'

He moved on to the next carriage. It was hard to get any information – I was simply told that we would have to wait, and that we would be wise to return home. No – impossible! This holiday was much more than simply a stay in the country. It was to be a fresh start for Edward and me. I would reach that farmhouse in Leddington somehow.

Edward would soon be leaving for Ledbury station to meet us. There was a telegraph office in the station – it would save him from wasting his time, something he hated. Had he heard the news? Would my telegram be the first he knew of it? I pushed my way through the crowds and sent my message.

A whole hour later a train hissed to our platform. All through the slow journey I thought about the fact that we were at war. I simply couldn't imagine what it might mean to us.

By the time we reached Malvern it was midnight and the girls were fast asleep. I heaved out the luggage, called Rags, and carried Myfanwy. Bronwen clung to my arm, miserable now.

There was no train that night for Ledbury! And the wretched station-master would not let us stay in the waiting room until morning! When I asked him what he suggested we could do he replied with, 'I've no idea. But you must leave the station.' Then he went into his office and slammed the door.

Was this man simply a brute to all his passengers? Or was it something about me? I had been travelling since early morning, a tortuous August train journey with children and a dog in tow. I knew how I must appear; my dress rather bohemian, informal, a simple crepe patterned with flowers, but drooping and soiled. My hair was coming loose from the plaits I looped at each side.

An old porter appeared on the night platform. He took pity on us, and found a cabbie friend who agreed to drive us to the Leddington farmhouse where we were to stay. I was worried about the expense, not having any idea of the distance, but I'd no choice.

The bare Malvern Hills were lit by a full harvest moon as we crossed them. Then I could make out a wooded, gentler landscape, the trees casting dark moon-shadows. Ledbury was utterly silent and sleeping under its spire, but a policeman was patrolling in the square so our driver asked for directions to Leddington and the farm. The policeman's head was clearly full of the war. He glared at me.

'Who are you, and where are you heading at this time of night?'

After the wretched day we'd had I struggled to be polite.

'I am Mrs Helen Thomas and these are my daughters. We are staying at a farmhouse in Leddington – my husband is waiting for us there. You may know Mr Frost, the American – it's near his house.'

Mentioning the name of a foreigner did not help. He insisted on taking down our names, very slowly and with a good deal of spelling out for Bronwen and Myfanwy. At last he gave the driver directions to the farm, another three miles away. Almost there.

Tall trees, two stately Scots pines away from the road. We turned off the narrow lane onto a track towards them. And then Edwy was there at the gate, waiting for us, a dark lean tree-like shape himself in the darkness. Then he turned and the moonlight shone bright on his hair and his beautiful face. I almost fell from the cab into his arms.

But I had to explain to him about the fare and why we were so terribly late.

*

Next morning I looked from our window towards the Frosts' house. When I was last here for a few days in June, the leaves on their fruit trees were a fresh vibrant green. They were darker now.

'We'll go across later,' Edward said. 'They're late risers, not like us. See if Merfyn is awake. Then you can meet the Chandlers again and have breakfast. I should think Bronwen and Baba will sleep till noon. And you must be tired too.'

I certainly was tired; it had been a hard journey. But I had no conception of what had begun that day. I was younger then though, younger and stronger.

Merfyn slept on a kind of open landing, and we'd carried his sisters to the far end of our room without waking them. Only a curtain divided us from the girls. That was a shame. The truth was I'd looked forward so much to our lovemaking on this holiday.

I bent over my son – at fourteen he didn't like to be kissed, but as he opened his eyes and grinned at me happily, I guessed what he was feeling: his mother was here and the exacting time of being alone with his father was over.

'So long as the plums are harvested and packed.'

The Chandlers' specialities were best dessert plums, thinned on the tree so that they were as large as a small apple. They took great care of these 'Covent Garden' fruits, dressing them up in little muslin jackets on the tree as they ripened, to keep them from wasps.

Their farm, Oldfields, was quite small, brick built, with oddly-angled windows tinted with green from the thick foliage of plum trees. The door to the garden stood open and black hens pecked at the earth between nasturtiums and chives. The kitchen was generous in every way: size, scents, colours. I envied the enormous table. Even in August the kitchen smelled of burning logs in the range and of baking.

I'd met Mr and Mrs Chandler when we visited the Frosts in

June and made our arrangements for August. I liked their friendly good sense. They were stocky and strong and remarkably cheerful; Mr Chandler was a reservist who'd been a sergeant in the Army for years, and he'd been recalled. He seemed philosophical about it and she was surprisingly unperturbed. They thought it would all be over in no time, quite possibly without him having to fight at all. I guessed that Mr Chandler rather looked forward to the humour and comradeship of the Army. But if I'd been his wife I wouldn't have been so calm. Her only concern was their fruit harvest.

It was odd for me not to be in charge of a kitchen, not to be able to cook and clean and arrange things the way I wanted them. I would have been happier in a tiny cottage that we could have made our own for a month, rather than being 'paying guests', with meals provided and beds made. I'd always fallen back on my talent for homemaking, to encourage myself and to try to lift Edward's terrible depression. Scrubbing, sweeping, polishing – something about gleaming furniture and dazzling brass always helped me at least. A table prettily laid, perhaps a cake on a plate, its promise and welcome. I was not good at the management of things; ordering, bill-paying, the business side of the household. That would infuriate Edward who was terribly methodical and thorough.

The previous year he'd stayed away from home so much, avoiding us, saying he could not work near us. Without him there, every day was like a tedious journey with no purpose and no reward. I had tried to manage, to welcome him home light-heartedly when he did come, to write cheerful letters. I'd dreaded he would leave us entirely and if that happened I could not have borne it.

I needed to spend time with Edward, carefree time, holiday time, have him see me as I really am, or could be perhaps. Make him want me, as he did want me sometimes. But I knew what was important to Edward while we were here – his friendship with Robert. Whether I wanted it or not, we two families would have to be great friends. Thomases and Frosts to-ing and fro-ing all day long between Oldfields and Little Iddens.

*

I knew I must call on Elinor the next day so around mid-morning I set off with Bronnie and Myfanwy, Rags tagging along behind. Merfyn declined to come and Edward was going to be out all day. He and Robert were meeting with their poet friends Lascelles and Wilfred. Robert had called in, still excited about Edward's reviews, and so I hoped that all the Thomases would now be favoured with Elinor's good opinion.

At the cottage we found her and the children out in the garden at the front of the house. The two older children, Lesley and the boy Carol, were working in the vegetable plot. Bronwen went to join them – she knew them from the spring and she made friends easily.

Irma and Marjorie were with Elinor on the long-grassed lawn. They ran over when they saw Rags and asked to take him for a walk.

'Just a short one. He's eleven, you know, he's an old gentleman and gets tired.'

They ran off round the corner of the house calling, poor Rags following with a resigned air.

Elinor was sitting in a battered cane chair, with a bowl beside her, shelling peas. I sat down next to her on the flattened grass – there was no other chair. Her greeting was polite, but without warmth. Her large dark eyes seemed to be looking through and beyond me as she spoke. She was so reserved, shy perhaps – not what I expected of an American woman. Silence soon fell between us. I talked to Myfanwy, showing her some long-stemmed daisies to collect; we could make a daisy-chain when she had fifty. Could she count that far? Her serious little face, with her new spectacles, was adorable.

Should I suggest helping Elinor with the peas? She was so slow! I offered, she coolly agreed and we worked on without speaking, other than to respond a little to Myfanwy about her daisies. The peas pinged into the white china bowl in the silence with a slow rhythm.

'You heard about our dreadful journey, I'm sure.'

'I did. What's more we had a mighty unpleasant visit because of it,' Elinor answered. 'A policeman came round yesterday, asking questions about who we were, how long we were staying, what we lived on. He had the nerve to hint that Robert was a spy.'

'Oh, that must be the same policeman who stopped us.'

'Quite,' said Elinor. 'He said you'd mentioned his name.'

'How did Robert react? I rather imagine he'd be furious.'

I thought back to a day in June when I'd witnessed one of Robert's rages. We were at Little Iddens when their landlord called and there was some dispute. I was shocked by Robert – suddenly he strode up to the landlord and punched one hand into the palm of the other repeatedly, close to the man's nose. Edward was surprised too, though I thought part of him approved of Robert's forcefulness. For myself, I thought his blustering and bullying on that occasion were not to be admired.

'He threatened to shoot if any policeman came anywhere near us again,' Elinor said. 'Of course, he doesn't actually have a gun over here. But Robert won't tolerate anyone questioning him. He won't be ordered around. So I guess they won't trouble us again.'

'I suppose this war makes these things necessary. It's such a dreadful thought.'

Elinor said nothing.

I tried to talk about things to do together over the holiday, with our two families. Did Elinor know possible places for picnics? I managed to elicit the information that Carol liked going to the River Leadon where he could skim stones better than anyone.

'Bronwen loves swimming and Merfyn likes it if it's hot enough – so does Edward. Perhaps we could pick a sunny day and do that.'

Elinor agreed without much enthusiasm. At last she finished her share of the peas, got up from her chair, stood looking at the house for a while and then asked me if I would like coffee.

I leapt up and offered to come into the house with her. Elinor, I remembered, kept an enamelled coffee pot constantly on the range and I hated its bitter taste. I'd dilute it with water if I could. Myfanwy was happy to stay on the lawn with her daisies.

In the sitting room I was astonished to see a mountain of shredded wheat and biscuit tins, but I said nothing and Elinor made no comment. Later Edwy told me that it was Robert's idea of preparing for the duration of the war and we laughed.

I remembered the pink-washed, heavily-beamed room from our visit in early summer. It had dear little lead-paned windows and a wavy brick floor, but only two chairs, a side table, no other furniture. No proper dining table! How did they eat their meals? Mostly outdoors on the grass perhaps. As I waited for Elinor to find two cups and rinse them under the pump in the yard my imagination was transforming the room. Somehow I would have found an auction yard and acquired some furniture and rugs for a song. After all, the Frosts had taken the place for a year. And there would be jars of wild flowers at the windows, and bookshelves – Edwy would have found some planks and constructed them within a day of arriving. Instead books were stacked on the window-sills, yellowing and curling, being spoiled and blocking the sunlight. And I would make those dirty windows sparkle.

I followed Elinor into the kitchen; there was a smell of something that has been left underneath a sink. I took my coffee.

'Oh, isn't it a dear little house, Elinor,' I said. 'Such fun to look after, a true cottage.' Elinor looked round vaguely.

'We're always out of doors. I don't pay much heed to housekeeping. I realised long ago that it's important to let things go. How would I have managed with my children when they were little tots if I hadn't?'

She looked out of the tiny window at the garden for a moment, touched her hand to her cheek for a moment and looked sad. She went to the door and watched Lesley and Carol uprooting the spent pea plants. Bronnie was just lying on the grass gazing up at the sky.

'Aren't your children good?' I said, wanting to praise her for something. 'And look at Irma and Marjorie, amusing Baba.'

For the girls were back with Rags and had flopped on the lawn, decorating Myfanwy with a bracelet, a necklace and anklet of daisies. Her face, rosy in the sun, was solemn with importance.

The strain of being with Elinor faded in my pleasure at watching the children. Irma was quiet like her mother, but Marjorie was talkative, asking Baba questions and making her laugh. I dampened my coffee at the pump – really I would have preferred a glass of that clear sparkling water.

The sun was growing hot as it neared midday and I asked if the children didn't need a drink or to wear their sun-hats.

'Why, they'll go to the pump if they do. And they'll find some shade if they're hot.'

'Well, Myfanwy's too little to manage that,' I said, rather annoyed. 'I think it's time we were going home anyway. A picnic by the river then. Soon. I'd love to do the preparations. There's such wonderful produce here, everything you could want, beautiful hams and cheeses, all the fruit you can eat—'

Elinor nodded. It occurred to me that she was glancing at her book and would be happy to have me gone. One last effort.

'I think you've chosen a perfect place, Elinor, coming to Leddington for your stay in England. And of course Edward and Robert love each other's company so. I'm looking forward to our days out together.'

I'd more than done my duty. I collected my girls and Rags, said good-bye to the children and took the field path towards home. Half-way there Myfanwy wanted to be carried so I swung her up onto my hip and hurried home, my dear Baba earnestly discussing fairy fare and holding out her braceleted arms for me to admire. Bronwen ran on ahead, hoping her Daddy would be back home by now. And so did I.

Three

'Edwy, what a shame – this would have been our first real day together. No help for it, I suppose.' But she sighed.

'Oh damn it, Helen! You don't have to cling to me all the time. Can't you find a way of occupying yourself that doesn't depend on me? Can you wonder I feel stifled by you sometimes?'

'I'm sorry.'

'I wish I knew there was something you wanted, for yourself? I know what you'll say – you just want us to be together and be happy. As if that's any help. Do you imagine I want to be indoors, slaving over that vile book, while everyone else is free to do as they please? Please let me get on now – and get the children out of the way too.'

There was a problem with his latest commission, *A Literary Pilgrim in Britain*, or 'Omes and 'Aunts as he called it. His publisher wrote that it was short of the required word length by ten thousand words. He would have to set to, interrupting his holiday with the family and his vital time with Robert. So often this compulsion to hack away at work that was not interesting to him and that did not deserve so much attention.

When Robert called, Edward was more apologetic about his unavailability, but Robert was not pleased. They'd thought of taking the train from Dymock to Newent and climbing May Hill. It tantalised them on their walks, the broad dome rising suddenly from low fields, promising such visions and distances. Robert had made friends with an amateur botanist who lived at its foot and wanted to call on him.

'Ed, I'm sorry for you. You're buried alive under that hack writing of yours,' Robert said. He left, almost slamming the door.

Edward slipped easily into the groove he'd followed for so long. He made the marble washstand into a makeshift desk in the bedroom and worked for two hours. At least, he thought, he could expand on Coleridge, the finest critic there'd ever been and a great poet. He had the *Poems* with him; he dashed off a postcard to Eleanor Farjeon asking her to send a copy of *Biographia Literaria*. Tom Chandler was about to leave for Ryton and was happy to post the card. Edward looked out to see if Helen and the children were in the garden but he could see no sign of them. She'd done as he told her.

Wood-pigeons cooed in the high Scots pines and the air was full of the scent of meadowsweet. It was a beautiful day, not yet too hot, and he couldn't bear to be imprisoned in the low-ceilinged bedroom with its one high window. The bench in the garden would work quite as well. He skimmed efficiently through the rest of his manuscript to see where he could pad out the text, making notes as he read. Then he took clean pages of manuscript paper and wrote, annotating where the printer should insert them. But while he worked, he felt the shadow of the pain he'd caused Helen. She would have been happy simply sitting there with him among the phloxes and hollyhocks, he thought.

By twelve o'clock he'd done a quarter of the ten thousand words and decided to take an hour off. He would make his peace with Robert – Helen would understand. He scribbled a note for her and hurried to Little Iddens.

He wanted to discuss his thoughts on Coleridge, but Robert clung doggedly to his theme.

'Like I said, you're buried alive under all that bespoken prose. I don't comprehend it. You owe it to yourself and to poetry to have your own work out to be admired. It's when you're writing as yourself that your prose has the qualities of poetry. Now wait, I do have your *In Pursuit of Spring* somewhere. In that box – just hold on.'

He rummaged through a box on the sitting room floor and pulled out a dark blue volume buried amongst papers, seed packets, dusty old magazines and children's exercise books.

'Right, let's walk, I'll bring it along and show you what I mean.'

'Well, just for half an hour.'

They took the easy path that led past Oldfields and up a rise before leading down steeply to Preston Brook. At the footbridge they stopped and Robert thumbed through the pages. Edward wondered what passages he would select – he was amused and rather excited. From his school-days, praise always had a powerfully physical, almost sexual effect on him and something about this man's praise meant much.

Robert read out sections concerning the Other Man who reappeared time and again during Edward's journey from London to the Quantocks. Certainly there was something uncanny, some uneasiness, about the contingency, re-occurring over and over, which might make a poem. Robert's own poetry, his 'books of people', could have accommodated such a character. But had Robert seen further into what the Other Man might be?

No, Robert was turning on. He read a passage where Edward had almost despaired of finding a bed for the night on Easter Day.

'Listen: *I found a bed and a place to sit and eat in, and to listen to the rain breaking over gutters and splashing on to stones, and pipes swallowing rain to the best of their ability, and signboards creaking in the wind; and to reflect on the imperfections of inns and life—* You see?'

Edward nodded – weather was a prevailing theme for him, like a perpetual descant to his life. He remembered the rest of the chapter – his long discourse on clay pipes and the Other Man's obsession with weather vanes. Unlikely that Robert would find much in them. No, he moved on, commenting on the passage on George Herbert at Bemington.

When he came to the chapter on Somerset he fell silent. Edward could hear the water murmuring below them under the bridge again.

'What are you reading?' Edward asked after a time.

'I guess it's everywhere, the poetry – just listen.' He read in his leisurely way, breaking the lines as though he were reading blank verse.

'*I went out into the village at about half-past nine in the dark, quiet evening. A few stars penetrated the soft sky; a few* lights shone on earth, from a distant farm seen through a gap in the cottages. Single and in groups, separated by gardens and bits of orchard, the cottages were vaguely discernible; here and there a yellow window square gave out a feeling of home, tranquillity, security. Nearly all were silent. Ordinary speech was not to be heard, but from one house came the sounds of a harmonium being played and a voice singing a hymn, both faintly. A dog barked far off. After an interval a gate fell-to lightly. Nobody was on the road.'

'And again – these images – see: *The pollard willows fringing the green, which in the sunlight resemble mops, were now very much like a procession of men, strange primeval beings, pausing to meditate in the darkness.* That's great. The music and the drama in it, working together. And the way it ends: *I felt that I could walk on thus, sipping the evening silence and solitude, endlessly.*'

Edward looked down from the footbridge into the dark brook. If Robert would just leave him alone for a while now, he thought. It was for him to evaluate his own work. If there was a possibility of him trying poetry, well, then it was for him to find his way, his sources and subjects. But he was grateful too.

'Robert, I think I have to be getting back to work. But thank you. Next time we meet, though, let's talk about *your* poetry.'

Four

Half a kiss, half a tear

Our two families set out together, everyone except Myfanwy carrying something – folding canvas chairs, rugs, baskets of food, cricket bat and ball, swimming things, towels, fishing rods. It was already hot.

We trooped around the Glyn Iddens orchards and I saw Ledbury church spire ahead of us. Two dusty field edges more and we crossed the railway to reach the River Leadon flowing towards the Severn and the sea. It was a little low from lack of rain. The astonishing raddle-red of the clay flushed bright on its banks. We were making for the bathing place that the Frosts knew, Robert and Edward ahead, talking away, Elinor and her children behind. The younger ones were whimpering about the heat. I was beginning to worry too as my dress stuck to my back and I knew my face would be an unbecoming red. Myfanwy wanted to take off her blouse but I said no, she would burn.

Merfyn had met the Frost children before. He'd shared the Little Iddens attic with Lesley and Carol, and written for Lesley's home-produced magazine. But they did not really enjoy each other's company.

Lesley was very like Robert – blue-eyed, tall and athletic. She seemed to see herself as one of the adults. She was fifteen but called her father 'Rob' and her younger brother and sisters 'the children'. I found it strange and thoroughly American. Although she was close in age to Merfyn she seemed much older, as girls do, and made him look awkward. And Merfyn wasn't being easy at that time; Edwy was inclined to blame him for not making better friends with the Frosts and for being too easily bored and this made matters worse between them. He had always been rather critical of Merfyn, sadly.

Bronwen and Carol were the same age but could not have been more different in temperament. Bronnie – so serene, popular and pretty, with Edward's corn-coloured hair. Carol was a rather solitary boy, handsome but sullen. I suspected that in character he took after Elinor and he was obviously most attached to her. He was unhappy in company. He went his own way, occupied himself but kept apart.

Irma was like her mother too, a little waif, nervous, yet independent. Detached. Marjorie, though, was a dear sweet nine year-old, dark-eyed like her mother, but so pale and unhealthy-looking. It was clear to me that she wanted to feel someone cared what she was doing, what she needed, for she wasn't a strong child.

How I wanted more children! Edward's children. Another boy, perhaps, who might have been more similar him in interests. But – there were so many buts, expense being the chief.

I'd prepared the picnic food carefully. Produce seemed plentiful as ever, but I noticed that prices were beginning to rise. I heard the Chandlers wondering whether they would have to increase our board and lodgings fee from three guineas a week. It was true we ate a great deal, especially Merfyn, at that growing stage.

In a sense we were also the Frosts' guests as we spent most evenings with them at Little Iddens, with the children munching their way through the wartime supply of sugary biscuits, so I felt we owed them this picnic lunch. And I enjoyed the work. Big fresh loaves, lettuces, tomatoes and a deep chicken and ham pie. And for dessert, yellow-skinned apples, which Edward loved for their scent as much as their flavour, and a big bowl of purple plums. Mary Chandler said they were not up to market standard but they were perfectly ripe, with that deep gold dew beginning to ooze sweetly in the little blemishes that condemned them.

But the Frosts were carrying lemonade and a tin of the wretched biscuits, although I'd said I would see to the food. The orderly lunch I'd planned was *not* to turn into one of the Frosts' haphazard free-for-alls. I wanted to show Robert and Elinor, especially Elinor, how it could be done.

The bathing-place was cool, the grass still a fresh bright green, enclosed by elms and with black alders and willows leaning from the banks. A little beach, quite sandy and gently sloping, was formed where the river curved and widened.

Further down-river the Leadon deepened enough to make a fishing swim. Edwy was always a keen fisherman, even in those Wandsworth Common pools when he was a boy, so if he wanted to escape from us he could go further downstream and fish. But he seemed happy to watch Bronwen, always his favourite, showing us her swimming strokes as if she were a golden fish herself gliding through the dark water. Merfyn was a good swimmer but he didn't revel in it. Myfanwy, dressed only in her white drawers, squealed with delight as the water reached her knees.

Carol enjoyed showing my two how well he knew the river – the tiny island in the middle, the mysteriously warm and the shockingly cold places that made them scream.

As for Elinor, she looked so tired. She fatigued so easily, I pitied her. I erected the two canvas chairs near the water and she sank into one, closing her eyes. So – it seemed I was expected to keep quiet. I took my shoes off and revelled in the pleasure of sand between my toes. Poor Elinor, it was as if she had never been young.

Dazzled by sunlight dappling the river, I saw our two men as golden figures; Edward's bright hair, his beautiful face, Robert turned towards him, talking earnestly, his broad full mouth emphatic, urgent. Robert was not as tall as Edward and a little more thick-set. His features were powerful – bushy eyebrows and a broad full mouth. They both had striking eyes, Edward's grey and steady under long lashes, and Robert's a startling jade blue.

I caught the words 'New Hampshire'. Robert was again trying to persuade Edward that we should all move to America! Edwy had told me of this idea of Robert's – he had a plan about starting something called a summer school and of us living near to each other in the country. The war, he said, might be prolonged longer than we knew and no one would be interested in publishing Edward's kind of work. Country writing, ramblings and leisurely travels – no place for them in war-time, he said.

'What do you have to lose?' I heard Robert say.

It was all I could do not to interrupt! We would have so much to lose – above all, our friends. We had good friends, friends who had known and cared about us for years. The Frosts were newcomers. Although it was plain to see how important they were to each other, Edward and he, how could we know their friendship wouldn't cool? And if we were in a strange country, knowing no one, how would we survive? And the family, Edwy's parents and brothers, my sisters, especially Mary and her children. The children's aunts, uncles and cousins. No, it was unthinkable. I suspected Robert of selfishness; he just wanted to keep Edward with him, for his own sake.

Edward would be unhappy away from his own country, from England. He called himself a Welshman who was just an 'accidental Cockney'. But he knew England, the English counties, better than anyone, their history, their people, both famous writers and ordinary people. He knew their lanes and byways and customs and legends. I could be happy anywhere if I was with him, but Edwy wouldn't be, I was certain of that. In fact I was afraid his writing would be over. And I couldn't believe what Robert said about no-one wanting his work in England now.

Edward was shaking his head, but smiling. I knew that look on his face. It meant he would be weighing the question in his mind, first one way, then the other, endlessly. I knew Robert had influence over Edward, and so did I, but I could not predict who would win, if it came to a contest. No, that was not right – Edward would make his own decision, but it would be a tortuous process, hard on him, and very hard on the rest of us. I would have to wait to see what Edward was thinking, almost powerless, but not entirely so.

The children eventually had enough of swimming; even Bronwen's teeth were chattering. When they were dressed Edwy proposed a game of cricket to warm them up. He always said he was a poor cricketer, yet it was something else that took him away from me a good deal most summers, playing with Eleanor Farjeon's brother and his friends. Merfyn played at school and even Bronnie had plenty of practice.

To the Americans, and to me too, cricket was a mystery. But Edwy was a good instructor and they learned fast, Lesley and Irma especially. Marjorie soon gave up and Carol was a thoroughly bad sport, going off with the hump the first time he was bowled out.

As for Robert – Robert was a dreadful sport too. The game went on and on, with him challenging every decision that went against his little team. I was astonished. Was this the American custom? It certainly wasn't the English way. Edwy, seeing how it was with him, let him off too lightly.

Finally the game was declared a draw and I could serve lunch. In the event I was pleased with my picnic. Robert and Elinor were indifferent to what they ate – not a single word of praise from them. Robert talked of other things throughout and Elinor pecked at the food saying nothing. But the children ate with a good appetite and the sugary biscuits were forgotten. Good food even put Carol in a better frame of mind and after lunch he showed Merfyn and Bronnie how to perfect their stone-skimming, the smack smack smack of stone on water bringing a smile to his solemn face. A growing boy needs a regular good meal and I'm afraid that was not something Elinor provided.

The day ended without Elinor and I having exchanged more than a few essential words. I could see she liked Edward well enough, but with me she was so reserved, more so than ever. It occurred to me that she would probably be no happier with Robert's American plan than I was, but it was impossible to talk to her about anything of importance.

Next day I knew I had to do something. We'd been in Leddington for ten days and I'd scarcely talked to Edward alone in all that time. I suggested that we Thomases go out together and leave Mr and Mrs Chandler in peace as they had a great deal to do before he left for his regiment. Edwy was cheerful and seemed happy to be with us that day.

We passed through the orchard where the tree branches were propped to support the weight of fruit. Giving the bee-hives a wide berth we headed for Ludstock Brook where Myfanwy could paddle. Merfyn and Bronnie were simply glad to have us all together.

I remember that I was happy that day. We were rarely alone at Oldfields. At mealtimes the Chandlers and the children were with us, and for so much of the rest Edward and Robert, and sometimes the other two poets who lived nearby, went out walking together discussing poetry. Well, I trusted they knew how lucky they were to have the best critic and reviewer in England with them.

I was glad to see Edward happy again, after the horrors of the year before, of course I was. Only – oh, I was disappointed with the holiday, but I didn't want to show it. Edward could be so cold if I importuned him like that.

My mind was full of – uncertainties. I could generally accept life and its changes without too much fuss. I'd had to the year before, when Edwy was so wretched and scarcely ever at home. I'd wanted him, longed for him. The loneliness ate my heart away, and yet I'd fear him coming home because I always hoped for too much. I'd have the house gleaming and a lovely meal and the garden free of weeds and so of course expect everything to be perfect. And then I would, over and over again, be disappointed and shocked by real life, the real life we were living. By his dark moods. The truth was, he had good friends who *could* work those wonders for him; their homes were opened to him, beautiful homes, which he described to me in letters, lovely houses by the sea or in the mountains. No wonder it was good for him to get away from me and our plain cottage life.

Still, in spring he had come home to stay and he was happier, although money was always an anxiety. We had the holiday boarders from Bedales and somehow we managed. We had worked together on the garden, planting things for the future: an apple tree a friend had given him for his birthday, some asparagus crowns.

But now the war and the idea of going to America with the

Frosts, Edward saying that there would be no market for his kind of writing in England – we had to talk about it. He would vacillate to and fro about America. I could foresee that – but not the outcome. Could he even be thinking of leaving us behind?

We arrived at the brook, poor panting Rags wading in first and lapping away. We sat on the bank amongst the willow and alder trees and talked. When Edward's mood was so light and untroubled I was loath to risk spoiling it with my questions, but I had to.

'This plan about America, Edwy – tell me what you're thinking.'

'Well, Robert's idea is that they will go back before much longer and get a farm working. And then he will maybe take up lecturing at his old college. He hopes his name will be made by the time he goes back. Those are his plans. I could come and join him and lecture too, or we would start some kind of a literary summer school – that's what he calls it. He seems sure it will go well.'

'I have the feeling Robert has had so many ventures in the past and they haven't on the whole gone well at all.'

'Perhaps that's true – but Helen, he's absolutely found his way now. His poems are quietly revolutionary. The way he simply writes of what he or some country neighbour in New Hampshire has seen or done and makes magic from it. Good natural English with just a touch of difference.'

'I know, but how does that help you? New Hampshire – who knows what it's like?'

'Robert says it's not unlike the country round here – or perhaps over that way, nearer the Forest of Dean – woods, rolling hills, villages. But with mountains to see in the distance. Perhaps that's why he can picture us there so easily; he thinks we're half-way there. But – all right Helen, tell me what you think.'

'I'd be terribly frightened for us and for you, Edwy. Uprooted, knowing no-one. And your work – what would it be? What about libraries? When you needed something, where would there be anything like the British Library? And then – Robert – well, I'm afraid he's so ambitious, so determined to be the head man.

You're known and respected here. Would he really help you if it came about that you were better known than he was? Even a better writer? I'm not sure he would. This summer school? Does he stick at things? You're dogged, you never let anyone down, you promise to do something and you see it through, no matter what it costs you.'

'Helen...'

'No, it's true, even with us. You've stuck by me and the children – it wasn't fair on you, so young.'

'You were young too.'

'Yes, but for a woman, for me anyway, it's different. I was simply overjoyed to have a baby, you know I was. But for you – oh, look at them, Edwy – just look at the "fruit of your loins!"'

The children were all in a line, Baba holding her big brother's and sister's hands, wading back towards us along the muddy stream. They were soaked and their legs were dyed with the deep carmine stain of Leddington soil. We laughed.

'Oh Edwy, we'll try America if it's what you want, but we must all be together. I can be happy anywhere then.'

'I know that, Helen. But then *is* it what I want? I have to think about what suits me and my work. It's for your sake too. And it's changing; I think I've gone astray all these years. But perhaps I'm getting nearer to finding myself, Helen, whatever that means.'

I put my arms round him, held him.

The children stepped out of the water.

'Hey, come here you scallywags and clean yourselves up on the grass. Your mother and I don't want you dripping over us. Rags, clear off – no – Rags!'

Rags shook a great deal of the Ludstock Brook onto us, the water-drops leaping and sparkling across the glare of the sun and falling like rain, or like a blessing, on my hot skin.

Five

Edward went out early. He wanted to walk, to look, to be alone and to think about his writing.

Twenty years of writing, millions of words, half-way through his life at thirty-six and he still could not be entirely pleased with what he wrote. Some work he'd done in the last two years was pointing to where he should go. *In Pursuit of Spring,* his childhood memories – they were in a new voice, individual, exploratory. But he felt like a hopeful musician, practising but never performing.

Frost's confidence in him confirmed what he already knew: that his best writing had the cadences of speech and that he used it as well as anyone. And he made use of all he'd read, writers of the past and present that he knew perhaps better than anyone.

He felt a degree of freedom, being away from his book-crammed study. No-one was commissioning him, no-one was paying him for being here on this summer morning. Usually in any new place he was at work, walking or cycling, stopping to note down his observations to write up when he came home. But this morning he was free – there did not have to be a book. It was both a freedom and a threat.

If he should try, what could he bring to poetry?

He looked around. A trickle from a smaller stream entered Preston Brook. White chickens pecked among the roots of an ash tree; they squeezed through the hedge from a farmhouse he could just see through the elms. The hedge was blackthorn skilfully laid, the clean scars of the labourer's hook still visible. He listened. The only sounds were of the stream, the birds and the trees – their own pure and individual languages, never straining for effect, never false. He thought about the many languages, man's one among many. Was it possible that a man's words could have that kind of truthfulness?

He sat on the short turf of the stream bank and listened and thought for an hour.

What it would be to find those words, to try to express the thoughts that arose from what he was seeing, whether in prose or verse! To write what it meant to feel a oneness with nature, with the kind of quiet ecstasy moments like these could bring. He knew there was so much that could never be fully expressed, or could only be expressed through absences and negatives. But perhaps the goal was to try, and at least not to betray the language in trying.

There was a commotion in the kitchen when Edward came home. It was the day Mr Chandler was to leave for training and he was quipping about the fact that he, an old soldier of forty-four, would be told what to do by 'Some whipper-snapper still wet behind the ears!'

He had a way with Merfyn, and Edward saw an aspect of his son he hardly knew.

'Right lad – you're as tall as me and not much younger than these officers I've seen. Let's see you give me me marching orders.'

And Merfyn responded right away, springing off his kitchen chair to attention, grabbing an ash walking-stick from the stand and barking out orders:

'Attenshun. Left right left right. About-turn.'

Tom Chandler stamped his boots on the flagstone floor complying, exaggerating. Merfyn's orders came faster and faster, until Tom had them all laughing by deliberately getting it wrong. Merfyn was flushed with happiness and Helen, holding on to Mary Chandler for support as she laughed, looked with love and pride at her son.

'Perhaps you should be a soldier, Merfyn,' Edward said. 'You plainly have a gift for it.'

Merfyn stopped laughing and looked abashed – he hadn't noticed his father there.

Helen stopped laughing. 'Never, Edwy, never. Don't say such

43

a thing. Merfyn knows what he wants to be.' She gave a little laugh again. 'I didn't have a son to have him shot at. Oh Mary, I'm sorry – but it's different for Tom – he knows what he's doing, he's an old hand, he'll be all right. You know what I mean.'

'Of course dear. If I had a boy I'd feel the same. But with your old man it's different, isn't it? Suppose Mr Thomas was to go – you wouldn't feel the same about it.'

'Oh but I would – just the same. What a dreadful thought! Edward a soldier! But it's only the unmarried men who go, isn't it, apart from professional soldiers like Tom. Isn't it Edwy?'

'Yes, I believe so – that's right Tom, isn't it? But you're so cut off here if it wasn't for you bringing us back news from Hereford we'd hardly know there was a war on at all.'

Helen was still looking shaken.

Tom Chandler said to her, 'Don't you worry, my dear. It'll soon be over.'

'Do you think so?'

'Course. Our lot are a match for these bullying Germans. It's that mad Kaiser's doing, wanting to take over the world. I doubt your ordinary German wants to go war, so they won't have their hearts in it. We're fighting for England, for our home. That's the difference.'

They were quiet then, until there was a sudden racket of voices from the garden path that led to the open kitchen door – Robert's deep drawl and Marjorie's chatter. It was the Frosts, come to say good-bye to their neighbour, Mr, now Sergeant, Chandler.

'Elinor sends her good wishes. I guess she's a little out of health today. But we're here to wish you luck.'

Soon Frosts were all over the house, the younger girls crawling under the table to reach a timid kitten taking refuge there, while Lesley and Carol accepted Bronwen's suggestion of coming up to the bedroom to try to see their own house from the window. Carol wondered if they might be able to wave to their mother and he stood on a chair to look out. But there was no sign of Elinor in their garden.

*

That afternoon Edward wanted to walk again and he decided to take Myfanwy. She rode on his shoulders, excited by the privilege of time alone with her father. She sang what she could remember of a song to fit her position – 'D'ye ken John Peel', jigging up and down and working her chubby little legs to make him go faster. He listened, fascinated, as she kept the music and cadences true but completely jumbled the words or invented her own.

'D'ye ken John Peel from far far away
Do'ye ken John Peel every single day
D'ye ken John Peeeeeeel in his coat so gay
and his hounds that get up every mor-ning'

And so on, with variations ever more numerous and inventive. But always the cadences were true to the original. Better than the original in fact, Edward thought. He tried joining in but was told firmly, 'No Daddy. My song.' And so it was, her song that was rooted in something else, in sound, pure sound.

They travelled so speedily that they reached a place they'd never visited, where a stony track forded the Preston Brook. Myfanwy paddled. Edward sat still on the bank by the glinting, murmuring stream. A dragonfly suddenly landed on a large stone by the water's edge and warmed itself, taking heat from the stone and sun together. There it stayed motionless and timeless, as he felt himself to be, sitting still in the sun.

Above the trees he could see March Hill, the last of the Malverns, prominent against the sky, a place of legends and ancient mysteries. He pictured Thomas Traherne, strolling in Herefordshire centuries before, meditating on the boundless potential of man's mind and spirit and enjoying the easy hours as a child did. He would have to read *Centuries*, again – such extraordinary and unconventional verses. Traherne's 'child' was a marvellous creature who could wander free of boundaries with no property to bind him. Edward shared his way of looking at the world; Traherne saw that we don't own the world or any part of

45

it, at best we hold it on 'an everlasting lease' and must care for it.

For a while he lost all sense of present time, of time itself. A walk like this, a place like this, could take him meandering through the centuries. It was as if he and the dragonfly were unchanged since Traherne's days. Or even since the long-dead chieftains were buried in the barrow up on the hill. This was England for him: timeless, the England that had roots far back in the earth of the ancient past and that still in moments like these could be found and would always be found.

A chaffinch flew down and perched on the wooden rail of the bridge, cocking its head a little and looking into the brook. How contained they are, he thought, the dragonfly, the chaffinch; these creatures aren't troubled like us, always reflecting and theorising. They have intuition and a wholeness of being. We are cast out from that – the Fall, there's a real truth in the story. These creatures are still in Eden, they're in touch with the world, with now, in some immediate way that Man never is. We have history – our awareness of history, those barrows, the past, what it gives us. And our own pasts.

And along with that is the fact that we're always thinking of the future too, he thought. Children escape that for a little while, before schooldays at least. He watched Myfanwy building a row of stones across the stream – even she had a clear plan, she couldn't leave the stream to be itself. It was the nature of Man. But then of course the stream would win. Within minutes of their leaving the little dam would be gone.

He could foresee that, but it was his belief that the only certain thing about the future was its unpredictability.

Six

Half a kiss, half a tear

I didn't see what happened. I ought to have seen.

Robert had made a swing in the orchard for the children by tying ropes up in a high apple tree. Myfanwy always wanted to come here and take a turn. It was so cramped and restricted at Mrs Chandler's, with only one room for our whole family. Without spending time at Little Iddens most days it would have been difficult for the children, but especially for Baba who was much too young to go out into the lanes by herself. Merfyn and Bronwen had bicycles here and could go where they pleased, but Baba had to be with me and we both needed more space, even though for me it meant the strain of being with Elinor. Her lethargic ways seemed to be infecting me, because I was feeling low and sad, discouraged; the holiday was not doing what I'd hoped for Edward and me.

I lay on the grass in the Frosts' orchard, shaded by a pear tree and listening to the drowsy murmur of bees. I took my spectacles off and without them I could see only a vague blur.

That hot day Elinor seemed particularly tired and pale; I began to wonder whether she was really ill with some complaint she couldn't discuss. I was the healthiest creature alive and I pitied her. She watched listlessly as her girls fought over their turns. Myfanwy was whining, waiting for the 'big girls' to let her swing. Irma was awfully crotchety, not at all fair to Marjorie. Elinor didn't interfere.

Eventually I had to ask Irma to allow Myfanwy to have a turn and with a bad grace she agreed. Now that Baba was within days of her fourth birthday she liked to say she could 'work herself' and it was true she'd grasped the idea. But to have a good swing she still needed a push. Irma offered to push her and, too glad for a little peace, I helped Myfanwy onto the seat and then lay down again under the tree.

Her sudden screams pierced me through! I jumped up. I had to grope about to find my glasses before I could go to her. I picked her up and held her, rocking her to and fro, while she sobbed and hiccupped, trying between wails to tell me what had happened. I hushed her a little and asked her to show me where she hurt. The worst damage was a bump on her head that was coming up into a great egg! We sat together quietly under the tree, rocking gently, until she stopped crying. Then I was afraid she would fall asleep, that she might have been knocked unconscious for a moment and so might be in danger.

I asked Elinor if she knew what had happened and whether Myfanwy cried out after she fell, or if she just lay still, which was what I feared. It seemed that Elinor had been dozing herself. But I couldn't blame her. I was to blame, for not watching my own child and being sure she was safe. I would never do such a thing again – one moment, that was all it needed, for what was dearest to you to be taken away forever.

I picked Myfanwy up – she felt so much heavier than usual, not springing to put her arm around my neck or lodging her little legs around my hip. The two burning fields between the Frosts and home never seemed so far, nor I so wretched. Myfanwy was suddenly sick and I half ran the rest of the way, stumbling across the plank bridge over the ditch, to get her out of the cruel sun. How I wished Edwy was at home, but he, of course was out with Robert.

Elinor sent a message enquiring how Baba was on the evening of her fall. She said nothing about what happened to cause it, and whatever had happened, I chiefly blamed myself.

Myfanwy was very poorly for a week. She needed to sleep a great deal and so I found myself trapped with her in a darkened attic room. The other two were annoying, being bored. Merfyn flicked through the old motoring magazines he'd brought with him, sighing and fidgeting, while Bronnie fretted over her copy of 'Home Fashions', complaining she couldn't make use of the dress pattern enclosed in it when she had no fabric. She was already becoming concerned with her dress and she tried on her few frocks, making alterations with my sashes and belts, but saying she'd much rather be in town with her aunt and cousin than here in the middle of nowhere. And I began to feel the same.

'You do have your bicycles. At least you can go out. Go for a long ride, why don't you?'

They sighed and shrugged and pouted but they went.

Mary Chandler was my best comfort. She made a camomile poultice for the dreadful lump on Myfanwy's forehead and within a day or two it subsided, so poor Baba didn't wake herself up from having rolled over in her sleep.

She slept uneasily and I worried about her. I wondered about a doctor, but both Edwy and Mary convinced me that a doctor would do nothing but prescribe what I was already providing: rest and quiet.

As she improved I could leave her sleeping and go downstairs. I liked to be in the cool farmhouse kitchen. The flagstones and lime-washed walls felt fresh after the hot attic bedroom, and the door always stood open. The range fire was low, just enough to keep a kettle of water ready. We drank a great deal of tea. I would bring some mending and sit at the big deal table while Mary kept her baking to the other end.

She was perhaps a few years older than me, thirty-nine or forty. Although she hadn't seemed to mind her husband going off to war, she was glad of our company. I enjoyed her country housekeeping – her once a week bread-baking with a mountain of dough pounded by her strong arms. It was even harder work, she said, than washday. I liked to bake myself but cakes were my speciality. We were content to work together around that kitchen table. If she had been a woman of my own class I would have told her, unwisely perhaps, how sad and disappointed I was feeling, how I wanted nothing in the world but a close and happy marriage and to be needed by Edward, but how it often seemed there was other company he preferred to mine. But of course it was out of the question with Mary.

So we talked about the village and village people. 'Would you believe that some Ryton folk have been to the police with their tales? They say the place is suddenly full of foreigners. Foreigners who sit up late at night so they're probably spies!' She laughed.

Our late arrival continued to cause speculation and the Frosts *were* indeed foreigners. The Abercrombies apparently had a Dutch lady with eccentric habits staying; she of course was believed to be a German.

Mary herself just laughed at these rumours. She said, 'It's the incomers. Them in the new villas round Ledbury. We folk believe in live and let live.' These were things I could tell Edwy when he came home from his rambles with Robert. People who lived close to the land: farm-workers, gamekeepers, labourers, even wandering peddlers and gypsies, his imagination was stirred by such chance meetings, with an exchange about the weather, trade, or the purpose of the journey. He could talk very easily with strangers – or rather, he could draw people out to talk to him, and he would listen and remember.

He wanted to know what people were thinking about the war because it occurred to him that there could be some material in it. He could be commissioned to write on the subject and have some paying work secured at least. So he wrote to an editor he knew with a proposal.

Since war was declared we'd all become patriotic, or perhaps aware of a patriotism that we'd taken for granted. In times of peace, it was not something we either thought of or even much cared for. But now we all subscribed to the new watchwords – 'Unity and Scorn'.

Over breakfast in the farm kitchen we three talked about these things. Edward, I realise, had been thinking a great deal about these matters, and I know he had talked to his friend Lascelles about the war.

'I suppose we normally think locally,' Edward said. 'Our own small unique places and their peculiarities and differences. And we quarrel between one county and another, like Yorkshire and Lancashire.'

'Even between one village and another too, like Steep and Sheet at home.'

'Yes, because we're secure enough to be able to. In fact, we've been so secure that we could be critical of England, quick to see her faults and weaknesses and very ready to point them out. But now that we're under attack that's all changed.'

'Yes, like a husband and wife who know each other through and through and quarrel, but dear me, if an outsider criticises either of them, or tries to come between them, well, woe betide them,' Mary Chandler said.

'Perhaps patriotism does come down to this,' Edward said, 'that we love England, the whole idea of England, because it's made up of all our own separate holes and corners and their odd ways, and they couldn't exist if England didn't.'

'To imagine England ceasing to exist – I can't bear to think of it,' I said.

'Oh, she will always come through, England. She won't be beaten, I know that,' said Mary. 'Not if Tom has anything to do with it she won't.' She laughed.

I could tell that the idea of an article about the mood of England at war was crystallizing in Edward's mind. Did that mean our holiday was going to be cut short? I asked him when we went back upstairs.

'I have to think of work that will pay, Helen, and I've so little in prospect. A possible idea about a biography of Marlborough and that's all. My plan would be to travel from here up into the Birmingham area and then further north. I'd go where I could eavesdrop on people, hear what they were saying, get into conversation.'

'So different from your usual journeys, I can't imagine you in a northern town. And would it mean going quite soon? Must you do that?'

'If I get the commission, yes. It's not what I'd choose, Helen. Have I ever been able to choose? It's a question of how I make a living for you and the children. But it does interest me more than you might think, the idea of England and fighting for your country. I know I always claim to be a Welshman and so I am by birth. But I suppose I've been steeped in England – English fields, English people, English poetry – for so long that I've become an Englishman too. I'm slowly growing into a conscious Englishman.'

'Well, if you can get a good contract that would be a relief. And no one, no-one at all, has described the English countryside better than you, nor knows more about English writers. And her history and geography and mythology and nature—'

He turned away, laughing a little.

'Helen, you are ridiculous. Right, I'm off now to try to get Merfyn and Bronnie involved in the magazine the Frosts' children are producing. The Bouquet – not exactly an original title.'

Edward often complained that he had to review enough garlands, wreaths, posies and bouquets of poetry books to fill Covent Garden Market.

'I'm sorry to leave you here again, but it will be good for them to use their minds a little for once. And Baba's much better, isn't she? She won't miss her birthday and we'll make it a good one for her.' Myfanwy would be four on the sixteenth of August.

When Myfanwy's better, I thought, I will come over and take an interest in The Bouquet too, if Elinor agreed. Lesley was the 'Editor', but Elinor was the guiding hand behind it. She'd been a teacher, but then so had I, only with the youngest children, though I was not college-educated as she was. That was one of the many differences between America and England.

I watched Edward and the children walk up the rising field, under the huge solitary oak, dip down into the ditch and up again Then they disappeared from my view behind the hedge – so I could only imagine them arriving at the orchard gate and entering into the Frost domain.

Seven

They had started out in mid-morning and were coming home towards a Western sky of turquoise with a few scattered gold-rimmed clouds. It was one of their 'talks-walking' days, as Robert called it. Edward mostly listened but put in his own comments occasionally.

'Exactly. That's it. Robert. The right language of poetry. I've been waiting for years for a poet to come along who will show, really demonstrate to the literary world what I've been saying, that the ear is the only true writer and the only true reader. So please see me as the Baptist to your Messiah.'

'Why, you know, I've no objection to that whatsoever! No truthfully, Edward, I do feel I've been understood for the first time in my life. You see—'

He stopped, looking at the sky, at nothing, looking inwards. Edward waited.

'What it is, what I always say – words exist in the mouth, not in books. Sounds have to be gathered by the ear, fresh from talk. Almost everyday talk. A sentence *is* a sound in itself, your little girl's lines from the song as you say.'

'Not that there was much sense—'

'No, of course, sense has to come too, words have to be strung along that sound, but skilfully, skilfully. There's the regular beat of the metre, like music, but that's just an abstract frame. It's the poet's own voice that gives it life, the drama in the meaning. Such possibilities! It's then that you discover what the poem wants to say, through its mood, its sound. Or so it should be. I don't like, for an instance, your Poet Laureate Robert Bridges – too regular a scansion, no natural cadences.'

'I know, though you could find far worse examples. And even myself – you don't know, Robert, how far books have formed me, much more than speech, and how *hard* it is for me to get free of them. I'm a nineteenth century man in the twentieth century; my head stuffed with bookish language I need to shed, like Yeats casting off his 'coat covered with embroideries'. But Robert, you really should write a book on speech and literature. If you don't I might do it myself. My ideas and yours, I use them every day now and I want to be rid of all that old bookish rhetoric.'

'Well Edward – what you say may be right, I guess. We came to the same ideas independently, by different routes. Maybe.' He frowned.

Edward sensed his reservation.

'But the difference is, you *make* something with your ideas, I only follow up behind and comment.'

'Why, you know the answer to that well enough.'

As they reached a hedge they could see beyond the next field to where a man stood high up on top of a cart, pitchfork in hand. Robert called out a question to him.

'What are you up to this fine afternoon?'

He was much too far away for the words themselves to be caught, yet the man called back an answer. And because of the cadence it plainly was an answer, as Robert's shout plainly was a question.

'There, that's what I mean,' Robert said. 'A sentence sound. And if we could hear the words, they'd fit just as a good shoe fits the foot.'

That night Robert strode restlessly about the living room. He told Elinor that Edward thought he should write a book explaining his theory of speech rhythms in poetry and what it meant for English literature. The idea appealed – having a scholarly book published to add to his poems. Something to show them back in America. But he was not Edward. The thought of sitting down to plan a learned book, the hours and hours of work. No, he wouldn't care much for that. But the *idea* of the book pleased him. If only he could simply talk and someone would write his words down.

Long after the children had gone to bed he would often sit up and work on a poem, Elinor keeping him company. He was working on one about the nest of fledglings he and Lesley found exposed after harvest. But he couldn't settle for long. He stretched his big body in his chair, chafed against the wooden writing shelf across his knees. Tonight it was something else he wanted, something to confirm him in his exhilaration and pleasure.

When they were in bed he sought it but he was refused, resisted. Elinor, pleading her horror of more children, her weak heart, refused him. It was an ill-advised time for her. He knew her feelings but part of him still believed that it was her duty to have him, as it was the duty of people like themselves, the right sort of people, to have several children for the good of the race. And he was roused.

'Don't, don't...' She shrank away from him, from his heavy hands and mouth.

The row exploded between them; it became a fight.

She turned on him with such a contemptuous look that he was daunted, then angry. He flung himself out of bed, threw on some clothes and left the house.

Out in the night he felt terrible loneliness, and rage too, that his pride in himself and his work should be cut down in this way. Elinor had such power over him, she always had. And they were like fire and ice. She was a little older, perhaps a little cleverer, and before he'd married her a good deal richer; he'd had to subdue her. Her opinion of him was crucial to him, and he could never feel sure of it, nor of her love. That anxiety was there, Elinor herself was there, in so much of his poetry.

He came to the yew tree at the front of the house, its trunk a denser blackness against the dark. Something glinted white at the foot of the tree; he could see some fragments of china and a little toy goblet and plate. The children must have been playing at 'housekeeping' there. He sat on the dry and dusty ground under the yew, put his head in his arms and wept for their dead first-born son.

And for himself. He knew that no matter what success he had, Elinor would never forgive him for that death.

*

They'd set out on what was to be a long trek in the Malverns, planning to take all day, through Bromsberrow and Hollybush, allowing for a stop at an inn for cider. They had bread, meat and cheese to sustain them on their climb up to the Herefordshire Beacon and the site of British Camp, said to be the scene of the last stand by Caractacus against the Romans. In part this was what Edward wanted to see. Though history, other than literary history, bored him, the thought of proud resistance to the invader interested him. And somewhere on those slopes was the site of Langland's Piers Plowman vision, as he 'slumbered in a slepping.'

'Well Edward, I sure trust you've made up your mind to come with me to till the soil of New Hampshire,' Robert said.

He was not ready for Robert's question; Robert should know well enough that he must reflect on such a decision. Today was for looking, for being out-of-doors and revelling in the beauty of the morning. *'Let us get out of these indoor narrow modern days into the sunlight and pure wind.'* Richard Jefferies' words and his own gospel since he was a boy. Today he didn't want to think. Often he found he could let the day, the sights and sounds, the wind, mist and rain, do some thinking for him.

But Robert wanted an answer. He seemed irritable.

'Well, come on, tell me will you?'

'I can't answer you. I haven't ruled it out by any means – some days it seems more and more likely. What I'm to do for a living, a writing living, I don't know. No response as yet to my proposal for a book on modern poetry. I put it to Cazenove last week, but my belief is it won't be accepted. So that leaves the possibility of the Duke of Marlborough, which I suppose is war-like enough for today's taste. After that, nothing. It is rather desperate I admit.'

'Well there you are – there's your answer. You'd much better come back with us in the spring.'

Edward stopped to consult the map without replying. He loved maps. They'd been the background to his wanderings for twenty years and he read the Ordnance Survey sheets

56

instinctively by now. This one was well-used, its folds and creases showing the thin canvas backing behind the woods, streams, railtrack and roads. Within those features he knew how to see the network of footpaths and old tracks, those ancient routes of drovers and villagers, some almost disappeared but with traces still to be found.

'This is the way, News Wood, Hangman's Hill,' he said, striking up a wooded track. They covered half a mile before Robert spoke again.

'And this old England of yours, this country – it's not so great you know.'

'What on earth do you mean by that, Robert? It's been good to you, I think you'll agree.'

'Well, I guess so. But I've seen plenty that disgusts me. Pitiful little kids, nothing on their feet and half-starved. And not only here in the country. My children went to school in Beaconsfield – for half-a-day. They couldn't mix in with such kids – ignorant, crushed little creatures, with no spirit of their own. They just couldn't understand each other.

'And your class system. Who decides these things? Who are these lords who own so much of the land round here? You won't find that in the United States. We value a man if he's independent, if he makes his own way in the world. But here I've seen old ladies, white-haired old ladies who deserve respect themselves, bobbing their knees at some young whippersnapper in his motorcar because he's the son of some lord or other.'

'But that's passing. The younger people wouldn't go that far.'

'And the worst of it is, it's backed up by your working man, your farm-hands and gamekeepers. Gamekeepers – what lackeys! That one whose boss owns Abercrombie's place. I've heard if he catches some poor hungry kids even picking a few blackberries in his woods he clouts them, tips their fruit out on the ground and stamps on it. And he's from the same class as them, but owned body and soul by your aristocrats. It's a sickening business.'

'It is, if that's true. But you know, gamekeepers have their place. I may not like their endless killing, but they're men with the woods in their blood and I respect that. The gamekeeper: his home is in the woods, he lives there just as another animal, a fox, a badger or a deer would and fights for his place. I hate the idea of owning land myself – much better to have a lease for a place, only for what you need. Private land is an abomination so I just walk wherever I please. But the gamekeeper doesn't own land either – his work is a lease on the land and his ways are country ways. Do you understand?'

'It's not our way,' Robert said. 'We believe in freedom and in independence. I don't care about politics or political freedom. All I want is the freedom to write, to decide my material. But I don't appreciate anyone lording it over someone else. And I'm damned if I'll be pushed around by anyone.'

The day was warm again, but by climbing the Malverns they were up where a light breeze blew. They fell silent, needing their breath for the climb. The British Camp rose high; its ramparts in wedding-cake tiers sharply defined with deep dykes. It was possible to see far into Wales in the west, and eastwards over the Severn to the Cotswolds. And there was May Hill and its distinctive clump of trees.

Edward was ahead again consulting his map, identifying places he'd heard of, recalling associations with them. Wordsworth, he remembered, said that we carry round with us a map of our world that was midway between life and books. It was quite true.

He began prodding the earth, looking for the remains of Roman horseshoes he'd heard could be found there. Then he sat, simply feeling the springy turf and enjoying the nodding harebells and the cooling breeze on his brow. A lark was spooling up into the pale sky, its song ringing down to him. He could feel the presence of the ancient inhabitants sharing the turf, hearing the lark, though rabbits were the only inhabitants now.

He told Robert when he caught up that Elgar had written an oratorio called 'Caractacus' about this place and the ancient British chieftain's battle.

'You know, Edward, I think you take too dreamy a view of your old country. See this place, the last stand, they say, before the Roman Empire conquered Britain. The way I look at it, history has a way of dealing with what's outworn, when the time comes. And that's usually through war.'

'What! Outworn things can renew themselves, they usually do. You don't have to be conquered by Roman legions for that.'

'Ah, but sometimes you do. You see how my country was made – you know my mother was Scottish, and before her my father's family came from some old place in England. It was time for a new empire to be formed, leaving the old country behind. And then that empire had to free itself from you – from the old master. Now we are becoming the strong ones.

'And Germany is in the ascendant too, creating its new empire. You folks don't accept it, but as I look at it, that's what history is. It's full of change and tears and grief. We can't avoid it. It's a question of looking out for yourself. So if you've any sense Edward, and you want to fulfil the promise you know you have, you'll get out while you can and join the new world.'

Edward couldn't speak for the passion he felt as he listened. Who was this man to tell him that his country, innocent of blame and at that moment losing her young men to a greedy unjust enemy, was inevitably doomed? And that he should abandon her.

He got up and strode down the hillside away from Robert, bounding down the ramparts until he reached the path running on the sharp lower ridge. To the side lay a steep wood of oak, ash and hawthorn underlaid with foxgloves. A mound of red soil on one bank marked an impressive badger set, the home of another tough old ancient Briton. He tried to gather his thoughts as he walked on. Looking back he saw Robert following, switching a stick angrily at the long grass and nettles to his side.

In a while Edward stopped and waited for him.

'I think you've just given me the best argument for *not* coming back with you that you could, Robert. Your history is misguided, I believe, and this emphasis on self, the individual rather than what is common to humanity, you take it too far.'

'Well, it's how we see it back home, I guess.'

'Well, it's not how we see it, I'm happy to say. Now please, will you change the subject and let's talk about something we can agree on.' For once he wished he had taken this walk alone.

Robert looked uncomfortable. 'I guess I'm tired, and in a bad mood today. I'm kind of homesick myself, Edward. We all are, truth be told. Thing is, I'm a real Yank from Yankville and I'm beginning to think of when we shall go home. This war is an ill wind for us – our game is up in England. There'll be no poetry published that isn't about the war. So we will be going home, if I can find the fare, or a job to pay the fare after we get home. I'm just hoping my reputation's been made back there.'

'I think from what we've heard you'll find it has.'

'Yes, and much of it thanks to you. The truth is I hate the idea of leaving you behind, because I've never had such a good friend. And I doubt I ever will again. You are my beloved blood-brother! I am truly sorry I offended you.' He held out his hand. Edward took it and they shook hands.

'And now, Robert,' he said, 'let's leave this prehistoric place or you'll be suggesting that ancient Redskin ritual for us to perform and I'm not too keen on the sight of blood.'

As they approached Eastnor Park the weather changed quite suddenly. At last there would be rain. The sky had turned an extraordinary dark blue although there was still sunlight in the fields.

'Look – you can see the rain over the hills and I think it's coming this way,' Robert said. He was right. A chill was in the saturated air and light misty rain fell and continued to fall as they trudged down towards home.

It was almost dark and they were aware that they would be walking by moonlight.

The strangest thing – they both stood still, silenced and over-awed. An effect of light through the moisture made an extraordinary ring, a kind of rainbow, but one that created a circle around them, so that the two of them stood as if protected, illuminated and marked out as somehow belonging together in a special way. Their friendship was noted by nature, singled out and lasting.

*

60

Twenty years later Robert would finish his poem about that moment.

And we stood in it softly circled round
From all division time or foe can bring
In a relation of elected friends.

Eight

Half a kiss, half a tear

It was her fourth birthday and Myfanwy was well enough to enjoy it. Our great friend, Eleanor Farjeon, sent her a jolly painted Russian farm and we gave her a doll's cradle and her first china-faced doll, which she loved. We had tea at Oldfields, with a cake I'd made, just our family. Bronwen and I, and Myfanwy too, decorated the table with cut-out and coloured place settings. Baba's face was a picture of pride and happiness as we sang the 'Happy Birthday' song. But I was rather sad to think that my last baby was four already.

In the evening we crossed the field to Little Iddens as usual, watching the rooks flying home across a rosy sky. We always crammed into the sitting room where some of us had to sit on the brick floor, dirtied to the same red colour as the earth outdoors. There we would rest with our backs to the wall playing charades and telling tales. The children would try to puzzle us with new riddles. Often on these evenings we would sing, with Edwy's beautiful voice leading us in folk songs, English and Welsh.

Some evenings we spent with the Abercrombies. Catherine was thoroughly unconventional, but friendly and hospitable, as different from Elinor Frost as could be. Lascelles was a small, spectacled, shy man and I always felt especially motherly around him. They lived in a thatched cottage three miles from us with their two charming little boys.

Then there were the Gibsons. Edward knew them both from Monro's Poetry Bookshop, as they'd worked with Monro and Edward was Poetry and Drama's chief reviewer. When we were in Gloucestershire in June quite a crowd of us had gathered one evening at the Old Nail Shop, Gibson's house – us, the Frosts, the Abercrombies, the Gibsons of course, and Rupert Brooke. He often visited us at Steep – a fascinating young man, I'd thought him, but perhaps a little dangerous.

Wherever we were we spent a great deal of time listening to Robert talking. He had a stock of opinions about everything; my chief impression of evenings in Gloucestershire will always be that the rest of us were an audience for Robert, his philosophy, his poetic theories, his quips, his anecdotes. Edwy seemed happy with this. He would put in a dry aside, which to my mind would have been at least as worth pursuing as Robert's train of thought. Elinor was inscrutable; if her face showed any emotion, which was rare, I would say she looked on as a mother might at a precocious child when she felt he might be accused of showing off.

On the occasion of Baba's birthday I sat on the floor with her already heavily asleep in my lap. The days were becoming shorter, so that by nine we were sitting in soft lamplight. Irma and Marjorie were in bed, but our older children and theirs were still up. Robert was talking about the Red Indians, native to America, and he held the children's interest. He admired these ancient tribes and knew some of their practices. He said he dreamed of finding an unknown, lost tribe of original savages in some hidden glen, a kind of Eden, where he would be welcomed in, protected, taught their ways and made a 'blood brother'.

I was thinking that this was all very well for children. I loved the history of our own ancient times, the barrows and standing stones, the marks man left over the centuries. But Edward and I did not make up fantasies about some paradise on earth that was and must always be a dream. Americans lack those ancient traces of their ancestry, so perhaps this is the best they could do. But Robert's fantasy had a false ring to my ears. Edwy listened in silence, but he caught my eye and I think understood me.

Then Robert turned the conversation to what he called the Negro question: whether the Negro, who of course was still enslaved in America less than fifty years before, shared our full humanity. Robert's remark surprised and distressed me.

He said, 'If my wife and I were in a gathering and a Negro came in, I should immediately take Elinor out.'

He went on to talk about racial purity and of his fears of the degeneration of the white race. And he denied any idea of a shared humanity or of equality between all people. Yet Robert was from New England, from one of the States which was surely of the Abolitionists' cause. I could not understand him. An awkward silence fell. Afterwards I wondered why Edward and I thought it best to drop the subject rather than pursue it. Elinor of course had that blank and nebulous look of hers which might mean anything. Apart from anything else, in her place I would not have liked the idea of being led from the room as though I were a child!

We left soon afterwards. A thin cloud veiled the moon and the fields were dark. For once few stars could be seen, so we took the longer walk home along the lane. Edward slung Baba over his shoulder and Bronnie leaned on me sleepily. We said nothing about the questions occupying my thoughts. America boasted of its sense of common humanity and condemned us as class-ridden.

Later in bed, I did talk to Edwy.

'Yes, it's inconsistent of him but it is not our country. He has theories that matter to him about differences and individuals who are naturally superior and must not be held back. In New England I gather that means the Anglo-Saxons like Robert – even the French are unpopular. I believe he misreads his Darwin. And remember, plenty of educated English people hold the same kind of views about Jews as he does about Negroes. Even about the working classes in the industrial towns. It's part of the eugenics cult, despising ordinary working people, calling them 'the masses' and wanting their childbearing prevented.'

'It's arrogant and ignorant.'

'Mmmh. I agree, it's contemptible. Well, I'll meet plenty of working people if my excursion to the north comes off. In the morning I'll have to write to Frank Cazenove about that again. Now, I'm tired, Helen – turn round and let's go to sleep.'

We didn't really talk about Robert's views after all. Edward had changed the subject.

I did try to involve myself in The Bouquet, but not only Elinor, Lesley too, made it plain that I wasn't much wanted.

Myfanwy and I had joined them in the shade of the walnut tree in their courtyard. This magazine was part of the children's home tuition, because they wouldn't go to English schools. Or perhaps English schools wouldn't have the Frosts? Elinor said she didn't want Myfanwy disturbing the older children. So after I'd admired the work I left Bronnie and Merfyn with their packets of sandwiches and took Baba away for a walk, disappointed but in some ways relieved.

I could see that Elinor and Robert would make a writer out of Lesley. Edward recognised another writer and talked to her as one. What a mystery it is, inheritance, talent. Why was Edward, the only one of six brothers, the writer he was? Why was I hopeless at school and my sisters so successful? And our children – only Myfanwy seemed likely to have inherited some of Edward's gifts. Bronnie charmed and amused him so much that he didn't much mind her lack of interest in learning, but with Merfyn it was different; his middling school reports were a source of unhappiness in our family. Though at last Edward accepted that his interests lay in mechanics, just like Edward's brother Theodore in fact, and we were encouraging Merfyn to apply himself and to be more responsible.

Of course Edward was such an extraordinarily disciplined, capable person; even in his times of terrible blackness he always fulfilled his commissions. He would do his research and keep all his commitments in mind and write, write, write. My scatter-brained approach to life, forgetting to post things when he'd told me to, losing things, infuriated him.

I wondered about Elinor – did she think me a trivial person, superficial for caring about keeping a comfortable home? I think she did. I knew she was far more involved in Robert's work than I was in Edward's; she even planned the arrangement of his poems in his new volume, Edward said. Edwy would never allow such a thing; he would read his work to me, but that was all. Robert appeared supremely confident and yet he was dependant on his wife.

I went back to the Frosts in the late afternoon. Merfyn was drawing a picture influenced by the war, I was sorry to see. He called it 'a French gun in action'. It was a pencil sketch of a convincing-looking gun, two soldiers in French-style caps and a swirl of lines representing the firing. An ugly shell lay ready to be fired.

Carol did two lovely drawings, one of a weasel on a tree-branch, its head alert, and another of a hedgehog, an un-English-looking hedgehog, in an orchard. When I asked him about it he said it was the orchard 'back home', at the farm that had been sold and where they would never be able to return.

Lesley's talent was in painting as well as writing; she made a professional-looking illustration for the poem, The Forsaken Merman, a favourite of mine. Marjorie drew some full-headed poppies, excellent for her age, and Irma another nostalgic piece, a sketch of the summerhouse at Beaconsfield, their home in England before they moved to Gloucestershire. I praised them all for their cleverness.

Lesley typed out a poem of her father's – it stemmed from a comment one of the children made about how the flowers at Little Iddens are locked out in the dark. One rather sinister line, about someone trying their door-handle in the night and a bitten-off flower being found on the step, made me shiver.

Dear Bronnie laboriously finished her story, 'The autobiography of a wolf', and then the children were done. They went outside to amuse themselves in the fresh air and Lesley went to find tomatoes for tea. They would have tomatoes, bread and the rock buns I'd brought back with me.

It was rash of me, but I felt I had to try to push against Elinor's coolness towards me. She seemed unwell. I had an idea it might be something personal, a sexual or bodily thing. I was always able to talk frankly about such things; in fact I gave talks to Bedales' parents on the importance of frankness to children on sexual matters, and had an article published in the Women's Liberal Foundation newsletter. I'd given a lecture to the suffragists. Even so, with Elinor I sensed I must be cautious.

'Elinor, please forgive me for asking,' I said, 'but are you unwell?'

She looked at me as though she could not have heard aright.

'I sensed that you were not strong, and this week it has been worse. The day Myfanwy fell—'

'Helen, please, I am well enough and I find your questions intrusive. I don't care for them at all.'

'Oh I'm sorry – but Elinor, we are women, women who have children and husbands, with all that goes with it. I have a sister to talk to if—'

'I have a sister too.'

'Oh, I didn't know that. I'm glad. And do you talk to her?'

'I write to my sister, of course.' She stopped and had that sorrowing look of hers. 'My sister and I,' she said, 'have shared the same sorrow.'

What should I say? She was so enigmatic in manner. I must surely ask her what she meant. 'Sorrow?'

'A child who died. Two children in my case, though one, the last, scarcely lived. But our son, our first child, Elliott.'

'Oh no Elinor, I didn't know. The worst, the worst thing that can happen.'

'It was the worst, because it should not have happened. It could have been prevented. If we – if Robert – had only fetched the doctor sooner. He blamed us.'

'He? The doctor? Surely not.'

'Oh yes, he was quite clear about it. And he was right. We were to blame.'

'What age was the little boy?'

'Just four years old. He was a year older than Lesley – he would be a young man. I will never never—'

She began to cry, hard cough-like sobs shaking her tiny shoulders. My heart was full of pity and womanly sympathy for her. I tried to hug her gently and although she stiffened at once, perhaps she didn't quite push me away.

Nine

Edward took a train to London, saw first his agent and then the editor of the English Review. His proposal was accepted. He was to write a number of short articles for the Review on what ordinary people in the Midlands and the north were saying about the war.

Helen met him at Ledbury station. She could not read his expression. He detached himself from her, for she had thrown her arms round his neck.

'Well, it's agreed, I'm to go, and for a good sum, I believe. The only caveat is that I must avoid anything that might hinder recruitment, as if I should.' He told her the fee he would be paid. Helen gasped.

'Edwy, that's wonderful, more than we'd hoped, how clever of you to have negotiated so much. We'll be able to—'

'*We* won't be able to do anything. I will be paying some bills. And I will be enduring weeks of writing at something I would not have chosen.'

Helen, only a little dashed in spirits, talked of his coming home to Steep and how she would work at the garden and be ready for him.

Their plan – to stay until early September – had to be abandoned. Helen would not be sorry to go, Edward knew. She found the place both too isolated and yet too constricted in one room. Their lovemaking could not be as free and fulfilling as usual. And he was so occupied with Robert and at other times, no doubt, irritable.

He would not be sorry to leave Helen. It was tiresome to him, her cheerful optimism, her enthusiasm for everything concerning himself. Worse, his sorrow at his own behaviour, the knowledge that he could not control his irritability, unless he could escape her for a time. Then he felt her loneliness.

Elinor was no sort of companion for her, even though the two families intermingled every day. Such a pretty woman, so feminine in her neat little body with her nipped-in waist and flowing skirt. Edward sensed that she rather liked and admired him, but she did not warm to Helen. Helen was much too demonstrative for her, used to winning people round with her interest and eager friendship. Elinor resisted.

Edward once talked tentatively to Robert about Elinor's nature, but he was silenced at once. Anger flared in his friend's face and his fist clenched.

'She's mine, my wife. And I'll thank you not to talk about her or to think about her.' Edward was astonished; he thought of how freely he'd told Robert about his own unhappiness the previous year. He was troubled; had Robert been thinking ill of him, then, for these confidences about his marriage? Even before her arrival in Leddington he'd talked about Helen again. Months earlier, when they first became friends, he'd begun confiding in Robert, telling him of his despair, how he spent much of his time living away from home, believing he had to be alone to fulfil whatever ambition he had left. How he felt he had been trapped and burdened since his youth. He told him that on the day they had met for the first time in London, he had been near to suicide.

Robert had said that he understood well both the horror of depression and the vicissitudes of marriage, 'But for me what you do is unthinkable. I've never been away from Elinor, not once, without feeling unbearably lonely. She somehow – she manages my lonesomeness. We're always alone, but a wife makes it bearable for us. You're making yourself more unhappy this way. You have to realise that running away, walking out, is no good. Look, Edward, don't look for a peaceful life, or a happy one even. There will always be suffering, always conflicts, always love and hate. You can survive these things. And you'll survive them stronger than ever.'

Edward knew how close he'd sometimes been to not surviving, not even wanting to survive, and how he could be trapped in wretched absorption with his own misery. He told Robert he believed that love, as he remembered it, had left him forever.

'Love – for pity's sake, you're married, aren't you. Of course you love her! She is yours – that is all there is to say. Love is like a poem, it begins in delight and ends in wisdom. Look, what you need is to set your sights on a goal with the intense desire to accomplish something, come hell or high water.'

He came back to the same theme often, the need for a goal. 'It's no good simply getting by with what some damned publisher will pay you for.'

It was good advice perhaps, but impractical for Edward, a father at twenty-one, who had to take what work he could. Robert had an annuity to rely on. And Edward knew that in spite of the compulsion he was under he wrote well. He created works close to what he wanted to say and in the last few years in the voice he believed was right. And he'd made a respectable living with his writing. But to Robert that was not enough.

'And what you could accomplish – what you've already achieve if you would but see it – is poetry. I won't complain if you work some of this out in poetry.'

They would miss seeing the September cider pressing, but there was no help for it.

In the Oldfields orchard the cider apples were showing rosy red stripes against the yellow. Mary had told him that they flourished because of the wassailing each New Year day. Well, perhaps, but the effect of such a perfect summer must have helped. He thought of Shakespeare's Justice Shallow, those comical ramblings in a Gloucestershire orchard – that sense of an eternal rural England. Animated by cider, surely? Ah, a long drink of cool cider on a day like this; what could be more delicious?

He had come to tell Robert about his leaving, and knew what his reaction would be.

Robert and Elinor were together in the sitting room, but Elinor left them and went upstairs. Lesley was typing out a fair copy of The Bouquet on the sturdy Blickensderfer they'd brought from home. Edward admired her efforts.

'Lesley,' he said, 'if your Daddy has his way and I ever manage to write a verse you shall have it for the Bouquet. Then I'll be able to say I'm a published poet.'

'I'll hold you to that, Mr Thomas. We'll probably bring out another soon,' Lesley said.

'Mmmh, I'm afraid soon will be too soon then. Robert, listen. I am going to have to travel north to write those pieces for the English Review. Then I have the blessed Duke to research. After that who knows.'

'What! Sheer journalism, quite unworthy of you. Any fool could do it. Tell them you've changed your mind.'

'Not possible – we need the money! And as a matter of fact, Robert, I do feel interested in the question of what it means to people, ordinary people, being at war. I find myself remembering how we were at Oxford – news came of the relief of Mafeking and we students went quite mad with patriotic zeal. What that chiefly meant was that we all got very drunk and behaved very badly. These are different times, I think. So, now I do need to get back and do some repair work on my old Humber if it's to take me as far as Newcastle, with help from the railways of course. But we've several days left.'

'Well, I reckon it's just too bad. I feel let down. And what about Helen and the children? What will they do?'

'They'll take the train back to Steep. Helen makes some money taking in Bedales' boarders who have to come back early before their term starts. I expect she'll write today to offer it. But Robert, don't imagine you've seen the last of me. Leddington's a second home to me now. I'll be back before long, either at Mary Chandler's or up in your attic again, if you and Elinor will have me. And besides, we've these few days left – let's you and I walk tomorrow; there are places I must go, to say my good-byes. And I intend to drink my fill of Gloucestershire cider while I can.'

The lane to Dymock ran between more orchards full of ripe fruit, the early morning sun casting long shadows across it and into the fields that sloped towards the river. They passed the two neighbouring farmhouses, mellow brick-built buildings like Oldfields. Mirabels Farm must of course be named for the little purple plums. But why Swords? Names of things, of places. He wondered if it was connected with the moated ruin of a building they saw as they struck out down a field path. Wilfrid Gibson, who lived at the half-timbered cottage on the corner, would know, but he was away. They crossed the railway bridge and the river and passed his rather fine cottage, once a nail-maker's house.

'I guess when you're gone I'll see more of him again,' Robert said. 'He was my pal here, until you and I met up. And Abercrombie too. But never as good a pal as you, my dear friend.'

'I do like Abercrombie,' Edward said. 'And Catherine. But I'm afraid, because I dared to put in a word or two of reservation about his verse in a review, she's cross with me. It is an error common in wives. But it does no one a service to have nothing to say but praise. If I read such a review I assume the author is a close friend or relation and I've no faith in what's written at all.'

'I know. You even managed to find a couple of faults in *North of Boston*! But Catherine Abercrombie has a good heart – she'll forgive you. She'd forgive you anything, I do believe, for being—'

'Being what? What are you laughing at?'

'For being "the most beautiful person she has ever seen." That's what she said to Elinor! She said it was a shock, until you got used to it. What is it with you and the girls, Edward?'

'Oh Good Lord. Really? And what did Elinor say to that?'

'I darn well trust she didn't agree! Anyway, about Catherine – you know, it's possible we may stay with them when the fall comes. They say they have room. And our house is so damned cold when the wind whistles through from front to back. So when you come to stay again, that's where we should be, and may it be soon.'

They went on into Dymock. Robert admired the half-timbered houses, very like Little Iddens, lining the street. Beauchamp Green, with its row of lime trees leading up from the road to the lych gate, invited them to rest. They sat for a while under the silvered oak of the lych, looking down the valley. 'You should have seen it early last April,' Robert said. 'A torrent of little yellow daffodils tumbling down to the brook. Beautiful.'

Two gypsies came up to them, a young woman smoking a clay pipe, with a baby in her brown shawl, and a thin young man with a concertina. The woman asked for money for the baby, but they'd scarcely any money and what they had was for cider at the Beauchamp Arms. Seeing Edward with his pipe she asked if he could spare half a pipe of tobacco. He looked long at her and smiled. Her brown fingers dipped delicately into the leather pouch he held out to her as she gazed back at him. Then she laughed, waved and went away, gracefully swaying across the green with the baby on her hip.

'They remind me of gypsies I saw at a Christmas fair last year,' Edward said. 'The brother had the blackest, wildest eyes. He played a tambourine and stamped his feet. Then he took up his mouth organ and played "Over the hills and far away". Everyone at the fair drew round and watched. That wildness, coming into our humdrum lives! Later I was walking on in the darkest of nights, only a sliver of crescent moon. I felt as if I were a ghost wandering in the underworld, but the image of him stayed with me, the wild bright spark in his eyes, and the memory of the tune. Ah, gypsies – George Borrow, of course, knew them best – but since his time they're turned away from the verges, the No Man's Gardens. Poor tired horses and sleeping children driven out by some officious policeman.'

They talked about gypsies, Edward's enthusiasm for Borrow and whether gypsy characters could be found in America.

'I sense from what you say that your people and ours – our country people anyway, are quite different,' Edward said. 'The people in your poems too; they seem to me to be rather without tradition and they don't quite trust themselves or each other. They show a good deal of competition and suspicion, you must admit.'

'Sure, of course – how else could it be? Each man for himself and his family.'

'Well, up to a point. But in England I believe there's a sort of native wisdom binding people together. My old Dad Uzzell from Wiltshire, who taught me about country life and started me off on Jefferies; no-one was more trusting and good to his neighbours than he, but no fool, far from it. Without the Dad Uzzells around me I think I'd find the country a sterile place to be.'

Robert was baffled. 'You're a strange man, Edward,' he said. 'I used to think you were a real solitary, thriving on being separate, like me. But maybe I was wrong. Even though it doesn't come easily to you, you really want to be connected to other people in a way I just don't understand.'

The talk took them through their cider-drinking at the Beauchamp Arms. They poured it from a height of a foot into their tankards to aerate the golden liquid with its faint tinge of green. It tasted of late summer and of ripeness, smelled of apples, grass and honey.

Edward leaned back in his chair and stretched happily.

'Perfect! Ah, cider apples – but think, the centuries it took to arrive at this perfection. Those iron-age men in the Malverns would only have had crabs. Then by the time of Robert of Gloucester they'd got as far as apple-jacks, the same as those Falstaff ordered, you know. And today, this. Perfection. Did you know you shouldn't tap the new cider until you hear the first cuckoo of spring?'

They both emptied and refilled their tankards.

'Does this Beauchamp guy own everything around here?' Robert said. 'Surely looks like it. I know he owns Abercrombie's place. Abercrombie's sister got it for him. She has that sort of pedigree, by marriage anyway.'

'Well, the Beauchamps somehow managed to keep their land in spite of Cromwell. Truly landed gentry. They're welcome to it, though, don't you think. Don't envy them, Robert. I know I'll never own land and I don't want to, always troubling yourself about it, putting up petty notices, do this, don't do that. Keep out. The land is mine to enjoy without any of those troubles.'

They got up rather shakily and held on to each other laughing.

'We'd better sit back on that seat by the church for a while. No hurry,' Robert said. 'There's all the time there is.'

The road stretched pale and empty when they did start out for home in the dusk. A low pink-washed farmhouse crouching at the foot of a great elm tree gleamed palely, lamplight yellow in one window. Edward stood looking, then spoke quietly.

'When we were here in June they'd almost finished hay-making, do you remember? The scent of it on the road. The wagon nearly fully laden, standing in the shade of that yew, and the men taking a rest, leaning on their rakes; they and the horses utterly silent and still. It was as if they'd been there since the beginning of time and would be always the same, older than everything, even older than the farmhouse. Utterly timeless. Immortal.'

'You're full of good memories today, Edward.'

'I know I'll never forget this place, this summer. The way the sun has shone on us, on our walks and talks. It's made some ideas clearer to me, and I believe that's true for you too. You have a great gift for talking about poetry as well as for writing it, Robert. That's why I think you should write that book. And as for me, you've given me a sense of something – of possibilities – that I haven't had before. Ambition even.'

'That's what I want to hear. Ambition is good – I have it aplenty myself and it beats me how a man can live without it. Only I tell you again, the place to be ambitious is in America. Progress and adventure, not always looking back. That's why I'm pretty near ready to go home and I'm damned if you're not going to come with me!'

'We'll see. Robert, you know how I waver. I do want to, believe me, but the truth is I have to depend on uncertain things. But look, it's getting late, we'd better hurry on.'

'No hurry, it's great to walk in the dark. All the time there is,' Robert drawled.

This is such a human landscape, Edward thought; every quarter of a mile or so another cottage or farmhouse. And always the high elms and the Lombardy poplars, reaching up into the darkening sky and sheltering each house. They passed a cottage in the dusk, seeing a faint light from the small square window and a thin line of blue smoke against the leaves of its sheltering elms. No-one could see that cottage and not long for his own home, or dream that this cottage was his home, he thought.

The silver sliver of a new moon rose near the horizon.

Suddenly Edward stopped. He thought of France, of the soldiers there. He wondered how many of them would be seeing the same moon – or would they be too blinded to notice it? Blinded by smoke, excitement, pain, or terror? Vividly he pictured them, their eyes briefly glancing at the same moon that he was seeing from a safe and silent lane.

He stood still, gazing at the moon, while Robert walked ahead.

Something essential was missing, he realised, in all his love and admiration for English landscapes, these cottages, farms and trees, the country life. It seemed to him that he loved England in a foolish superficial way, only in terms of charm and aesthetics. As though he were just a detached observer. It was as if he hadn't acknowledged it as *his* country.

To acknowledge it, perhaps – did not that mean he should be willing to fight for his country? To do *something*, at least?

'What's halting you, Ed?' Robert called. Edward didn't hear him.

Would something have to be done, he thought, before he even had the right to look again with appreciation and composure at English landscape? At the elms and poplars around the houses, at the white campion flowers in the verges each side of the lane, the verges known as 'No Man's Garden'.

Ten

Half a kiss, half a tear

It was nearing the end of August and we Thomases would be leaving Leddington next day, just as harvest was over and before the apple and perry pear picking began. The air was still warm late into the evening, but darkness came earlier.

I watched from the window as Edward stood below in the orchard. He was leaning against an apple tree, filling his clay pipe. I could see that he was looking and listening, committing everything to memory. The night before we'd talked about the war, and Edward, always so insistent on his Welsh origins, told me again that he was finally becoming a true Englishman.

He looked away across the fields towards Little Iddens. I knew that he'd been as happy here as it was possible for him to be, but that the children and I played only a small part in his happiness. I'd rarely seen him so exhilarated, so sociable. And because he'd been happy, so sometimes had I. It was selfishness, I saw it now, to expect Edward not to take every possible chance to be with his friend while we were here. After all, that was why he had come.

Now I must go home without him; I was used to that but wished it could be otherwise. I knew that Edward already wanted to be solitary again, after so much company and such close confining with the children and me. His restlessness, his longing for new scenes and for solitude, was back.

Perhaps I would like to be alone, I thought. I grew tired of the children's company too, sometimes.

I sensed that something was about to change. It may have been because of the war, of course, but it was more than that. Edwy would perhaps start to try out this ability to write poetry that Robert saw in him. It needed the opinion of a man, and especially Robert, to convince him. Perhaps that would make him more contented, and that was all I wanted. But how could we live if he were to stop writing his country books and criticisms? I knew enough about poetry to know that one could not live by it alone.

I looked across at the roof of Little Iddens, thinking about the Frosts.

Robert had wanted Edward to stay longer, even if the children and I went home to Steep, and although we needed the money Edward would earn. Robert was not used to anyone defying him. And it was necessary for us to escape from the war by coming to America, he believed, as if he knew what we needed better than we did ourselves. But I knew that Steep was the right home for us, and I would do everything I could to help Edward feel that, when he came back from the north. And with Robert a hundred miles away he would surely be a lesser force.

And Elinor? How hard it was to know her. She was so utterly different from my idea of what a wife and mother should be. Such a hopeless cook! The whole summer it had been me who made sure the men were fed, and the children, whenever they spent the day at Little Iddens or when we went for picnics. As for Elinor and her potatoes! The way she sat, so upright on the grass, her skirt neatly tucked under her, but with her little hands fumbling a great muddy potato and a blunt knife. No bowl of water to work in! It was as if she'd never been shown how to manage her home, and that it was completely beneath her to try. And she was so wan, so cool in her manner. I suppose you could say she was imperturbable – certainly nothing disturbed her indifference to me! But I was sorry for Elinor – to lose a child, a four year-old, just Myfanwy's age. A real person, and a first-born, with his own loveable ways. And to be told that it could and should have been prevented. How could that be borne? Could the sight of Myfanwy be painful for her? It might be so and it might account for Elinor's coolness towards me.

Yet Elinor did have her four children. I ached to have another baby. But supporting three had almost broken Edward, as he told me often enough. If only he could be sure of a steady income he might agree to more children. He would complain that it

78

burdened him, that I had no wishes or desires of my own unconnected with him, but he was wrong – my longing for another baby, that was my own.

I had to start thinking about packing and about presents for the Frosts, and for Mrs Chandler too perhaps. Did you give your landlady a present? Perhaps the girls could make her a posy of wild flowers and grasses. But the Frosts? I'd have to think of something for them before the evening. Perhaps a cake, if Mary would let me use the kitchen. Oh, to be home again and have my own table and stove. What would Edward think about a present? I leaned out of the open window, wanting to call him. But I didn't call; I would wait until he was ready to come in.

Eleven

Edward knocked out his pipe on the apple-tree trunk and put it in his pocket. He would go and see Robert, who was still unsettled by his leaving. Helen would guess where he'd gone. They'd worn such a path between the two cottages during the past month that the dark red clay was pounded hard, a firm line drawn in the earth itself.

The remnant of a mist hung over the fields that morning. It was already turning from white to gold by the sun, and would soon be driven away, but it meant the beginning of autumn, the end of the season of clarity and sharpness and the beginning of what he always preferred, the fluidity of a changing season. Oats reaped the day before stood in stooks drying to pale gold, those furthest from him hazed in white. They were shaped like bivouac tents such as gypsies had and as he sometimes made on his travels. Ah, he would soon be gone, travelling again, on the road. Always going on, that need he had to be elsewhere. And yet at the same time he wanted to be settled, to go home, to be in one place and to be content with that.

At the cottage gate he noticed three fat walnuts lying between the cobbles of the yard. He would take them in as an offering.

Lesley and Marjorie were in the sitting room and he could hear Robert crashing about in the kitchen among the unwashed dishes from the night before.

'Morning Robert – am I too early? Sorry, you haven't eaten. Look – autumn is here.' He handed over the nuts.

Robert cracked an egg into a bowl of milk and whisked it with a fork. 'Thanks – good to see you. This is my breakfast today.' He cut a hunk of bread. 'Elinor's still sleeping. I was up late last night writing and she kept me company.'

Edward stood by the window and looked out at the rear

garden.

'Those plums are ripe, ready for picking. Look, they're perfect. A few more days and they will be oozing and the wasps will attack them.'

'Maybe Carol will pick them, he's our fruit man. Now tell me, if you really have to leave tomorrow, have you thought some more about New Hampshire rather than old Hampshire. It must mean something, don't you think, that coincidence. The new, not the old – whatdysay? It needn't be for too long, a year, a few months even and the war will be over. And I want you to see my country.'

Edward came to sit opposite him at the little table.

'I want to myself, but it's not easy, Robert. What would we live on? Where would we live? If it were just for me perhaps, but for Helen and the children – and then, England is where I live. England, and Wales – they are what makes me what I am. You know my writing, my subjects.'

'Your subject is the natural world and yourself in it, Edward. You would find that wherever you travelled, in New Hampshire as much as in Gloucestershire. And I've told you about my summer school plan.'

Edward shook his head. 'No, there's much more to it than that.'

Robert thumped his fist on the table. 'Always no from you! No, I'm condemned to a life of hack work. No, I can never be happy tied to a wife and children, and Helen such a fine wife for a man like you. No, I couldn't leave England and try my luck in New Hampshire, even with the best and closest pal I ever had to give me a hand. And no, I can't write poetry to save my life, never wrote a line of it, when you've been writing poetry always and couldn't see it.'

Edward frowned, then laughed. 'I think you've bullied me into seeing that you may be right about that last at least. I was in a way ahead of you there. I'd begun to have a presentiment of it myself and made a few attempts a year or so ago, but you can have the credit, should there be any. As for the rest – you know I'm trying to stop glooming around where Helen and the children are concerned and I'm better for it. I thank you for that. But to leave England; I would have to go on my own first, to look for a place and some work. I'd feel I was abandoning them, with this damned war starting. I can't do it, Robert, you must see that.'

'On the contrary, the war is the best reason for leaving. Who will publish your kind of work now over here? Literary criticism, country rambling? And then, there's your boy. What is he, fourteen? I guess you think this war won't last more than a few months, but that's what they said about our war and it lasted five long years. It's what they always say.'

'Merfyn caught up in it? That would move Helen more than anything, and me too. But you know, I've been thinking about my own position. I do *believe* in England and Englishness. What does that mean if I'm prepared to abandon her? Look Robert, I'll think about it, I'll talk to Helen. Now, can we please just go for a walk, and look, look at the summer ending, let me hold it all in my head, in peace. Shall we take our old path to the stream, or head for the woods? Which would be best, I wonder?'

'Why Edward, I know full well that whichever road we take you'll fret and sigh at what we missed on the other, so it won't make any difference! Let's just get going!'

Their last night with the Frosts in the orchard at Little Iddens; Robert roasted potatoes in the bonfire and they drank cider – not too much, because the Chandler's cider was mighty strong. And they sang, Edward especially, so much that his throat was raw from it.

Next day the Thomases were up at dawn.

Again a mist hung over their field like milk and there were touches of yellow in the plum trees leaves. Edward resolved to have a good parting from Helen and the children. He was ready for this new venture; perhaps he would discover what he himself felt about the war by listening to other people. Since the evening of seeing that new moon he had found that he could not stop thinking about soldiers and about England as though they were connected with him, not as something apart. He had that sense that he must do something, but what that was he did not know.

He oiled the Humber and loaded up its pannier bags. By the evening he would reach Coventry. It was a commission, and with work suddenly so precarious he had no choice. He would strive to do it well; perhaps even that would be a contribution of some kind. Then he would be ready to go home to his hilltop study at Steep and possibly try to write poetry.

Book Two

One

Birmingham. From New Street station Edward pushed his bicycle along the narrow terraced streets. Hot, hard unforgiving pavements underfoot; he was a man for green roads, footpaths, barely trodden tracks through the woods. After a month of seeing nothing but the gentle hills, lanes and streams of Gloucestershire he felt uneasy and he looked out of place in his loose tweed trousers and linen jacket.

The scale of Victoria Square with its towering municipal buildings diminished the few people crossing it. A few black motorcars glittered among the horse-drawn traps and hand-carts. The new statue of the old queen glared white and stark. He wondered where he should go, how he should begin finding people.

He took Paradise Street because of the name, but soon he was in the din of iron-works, their high gates proclaiming the name of each business. It was six o'clock. Factory hooters blared and soon the people found him; out they came in hundreds, chiefly men and boys, small statured in open shirts and dark worn jackets. A few head-scarfed women, sallow or pale, walked close together.

He stood on the edge of things and listened. People glanced at him in his old tweeds and cycle clips and then ignored him. He followed some men into a public house and listened there, even managed to talk a little. The ale was good and the weather hot, there was a thirst for talk as well as drink, and the pubs were thriving.

He rode along another street at random. It seemed a harsh city, worse than London. There when he was growing up he inhabited parks and commons whenever he could, living like a country boy in his imagination. Here he could find no green park or even an unused space other than the dirty towpaths of the black canals. One small brick street led to another identical to it. It was a relief to find a cemetery. He could sit down on some grass at least and rest for a while before facing the streets again and finding lodging.

Everywhere were the posters. He'd had no idea what was really happening but here it was unignorable: the Government was desperate for recruits. Billboards were covered in official notices and even cinema newsreel posters and music-hall bills reflected the war. One of them drew his attention, and he asked a man standing near about it.

'What, haven't you heard of Edna Thornton's song?' he exclaimed. 'Goes like this:

We don't want to lose you but we think you ought to go,
For your king and your country both need you so.'

He stared at the posters, bemused:
'Women of Britain say – GO'. A mother and sister, pointing gracefully.

'There's room for you! Enlist Today!' This with a picture of a truck-load of cheerful youths having the time of their lives. War as an adventure, a great game, and one that took you overseas too.

A frowning young woman, with the words *'Girls! Is your "best boy" in khaki? If he doesn't think you and his country are worth fighting for, is he worth much?'*

Shiny new posters of Kitchener: a powerful, clever image – those eyes, and the finger pointing at you wherever you went. 'Your Country Needs YOU'.

Next day he took a street past the noxious gas works to Aston Park; he watched thousands of young men pouring out of a football match without giving the posters near the gate a glance. What were *they* thinking about the war and their place in it? *'Is it football still and the picture show?'* He was thinking of Begbie's poem, Fall In, which he'd read in the Chronicle the week before. Now everyone was quoting it. He and Robert had groaned as they read the shameless appeal to shame itself. He'd cut it out with a critical article in mind.

Where will you look, sonny, where will you look,
When your children yet to be
Clamour to learn of the part you took
In the War that kept men free?

Why do they call, sonny, why do they call
For men who are brave and strong?
Is it naught to you if your country fall,
And Right is smashed by Wrong?

Is it football still and the picture show,
The pub and the betting odds,
When your brothers stand to the tyrant's blow
And Britain's call is God's.

He merged with the crowd although crowds alarmed him; the match was their theme, but then the war was mentioned – as a joke. An iron barrel fell from a cart with a deafening clang of metal onto the stone of the kerb.

'Watch out, the Germans are coming!' someone shouted. They laughed. He laughed with them, but he sensed that there was some awkwardness as if laughter concealed a moment of fear.

In the public houses he got into conversation easily enough after a few ales, just as he had with country people he met in the South. More easily, in fact; people needed to talk.

'What you find is that the young unmarried lads are getting the push, to drive them to enlist.'

'Of course them motorcar-workers are on short time. Be looking to start on things for the Army I reckon.'

'I know who's doing very nicely thank you – the harness and the boot-makers.'

'And the explosive makers. The luxury trades, though, they're folding. It's a shame, the jewellery industry, Birmingham's pride.'

'And them who relied on trade with Germany are having to think again. Serves 'em right, I say.'

'Of course, for a poor lad, to get into the Army is to better himself, but for the respectable working man it's not. How can he be sure he'll get his job back? He's got a family to take care of.'

He went back to Aston Park on Sunday, finding the place thronged with people. Crowds encircled men on soap-boxes; it was a kind of Birmingham Speakers' Corner. His notebook was rapidly filling so he endured the crowd.

A socialist was shouting that the working-class were making fifty times the sacrifice of the rest, but he had no support from the crowd. Another man was cheered when he said they must sink class feeling, fight together, and cease all quarrelling. 'Unity and Scorn' were the watchwords.

A thin sneering man despised especially the middle class clerks and the like – 'neither men nor girls', who stayed at home thinking about their socks while the toffs and the working men did their duty. He had some support, but not much. The mood was much more for unity. Someone said that the Irish had responded manfully and that the war seemed to be binding people together.

They were sober and moderate in their language, philosophical in their position that the war had to be seen through to the end – until the Kaiser was mentioned. If they got hold of him they'd choke him with his own balls. That Kaiser must be mad to declare war on every nation. Some blamed the generals too, German and English, for rushing into war before any negotiation could be tried. They had not wanted a war and they were glad that England was not responsible for it.

As for the soldiers, the English in contrast to the Germans were good-hearted and rather casual about things, not ruthlessly and unnaturally organised. And the German politicians – a lying, treacherous, barbaric lot, a rotten lot.

In the Coventry Tavern he brought up the question of joining up and what it meant to 'fight for your country'. An awkward silence followed; no-one wanted to talk, but when they did it was to mutter phrases they'd read on the posters. Edward wished he had not asked. He found he was as discomforted by that question as his companions. These were an older crowd, his own age in the main, family men.

On his last day he saw some recruits, lean pale young men in their dark clothes and caps, with occasionally the tanned face of a farm worker among them. Why had they enlisted – because of the posters, urging them to fight for King and country? Under pressure from employers? From girl-friends? Or to follow their friends?

He had a sense that a man joined up for inexplicable reasons, making a leap beyond rational thought. Then afterwards he would explain himself to his parents and friends in the old conventional terms about fighting for king and country – but surely that was simply too poetical and too self-conscious to be real?

Enough of Birmingham. He took the train, stowing the Humber in the guard van, and travelled north to Manchester, then a day later to Sheffield and on towards Newcastle. He was happy on the train, watching the rocky coast north of Hartlepool, little steep valleys cutting through, and the great innocent-looking sea, blue-green and empty of ships. Train journeys were a great part of his life, a good part; brief stops at unexpected places you may never see again, a moment out of time that could contain something everlasting, a rapturous moment, always remembered.

Newcastle. Strange for him to be so thrilled by the sight of a city, but this city was beautiful. In Grey Street he thought of Hazlitt's words – you expected a coalhole and found a city of palaces. He stood at night looking down at the shining black river, the High Level Bridge far below, the Swing Bridge opening to let the steam tugs come home. The lamps were lit and the glitter of their reflections all along the quays was entrancing.

Of course, he thought, this is England too, as much as the quiet woodlands and lanes of his own corner. For some this city was home and was rightly loved. That was the meaning of England – the corner that was home, and then a whole set of concentric circles widening out from that. This *was* how people loved England, because without England, the whole of England, their particular corner could not exist.

The night sky and the moon, which was almost full, reminded him of the moment when he saw it new in Gloucestershire and thought of soldiers in France. Back at his lodging he opened a new notebook and wrote about that moment and the sudden conviction that followed:

'All I can tell is, it seemed to me that either I had never loved England, or I had loved it foolishly, aesthetically. Something, I thought, had to be done before I could look composedly again at English landscape, at the elms and poplars about the houses, at the purple-headed wood-betony with two pairs of leaves on a stiff stem, who stood sentinel among the grasses or bracken by hedge-side or woods-edge. What he stood sentinel for I did not know, any more than what I had to do.'

Two

Half a kiss, half a tear

We took a cab home from the station as it was far too hot to walk with the luggage. Merfyn wasn't with us as he was cycling back.

We were home! Up the long path to our front gate, tendrils of goose-grass catching at my skirt, leaving little burrs trapped in the threads. How could everything have grown so much in our three weeks absence? It is as if simply being there, strolling round a garden, patrols it and makes it keep order. As soon as it's left to its own devices, Nature gleefully seizes her chance to show what she can do.

The grass was knee-high, the damson bushes more straggly than ever and bending with deep purple fruit. On the cottage wall our trained William pear had broken away from its fastenings with the weight. The luscious smell of ripe pear was in the air so they must be picked at once. The vegetables had taken care of themselves – masses of runner beans, and the carrots' tall fronds looked very promising. The last of our lettuces were bolted though and the vegetable marrows were almost as big as Myfanwy. I was going to be busy.

Bronwen was excited to be home and as I unlocked the door, pushing it against the swishing heap of post on the mat, she squeezed by and ran through the whole house. Then she was out into the garden again to check her own little flower patch. I was happy to think of the pleasure of putting the garden to rights, the thought of autumn coming and Edward coming home soon. Rags ran a little circle of glee to show that he was glad to be home too.

'Bronnie – look at the garden! Do you remember it last summer when we moved in – just weeds, weeds, weeds?'

'Except for the yew tree and the damsons,' Bronwen reminded me.

We'd moved down to Yew Tree Cottage the summer before. Now I could hardly imagine us being high up at the big Wick Green house, looking out over the South Downs – when there was not too much mist, that is. Myfanwy would have forgotten it, the house where she was born, if Edwy hadn't kept on his study up there.

He was never happy in that house, even though it was built specially for us. We were tenants of course, but at first I was as proud as if it were our own house and I did all I could to make it our home. But it was a strangely inhospitable place. And the wind! You would not have believed the difference in the wind on the hill and the gentle winds down in the village. That made it expensive to heat; and then our rent was increased. We simply couldn't afford to stay.

Yew Tree Cottage was quite different, just a newly-built semi-detached workman's cottage in Steep, without much character and less charm, until we made it home. Its good feature was that it was set back from the road between the other pairs, peeping out down the long path between them like a shy child hiding behind its parents' legs. We had gardens on three sides and at the back of the house was the openness of a meadow and the hill with its beech hangers.

The six cottages had no bathrooms, yet the rent was more than a working villager would be prepared to pay. It was cheaper than Wick Green, though, and better for the children, because Bedales was close by and they could join in more school activities. When we moved in, I'd hoped for so much. I always did when we moved house, hoping above all that Edward would be happier.

He kept on his Wick Green study for a rent of only a shilling a week. It was separate from the house, a long low building called the Bee House, perched at the steepest point of the hanger on Cockshott Lane with a grand view down the hill towards Steep. So if I stood in our garden and waved a linen-cloth Edward could see me when the trees were bare. Or I would walk up to the start of the hanger and call 'Coo-ee' for him to come for his lunch.

Up in the study he had a fire, a desk and chair and his books and papers. He would have breakfast and then set off up the hill, coming home at noon. Then he would work in the garden, or walk until tea-time. Sometimes he went up to his study again until supper at half-past eight, or would read through at home what he'd been writing.

Yew Tree cottage pleased me, even though it was so small, and I worked to make it a real home. The kitchen was simply a corner in the living room; there was a tiny back room and three small bedrooms – that was all. We bathed in a tin bath in front of the big fireplace. But I loved the built-in dresser in the kitchen, and my solid kitchen table, which had moved from one home to another with us. Edwy had given me a decorated cottage tea-set to hang on the dresser, white earthenware, with a wreath of flowers and leaves in red, blue and green.

An ancient yew tree stood in the garden, leaning over the gate. The six cottages were built on the plot of an old house that had been demolished. The garden, worked for centuries, was fine and fertile once we had cleared the building rubble, the soil a beautiful rich brown crumb, not white and stony and dry as it was up at Wick Green.

Edward and I gardened together, mostly growing vegetables. He found so much satisfaction in digging and seed-sowing. We wasted nothing, preserving our vegetables and fruits as if our lives depended on it. But we had some flowers for their beauty and climbing plants that we brought home from the wild to clamber up the straggly hedges.

By the front door the grey-green bush of Old Man grew, and the other herbs we brought from cuttings whenever we moved house, lavender and rosemary. We hid the harsh pebble-dash walls with trained fruit.

Edward built a porch around the front door and it was soon covered in jasmine. It had a seat on either side where we could sit talking in the evenings, listening for the calls of our own blackbird and thrush. Just once a nightingale spent a few nights singing to us from the damson hedge, first on one long rising note, then with a stream of round, liquid notes, so wild and pure. Oh, to think of it – we could be so happy together, we really could.

Our closest neighbours, the Dodds, had a little boy of Myfanwy's age. They were village people who could just afford the rent by taking in a lodger. We had a gate in the fence and Tommy and Myfanwy went to and fro between our houses all day. The Dodds were good people. Life was hard to them and yet they were full of humour and tolerance. They had time to talk and they were generous. Our other neighbours too were good people, some workers, some more like ourselves, poor gentlefolk.

The truth is that we were poor again ourselves, after a few years when Edward had earned well. His friends had persuaded him to apply for a Literature Society grant to eke out his earnings, because he had struggled to manage any work the year before, being so wretchedly low and unhappy. That hundred pounds made a little difference. But nonetheless we had moved from our grand house, not really because of the wind and mist up at Wick Green, but to save money.

Our acquaintances in the neighbourhood were mostly Bedales teachers. I had given talks at the school to parents and staff about sexual matters and the need to be frank with children about them. I suppose I'd always been quite advanced and enthusiastic about the sexual relationship. My own mother was a dreadful example – my innocent first query was met with a grim, 'All men are beasts, including your father.'

My father, who I adored! I never quite trusted my mother after that. But I wasn't a bit influenced by this and Edwy and I – well, our lovemaking was heavenly from the beginning, but we were both ignorant. I was against marrying; it was our friends who persuaded us that with a child coming we must. Then I came to believe in marriage after all. Some women suffragists I knew – I was a member of the local branch – were opposed to marriage. It was clear to me that they had simply not found love. Of course the war had put all the suffrage drive aside; Votes for Women would have to wait.

To think of Edward in the north of England, a simple journalist! The war had begun to change our lives a little. Imagine – when I'd left Steep there was no news of it. I would soon hear what my neighbours in the village were making of the war. Mrs Dodds next door saw us coming up the path and waved cheerfully. I had a feeling that for us country people life would go on very much the same and that was what I wanted.

Leddington began to feel far away, merely an episode in our lives and one that I had not altogether enjoyed. It was over for me and I was glad to be home. But as long as Robert was there, I knew that Edward would be drawn back to Gloucestershire again. And when the Frosts did go home to America, what then?

Three

Eleanor Farjeon was in the library of her home in Hampstead. It was a long room on the first floor with tall sash windows on two sides. She sat at her father's old desk, now hers, working on a sonnet. Edward was its subject, Edward and love. She propped her head on her hand above the green leather of the desk, pushed her glasses back more firmly on her nose, thinking of him. But then wherever she was she was always thinking of him. When she woke in the morning, as she breakfasted with her mother. As she worked on her stories thoughts of him with his children would intrude and as she closed her eyes to go to sleep she thought, finally, of him sleeping too.

Her arms and hands were a little tanned from her few days in Leddington, but the wide hat she'd worn protected her face and her wiry brown hair from the sun. She thought of the one walk she'd been able to have alone with Edward. She thought of Helen and the Thomas children and of the Frosts too. What did Robert and Elinor make of her friendship with Edward?

Perhaps she couldn't work on the sonnet, with so many vivid impressions in her mind; she would go and talk to Bertie. She'd hardly seen her brother since he'd enlisted a few days earlier, while she was away. He would be up in his room.

She tapped on his door.

'Nellie, come in. Tell me about rural life in Gloucestershire. How were Edward and the charismatic Mr Frost? Is he as fascinating as Edward says?'

'I suppose he is. I'll tell you in a moment. But Bertie, what about you? Surely you're not well enough to fight. Really, why have you enlisted?' But she knew why from his letters; it was his unhappiness over a woman, the woman he adored who was engaged to marry someone else.

Bertie looked at her.

'I simply want to get away to France now. Oh Nellie, Nellie, what an utterly hopeless pair we are. How do we bear it?' They hugged each other until Eleanor broke away.

'This won't do, Bertie. Let me answer your question about Robert Frost. I liked him. I suppose our American side responds well to other Americans, but I really liked him. Very direct and shrewd and a great talker, with his own ideas rather than from books. He's done all kinds of jobs, but as he says, "When a man has learned to make a metaphor he is unfitted for other kinds of work."'

'Ha – I like that.'

'And he is really good for Edward. It's wonderful to see them together, they enjoy each other's company so much. Edward told me that Robert is the only person he can be idle with. As for his wife Elinor – I don't know. Certainly not a homemaker, and not robust. Clever, and interesting, though, but reserved. The only boy, Carol, I liked. Very intense and absorbed in what he was doing.'

'And Edward and Helen?'

'Oh Bertie – you can imagine. Do you know, Edward said, "My wife could be the happiest woman on earth, and I won't let her." It's so true. He spent most of his time with Robert, and Helen was – well, she was worried about Baba when I was there. She had a nasty fall at the Frosts. I preferred being with the Frost children really, and I don't suppose Helen liked that. It's as though she's a little on edge when the Frosts are there, a little jealous of Robert but trying not to be. She agreed with me that Robert was good for Edward, that she had rarely seen him enjoy anyone's company so much or feel himself understood so well. I had a few walks with Edward and Robert myself, listening to them mostly. Especially to Robert.

'And we had one hilarious evening, all of us, and the Abercrombies and the Gibsons. My landlady invited them for supper, on my account I suppose. It was kind of her, but she was so determined to be genteel and her husband so determined to be himself. So, between the two of them – well, you can picture it. It made us quite hysterical. And I was used to Mr Farmer's cider but they weren't. Frankly, I drank them under the table – all the poets in Gloucestershire. I'll tell you the full story one day.'

'Good for you, Nellie. But come on, how are you, really?'

'Bertie – I was with him, that was enough. He was as friendly as ever and I was as useful and companionable to him as I always am. He counts on me for friendship. There isn't any more to be said.'

He saw his sister's eyes, magnified behind her glasses, swimming with tears and he put his arm around her shoulders. She gave a desperate laugh.

'Oh Bertie, you're right – what a pair we are. And have *you* really given up all hope of Joan?'

'I have. It's over.'

Eleanor was thirty-three, but she felt as though she had not long emerged from childhood. It was one of those strange inward-looking childhoods, full of books, writing and mystical games, rather like the Brontes, though she herself had only brothers. She had never been to school and was shy, naïve – and virginal. When she'd met Edward almost two years before, she was overwhelmed by him. So beautiful – his face, and his voice. And his mind, she felt sure.

'He was so kind to me,' she'd said to her brother. 'He asked to see some of my writing. Do you think he meant it?'

'I'm sure Edward doesn't say anything unless he means it.'

So she wrote him a friendly note, rather a witty one, and he replied in the same vein. After that they wrote and met often. She knew that he was habitually melancholic – after all, their circle of friends thought of him as 'The Patient' by reputation before they knew him. They'd been quite cross at the way this mysterious 'patient' absorbed the time of their doctor friend, Godwin Baynes.

She fell in love and she continued to love him when that first 'in love' phase passed. He knew, of course, but she sensed that she must never speak about her love for him. Bertie and a few close friends knew – and her mother, who was dismayed and disapproving.

On the first occasion that she went to visit the Thomases at Steep, Helen realised it at once. Seeing that Eleanor loved her husband, her response, her strategy perhaps, was to make sure that she became Eleanor's loving friend too.

Four

He was glad to be home. September, and the beech leaves beginning to turn yellow-green. Those autumn scents: leaves, bonfires, fruit and something more – the earth itself, an indefinable scent a little like mushrooms but fresher.

He climbed the stile in their back hedge and started up towards his study. It was a bright morning with a few scudding clouds. He crossed the rising meadow of Island Farm, hard and whitened with chalk dust after the hot summer.

The sunken lane alongside Ludcombe ponds was green and cool, though the brook was low. Harts-tongue ferns flourished on the lane's high banks. At the foot of the hanger he looked up at the climb that he always enjoyed, the path through the wood forking by the ruins of a woodman's cottage. To each side were mosses, emerald and olive, together with dark ivy, covering the ground below the beeches. It was where Myfanwy liked to collect tiny pieces of broken china with their blue-and white flowers hidden among the moss.

He stopped to look down before he went into the study. There was Steep village and the cottage far below, and nearer the beeches dashed with pale whitebeams and dark yews. So different from Leddington, where the fields were gentle and rolling, where you were always among cultivated land, orchards and wheat fields. Here you were up in the air, in the sky. Only at May Hill, that strange anomaly, had he had a sense of the beautiful curve a steep hill makes against the sky.

The earth here lay lightly over the chalk with a nut-coloured brown gleam to it and a complexity that he loved. Even when it was muddy there was such a blend of leaves, twigs, creamy earth, earth the colour of a woman's light-brown hair.

But to work: his new-moon piece, as he thought of it, must be revised and polished. It had been a private note to himself, but he had decided to include it in an article – why, he was not sure, it was as if it was decided for him.

Then he had to make a worthwhile article out of what he had collected on his northern expedition. The contract was negotiated well by young Cazenove's agency. How wise he was to have an agent, even if the work he was offered wasn't always what he would have wanted. Three articles for the English Review in all, twenty-five pounds for five thousand words. Including expenses. It would do. He remembered that Cazenove himself was not in his agency any more. He had enlisted. Wherever he is, Edward thought, I wish him well.

It was a question of getting all the material into some sort of order. He wanted to write in a style that spoke directly to his reader. He would simply show England and the English as they were, not sentimentally, and not introspectively. In later articles, he thought, he could probably be more subjective, closer to his own intimate style that Robert had seen in *Pursuit of Spring*. Then he would be more personal, exploring what England meant to him.

So he worked, his brown hand crossing and re-crossing the page.

Hours later, stiff, his eyes tired, he got up and stretched his long frame and flexed his aching fingers. Well, he was back with his nose to the grindstone again. He looked through the study window and down Shoulder of Mutton Hill, just wanting to walk outdoors in the September sunshine. But Helen would be expecting him home for lunch.

When this was done he must travel again; it was too long since he'd been to Wales, to see his cousins, and Gwili at Amanford and other Swansea friends. And for the last article he needed to find more material, a wider sweep.

He had a thought, too, half-formed: perhaps he *could* try writing a poem. But that would have to wait.

Early in October he set out. As the train came into Swansea at dusk he saw the hills black and velvety, the lights of the city crystalline among the blackness. He wrote to Helen about some gypsies he saw by the roadside. He enjoyed the sight of them, their gramophone and their hooped and lighted tent so near the wind and stars. But again came the critical thought – that this purely aesthetic pleasure he took in the mere sight of things was not enough, or was wrong.

It was the same in the mountains next day. He should know more about the lives of those he met – the shepherds and stone-quarrymen. Even that black-suited white-collared minister. Something had changed him and he could not turn back.

He hoped for a letter from Robert asking him to stay with them on his way home. He could spend some time in Gloucestershire collecting material for an article about country people's attitude to the war, and spend more time with Robert while he could.

But Elinor was not well, Robert wrote. Then an invitation did come from Elinor herself. The Frosts had moved out of Little Iddens as they had planned, and as the Abercrombies were often away from home; there was room for him at The Gallows.

So, he thought, as he strode up the rise to where he could see the cottages, Elinor is at last living under thatch. That was her dream when a toss of a coin decided them on coming to England. Two cottages were joined at right-angles and the smallest of them was thatched. From its chimney smoke was blown along its low decorated roof ridge.

He saw that the seven tall elm trees surrounding the garden had lost most of their leaves and the blustering wind was threatening the last. Yellow-brown sunflowers and a few late dahlias were left in the garden. He wondered how the Frosts were managing there, with that most primitive bathroom, simply a curtained-off shed, with water coming from an iron-handled pump in the yard. Cold lurked behind the sunlight; it was only his fast walking which kept it at bay. Catherine Abercrombie was a great deal stronger and bolder than Elinor was.

He climbed the steep steps from the lane and rapped with his holly staff on the studded door. In a moment Robert threw it open and flung his arm round Edward's shoulder, drawing him in. 'Ellie,' he called up the stairs, 'he's here. Why, am I happy to see you!'

He took Edward into the sitting room. Their part of the cottage could be kept warm by keeping plenty of wood burning in the fireplace and the Abercrombie's study-cum-sitting-room was neat and attractive; some easy chairs, a worn sofa, a piano, a desk and a wall full of books. It was much better than the Little Iddens bare room; their move was a wise one. He sat and stretched his long tired legs with pleasure. Robert was flushed and talkative.

'Do you know, Ed, it's exactly a year ago that we met, in London. But I feel I've known you all my life – you're the nearest thing to a brother I'll ever know.'

'I have a superfluity of brothers, so I won't join you in that sentiment, but – well, I'm really glad to be here and see you again. And you, Elinor.'

He'd stood up as Elinor came in smiling; they shook hands, hers feeling cold and frail in his. He could see that neither was well and that Elinor as well as Robert was very glad that he had come.

'How are you, Elinor?'

'Oh, I do fairly enough. We like this place fine. But I'm teaching the children again, now that summer is past, so they're indoors more and that tires me out. Lesley is a help, but still – the truth is, I'm more than ready for us to go home.'

He soon saw that she was always tired, depending on a continual flow of coffee from the enamel pot on the stove to keep her going. The children, who were visiting a nearby farm to buy bread, came in soon after he arrived. The three young ones were lively enough and wanted to tell him what they were doing and show him the completed Bouquet. Lesley had become absolutely a young woman and Edward treated her as one.

The children talked about going home much more than they had – Carol especially said that he had had enough of England and wished they could go back to their old farm in Derry.

'We all wish that,' said Elinor, 'but it can never be.' Robert had sold the farm to pay for their passage and their stay in England.

At supper Robert complained of having no appetite. The noise of the wind in the seven elms in the Gallows' garden troubled him, he said. Wind always made him restless and dissatisfied; he felt that the trees had more to say than he had, he told Edward.

'Why do we always want them so near our houses, I ask myself. I always seem to be listening now to those damned trees, or watching them swaying in the wind till I feel as if I'm rooted to the ground and can never move on.'

Elinor seemed too lethargic to be anything but indifferent to Robert's health. Without the summer vegetables they had at Little Iddens they lived more poorly than ever. Bread, potatoes, eggs and dreadful cheap 'raspberry' jam – which Edward thought contained almost nothing but apple, red colouring and wood-chips – formed their diet.

Well, at least Elinor certainly isn't 'on at' Robert all the time, he thought. That was Robert's expression. Not like Helen, so insistently loving, as if whatever he did concerned her and was her greatest interest. But would he really want such apparent indifference?

He wondered whether he ought to have come, as he was warned that Elinor was unwell. Why had he been so eager for an invitation? An uncomfortable sense, a familiar one, came to him: Was Robert more important to him than he was to Robert? Although he was more able to be himself with Robert than with anyone else, he was aware that he always wanted to impress him. He knew that when they were apart, he wrote perhaps five letters to Robert's one. But no, that was just the difference in them, he being too punctilious.

He thought it best to go out early next day to Leddington to call on Mary Chandler. He walked through a dense mist lying over the valley of the Leadon and along the lane, so that his path was altered yet familiar – just visible were blackberries, bracken turning amber and heavy rain-clouds gathering.

She was in the kitchen as usual. She waved and smiled through the window and gestured to him to let himself in as her hands were covered in flour. He thought she looked thinner.

'Tom's doing real well – promoted already. I'm not too worried about him, even if he does go out. He can look after himself, I know that. He's been home just one day, and I must say I could see he wasn't sorry to be off. Well, that's soldiers for you.'

'And are you managing all right, with the farm?'

'It was right hard straight after you and the family left – the harvesting – such a crop as never was and only me and a few casuals to pick and pack it. But my sister came over from Hereford and we got it done somehow. I'm tired out now, I won't say otherwise. It's the same for everyone, so many men away, it's hard to get things done that must be done. But how is Mrs Thomas – and the children? Little Myfanwy – what a little sweetheart!'

Next he called on Mr and Mrs Farmer, the fruit-growers and cider-makers in the neighbouring farmhouse where Eleanor had stayed when she visited them. They and their neighbours thought that the Forest, the Forest of Dean nearby, would be attacked by planes to destroy the pits. Mrs Farmer had strong views about the Kaiser.

'That Kaiser's ambition is to eat his Christmas dinner in London,' she said. 'But we had those German guests, didn't we, father, the year before? They were such nice polite people...' They didn't believe stories of atrocities, and they both thought, 'the Americans will come to our rescue if by any chance we looked like being beaten.' They'd had very nice American guests in the past too.

When he mentioned that in a battle recently thousands of German soldiers were lost, she said, 'God bless every mother's son of them.'

Their two elderly labourers were in the yard, and Edward asked them how they thought the war was going and what people in the village were saying. They were glad to shelter from the rain in the open barn and talk. He found that country people abused the Germans even less than in the cities. They were disinclined to believe the stories of mutilation – of children thrown in the air and stuck on bayonets, of women having their hands cut off.

About the end result of the war, they were stoical but optimistic.

'All the other nations are coming in – Canada, India,' one said. 'They won't let England be beat. Oh no, sir, England will win, you'll see. Oh yes.'

Everyone seemed to have grasped the idea that this war concerned the whole world; they talked quite familiarly of places they would never have heard of two months before – Kandahar, China. And of France as casually as if it was the next county.

Five

It was November and his second visit to the Frosts at The Gallows. Robert was warmly friendly and welcoming, but he and Elinor continued to be far from well and Edward would rise early to light the fires for them and chop more logs. Then he would walk for a time alone.

'Right, Edward, I feel up to a walk if you do after trekking about in the rain.' Robert said. Edward loved rain – heavy rain or light showers, rain's cleansing power, the sight of it foaming down the lane sides. He'd come back to the Frosts invigorated and happy. The rain ceased at about three.

'But you must forgive me, Ed, if I'm inclined to be irritable. I'm just none too good at present – that damn wind! And the mud. Your darned mud and rain! What a climate! Three days without rain in this country and they declare a drought.'

Lord Beauchamp, the Abercrombie's landlord, owned the ancient woods of Ryton Firs where Robert had planned their walk. The afternoon was bright but clouds built to the south and they sensed that more rain was not far off. At least the wind was quieter away from the exposed elms.

Those few miles distance from Leddington meant a surprising change in the landscape. The soil was an even deeper red – it was known as Redmarley country. It was stony and the fields were rougher and steeper. Instead of orchards, sheep grazed on short-turfed hill-sides, while the valley slopes between were deeply covered with dense beech and oak. The paths through them were lined with the spent stalks of foxgloves and with brambles turning crimson. They turned into Ryton wood where larches waved overhead, murmuring like the sea and showering them with raindrops.

Edward had told Robert about his northern tour. He was still enthusiastic about what he saw.

'People see me as a country mystic, you know. But they'll find they're wrong. I grew up in London, after all, and it draws me still because my work and friends are there. Bricks and iron aren't related to me in the way flowers and trees are, but I can't bear the purple passages of so-called 'country writers' – they write as if there were no such thing as the Tube. Cities, towns, villages, hamlets, they are all part of the whole, part of this country.'

But Robert wouldn't enter into his thoughts for long. Nothing urban interested him.

'Tell me about Wales and those Black Mountains of yours,' he said. 'I'm real sorry we never got there. Thanks to that darn book of yours you had to finish.'

Edward told him about his Welsh cousins, their pigs, their fishing, and their apple growing, and how time there always helped him to feel well.

'Sounds like back home to me,' Robert said. He started to tell Edward again about New Hampshire people and what he called their democratic character, unencumbered by the constrictions of class that Robert always sensed in England. He extended his argument to poetry.

'I want to be a poet for the general reader, to reach out to all kinds—'

At that moment they came out of the woods onto a lane and were face to face with a man holding a shotgun; a short pugnacious-looking man with a thick neck, red ears and a mean mouth. It was Lord Beauchamp's gamekeeper, Bott.

Bott had unwillingly tolerated Gibson and Abercrombie on his preserve because his lordship had told him to. Abercrombie was well-connected and a tenant of his Lordship. Robert hadn't even thought about it, but if he had, he would expect, as Abercrombie's guest, that he had the same rights. But Bott didn't see it that way at all. He saw two men who were disturbing the birds and could even have been planning some poaching. His dark face reddened and his eyes expressed something between triumph and rage. His snarling gun-dog seemed to be about to attack and Bott was doing nothing to quieten it. He raised a long-barrelled shot-gun and jabbed it in their direction, spluttering threats and insults.

'Oh Lord!' Edward exclaimed. He tried to quieten the slathering dog. 'All right boy, all right, all right.'

Bott was shouting, almost incoherent.

'Oy— You— What you think yer're doin' in these woods – disturbin' my birds – I'll have the law on yer.'

Robert shouted back. 'Don't you go pointing that gun at me – clear off and leave us alone – I'm Abercrombie's tenant – he's been told he can walk here.'

Bott smirked. He was enjoying this.

'So what – if it's up to me he bloody wouldn't, but yer're not him, yer trespassing – yer look like a bloody cottager to me, and your friend skulking behind. Get going back the way you came or I'll set the dog on yer.'

'Who do you think you are, telling me what to do, you lowdown—'

'Robert, come on, come away, for God's sake, he's crazy, look at him – the gun.' Edward turned to Bott. 'OK, we're going, it's a misunderstanding, that's all, we're sorry, no need for all this. Please quieten your dog. Robert, come on—'

'Let go of me, Ed. OK, I'm coming but he's not heard the last of this.'

'I'll have you next time. Yes you, you damned cottager.'

'Why you—'

'Ignore him, Rob, for God's sake. He's dangerous with that shot-gun.'

'If you'd backed me up, Ed. You let me down – letting yourself be pushed around like that. What – are you afraid?'

Back home Robert could not calm down. He punched one hand into the other, prowled up and down the garden and snarled at the children when they wanted to know what had happened.

After their meal – one of Elinor's bread slices and potato suppers – he leapt out of his chair.

'Right I'm going round to see that swine game-keeper. Are you coming, Ed? Or are you leaving it up to me again?'

Elinor was pale but her expression was quite impassive. Edward had expected her to try to argue Robert out of this rashness, but she gave no sign.

'Well, I'll have to come with you to try to keep things on a civilised basis, but I think this is a great mistake. You're not in your own country. Things are done differently here.'

It was dusk as they took the sunken bridleway, then the field path to the edge of the wood where Bott's cottage stood. The dog started barking menacingly as Robert thumped on the door. As it opened he gave Bott a shove to his shoulder, pushing him slightly back into the room. He bellowed at the man.

'You ever again tell me or my children where we can walk in these woods and I'll beat the hell out of you.' He started to say what he thought of gamekeepers, lackeys who turned on their own kind, men who begrudged hungry children a few blackberries.

Bott was not listening.

'You've 'ad it now. Yer going to get prosecuted for trespass. You an' your friend lurking there behind. Yer trespassing again, comin' here.'

Robert laughed.

'Just you try it, you stupid oaf,' he shouted.

At first Edward hung well back, thinking that one man was enough, that two tackling Bott together would be too much of a confrontation. He hated this sort of thing, but Robert was just making things worse. He stepped out of the shadows and came to try to urge him to leave. Suddenly Bott ducked back inside the house and charged straight out with his gun. He ran at Edward and Edward ran away.

Robert followed him, but was still for going back. He caught up with Edward on the main track.

'You just ran off again Ed!'

'The man had a gun,' Edward said. 'And I have no desire to get myself shot, even if you have.'

Next day the local policeman called; Robert was to be charged with threatening bodily harm. Edward succeeded in dealing with him without too much intervention from Robert. Then they both tried to make light of it, saying that to be called a damned cottager gave Robert still more right to be known as the People's Poet than Gibson, and that he could use the phrase in his advertising.

It was Gibson, he thought, who could help him, and he sent a hurried letter. But fortunately it was unnecessary. A few days later a letter came from Lord Beauchamp to Robert, apologising for his gamekeeper's behaviour and giving them permission to walk in the woods. The charge would be dropped.

'I have told him that if he is so keen to fight he had better enlist,' the letter ended.

That ought to have been the end of the matter, but for Robert it partly soured their stay in Gloucestershire. The appeal he made to Gibson to help was pompously refused and Robert never forgave him. He was more determined than ever to go home, away from this class-ridden country. And then, he had a shadowy, lingering sense that there was madness surrounding him. His sister was threatened with an asylum. He banished from his mind a recurrent fear that madness might be within himself as much as in the world.

For Edward the gamekeeper affair was something that stayed with him like a sore; he had to keep touching it, worrying at it. Time and again in the months that followed that gamekeeper appeared in his letters to Robert. He would joke that he feared editors as much as 'that keeper'. One day he wrote 'I have missed a chance to fight a gamekeeper.' But confronted one day with dangers that his friend would never know, he could write to Robert, 'You can only face what you were born to face. So I worry less and less about that keeper.'

Six

Helen was eager for night to come, the children to be in bed so that she could have Edward to herself now he was home. They made love on the rug in front of the fire and afterwards they talked – about the Frosts and about the gamekeeper.

'But you were absolutely right to act the way you did – Robert has that side to him I don't trust at all. He doesn't understand how things are done here – he doesn't want to understand. Well, perhaps we would be like fish out of water, too, in America.'

Next morning they were both full of energy. They saw Merfyn and Bronnie off to Bedales and then dressed for the garden. The low morning sun shone directly onto the east side of the cottage where they grew vegetables, melting the light frost and making the soil gleam.

Once the last carrots were lifted they would turn over the whole plot. The food shortages wouldn't defeat them. They worked together all morning, Helen pink-faced and with her back beginning to hurt, but entirely happy.

Edward loosened a particularly long orange root in the soil and called out,

'Baba, Tommy – look at this.' He slowly drew the carrot as if it were buried treasure coming up from under the ground and the children squealed, half afraid, half excited.

Helen remembered something.

'Edwy – that day in Leddington when Robert had us all digging up his potatoes at Little Iddens – how he allotted everyone a patch to dig – except himself! And how we all toiled away while he just strolled up and down, and you pretended to be his farm-labourer, pulling your fore-lock and taking orders?'

'Yes, I remember. It was just a joke.'

'Well, I wasn't particularly amused. Don't you think, maybe,

114

you look up to him rather too much? After all, who is Robert, compared to you? A couple of books published. But you've published dozens of books; you've been a well-known writer and critic for years. I think—'

'I know what you're saying, Helen, but – it meant nothing, that playacting of his. He likes to tease and fool people a little but he has a good heart, a generous heart. I admire him and you should too. Robert does what I wish I could. He dares to write only what he wants to write, and do only what he wants to do.'

Helen had nothing to say to that.

Edward enjoyed digging for its own sake – the pleasure of the earth itself, his fork loosening and refreshing it which was all the rich loam needed. The robin hopping close looking for wireworms, the scents of currant and raspberry prunings on the bonfire. It pleased him to think of what the earth could give them in return for their cooperation and nurturing of it. There were leeks they sowed in spring – 'We must have leeks – my national dish.' They would soon be thick enough to fork up and eat.

When the soil was as it should be he ran a line across and scooped a shallow trench, Helen coming along behind with a hen-scoop of broad beans. By mid-day the plot was done, the rows of beans watered well to encourage them to put down their roots first and then, when the time was right, to try out their first pale shoots to endure the winter.

After lunch he hurried up through the hanger, where the beeches were just beginning to bronze overhead and a scattering of crisp freshly-fallen leaves lay on the soft brown mulch from the previous autumn. Yew trees, threaded among the beeches, were taking up their winter stance, looking like black caverns cut into the green-gold of beech and the pale whitebeam.

He set to work to light the first of the autumn fires. His desk looked friendly to him, not burdensome as it sometimes did. He had a head full of impressions for the two reviews he must write, and there were two more articles to be written.

Tipperary, about his experiences in the midlands and the north, would be published at the beginning of October. The next was not due yet, but it would be far more ambitious. His mind ranged around the subject of what England meant for his readers and for himself at this time. 'England' – not Britain, Great Britain, Britannia. They were words without humanity and meaning for him. He trusted that his readers would gain more from the real, the local, in his writing, wherever they lived, than from some hollow concept of Britain and her Empire.

It was all fragments as yet, drawn again from the city people he met in the north and the country people here and in Gloucestershire. None of it formed a coherent pattern, any line that he could follow. Snatches of conversation. The conversations with Mary Chandler at Oldfields and the way Mary always called England 'she'. And in the north someone who said that love of your country was all about self-interest, self-preservation. Another who thought that England was where you were free, not forced to do what somebody else wanted.

To be free was above all to be secure – for instance, a woman with children able to cross the country safely, he thought. Helen, the girls, and that journey on the first day of the war. Unpleasant but never endangered. How free would she be if England were occupied, as Belgium and France were?

He remembered Wordsworth on the Tyrolese people – that phrase, 'the land we from our fathers had in trust.' And on home, the place where 'you have your happiness or not at all.'

He wanted to celebrate England. Hazlitt, with his 'England is a place of bells and nonsense,' and 'We are the only people who can understand nonsense.'

He thought of Isaac Walton and the *Compleat Angler*. There you had the sense of England, more than in a dozen so-called patriotic writings. Walton was a free man who wandered wherever he wanted and wrote what he wanted. Edward took up his copy of the book, read for a while, then made a note. In Walton you had *'The antiquity and sweetness of England, English fields, English people, English poetry, all together.'*

He would probably just call the article *England*. It was still a confusion of fragments in his mind, but he was slowly forming in his mind a definition of what England meant to him. Hazlitt again was right on patriotism when he wrote that love of your country does not consist of hatred of the rest of mankind.

He thought of ancient Robert of Gloucester, who probably was the first to call England merry.

England is a right merry land, of all on earth it is the best,
Set in the end of the world, as here, all in the west.

He smiled and said the lines aloud. Well it's ours, he thought, so of course it has to be 'the best'. But he must be more rigorous than that. Even so, those are such evocative lines. Maybe he would use them in the introduction to the anthology he was hoping to negotiate. He could begin collecting for it seriously when these articles were done. In homage to Shakespeare it would be called *This England.* But it would not be about kings and queens, empire or perhaps even about war. Though he thought he would include Coleridge's Fears in Solitude, which expressed his own suspicion of institutions and politicians. Like him, Coleridge loved his own landscape and community, the places that had nurtured him and his writing – his particular corners of the 'mother isle'.

Of course Shakespeare would be important. But there were so many Shakespeares; he looked forward to making his choices.

It was a relief that a little work continued to come in – reviews – Masefield and Gibson – an article for Poetry and Drama and his war articles, still the third article to do. Perhaps *It's a Long Long Way,* as it followed from *Tipperary* but with a broader sweep.

In his article about the August Ledbury weeks he'd written as well and as honestly as he could how that thought had come to him about the new moon and the soldiers who might not be able to register it in their minds because of what they were undergoing. He knew that it was a confession, or a pledge, those lines about feeling that he had to do something. He meant it, but still what he meant by it he was not sure. Was there anything a man like him could do, a man over thirty who knew war only as part of history? Writing was all he knew.

No one seemed to doubt for a moment that England would win the war. But in reality, he thought, weren't we fragile and unready? People talked of a stalemate and were beginning to understand just how many lives were being lost. The authorities were eager to recruit more and more men; the requirements for height, health and age were being relaxed all the time.

He remembered recruits drilling on the Welsh shore, in a ghostly mist and in utter silence, their feet making no sound on the sand. The sea sucking at the rocks drowned the shouts of the sergeant and all other noise except for a dog nearby barking at the waves. Were they almost ghosts already?

Seven

It was December, a day of grey-yellow skies and the promise of snow.

Another fire lit in the Wick Green study. There was time for him to allow other thoughts to come to the forefront of his mind. Thoughts that seemed to surround him like trees in a wood, becoming unignorable. But he was afraid.

In the latest notebook he'd been writing differently, in short, impressionistic lines set out almost like poems. He was aware of the difference, and that more lines, more thoughts, were hovering as if waiting for him to let them in.

Try writing a poem. What is there to be afraid of? No-one need know that he had tried and failed. But he would know.

His pulse was racing and his mouth was dry.

He looked at *North of Boston* again to calm himself. It confirmed for him the excitement he'd put into those reviews. It was Robert's verses more than his urging that had changed him, made him feel he could try to be a poet. He knew, had known for years, that he wanted to use words that were familiar and necessary to him, but now he saw more clearly how it could be done. His language was not Robert's – sometimes he might want to use a more subtle, educated language. The truth was, though, that the poetry he liked best was not written by an Englishman but by an American. He had better try writing what he wanted to read himself, it seemed.

He would follow Robert's advice and take things from his notebooks, to see what could be done with them. His latest notebook, a Letts pocket book in green, was beside him; they were all there in the study, twenty years of notebooks. He found what he wanted, something he had written just a week or two before.

There was an inn a couple of miles west of Wick Green where drovers' green roads had once passed when the land was common. Now it stood in too isolated a position, off the little lane that was itself off the busy main route. No houses could be seen for several miles, nothing and nobody nearby. The high beeches concealed the inn, and the empty iron inn-sign intrigued him. No name or picture hung inside the frame.

It was a rather dirty white house, with a tumbledown disused forge in front and a muddy pond, but inside, with its ancient settles and Windsor chairs, it was, he thought, one of the pleasantest inns in Hampshire. Edward had always liked the wild girl, the landlord's daughter. Those chairs, she told him, were the work of her great uncle who'd come to cut the beeches, married the farrier's widow, and stayed to be an innkeeper himself. The beeches had mostly been spared.

The girl had once broken away and worked in London, but she came back and stayed on, a reluctant part of the place. He remembered their first conversation about the 'old girl' who'd been mad enough to start an inn beside her husband's forge.

'And don't get me started on the wind!' she said. In that she was like himself at the Wick Green house. But on his last visit a few weeks earlier he found that she'd left again; he wanted to remember her, the inn and the changes it had seen from the old days of commons and drovers.

And so, with his heart curiously thumping and the rhythms of speech in his head he wrote her words:

> 'I could wring the old thing's neck that put it here!
> A public house! it may be public for
> Squirrels and such like and ghosts of charcoal burners
> and highwaymen...but I call it a hermitage.'

No, she wouldn't say those last few words. He crossed them through.

> She laugh... No – The wild girl laughed. 'But I
> loathe it and since I came back from Kennington.'

Oh, it was difficult. Perhaps 'hate' not 'loathe'. And should it be 'there' rather than 'here'? The first few lines had come so easily but then he struggled to find any rhythm.

It was difficult but somehow absolutely compelling. There was nothing quite like this exact honing of each word for naturalness, for rhythm, for rightness. Deciding exactly where to break the line. He read his words aloud, made some changes. Later he realised that he had let the fire go out, and looking up from the page he saw snowflakes whirling across the window.

All day he worked on the poem. Next day he went back through the snow, ducking under the bent-low branches of the laden yews. By the end of that day he thought it would do.

Next day he thought it was rather too 'Frosty'. He wouldn't always want to be writing so much dialogue, or perhaps in blank verse, or at such length. Nor did he have, or want to have, Robert's gift for entering into the minds and voices of women.

What would he write? Weather, old men, inns, roads and journeys – he had always been intrigued by them and had put them in his prose. It was the place of such things within nature that he wanted to explore. He saw nature as what was other than human, and that was – almost everything. People seemed to see themselves as the centre, and nature as only what surrounded them, that tree, that bush, as if they were in a house with furniture. That was not his belief at all. Nature was not separate from Man; Man was one small part of nature, and not the best part. The landscape, the wind and weather, the seasons, the wild creatures, these could enter and change a man, if he would allow it, be open to it. He had felt that in himself and in others too. The wind itself – how much older than mankind, than the gods even, was the wind? Yet it was always new.

We should teach our children our responsibilities to the other creatures around us, he believed. We are only one of the inhabitants of earth and latecomers at that. Think of the badger, a true ancient Britain, its home delved from the soil, maltreated, dug out and given to the dogs. The weasel, hung up on the gamekeeper's gallows.

He was surprised to find that he trusted that ideas for poems would come, perhaps from his notebooks, from the day's events, the weather, or the children's doings and sayings. Sometimes he would return to his prose – what he'd written in *Pursuit of Spring* about March, for instance. And then – harder to define, there would be something of himself, his own dilemmas and meditations, his own experiences and sorrows, just grasped, or just eluding him. Robert believed that artless self-expression is not poetry. He agreed, but he would manage it differently, in his own way, with his own distancing.

He would find his own way; no danger of him being caught up in the latest fads because, after all, he knew them and their faults better than anyone did – Pound, and the so-called Imagists and Symbolists. If he used symbols they would emerge naturally from the poem and they would not be obscure or private. They would be understood by any intelligent reader who shared the world they all had in common. Such things as wind, mist and rain, the sun. Trees and flowers. Houses and roads. And the seasons. Night and day. Those moments of transition as one season merges into another, and as day turns towards night. Birds and birdsong, always unaltered and perfect. The war made these subjects no less vital. If what he had heard about the destructiveness of the German advance was true, France, only a hundred or so miles away, was being reduced to a wasteland. And at home the mines, the mills and factories were part of a great greedy machine, eating everything up. A machine to turn young men to dung.

He needed to spend more time on the garden. He was considering whether this was a good time for winter-pruning the William pear. It had survived having been pulled off the east wall by the weight of pears and he wanted to work at a stronger structure.

Myfanwy was watching him from the porch. She reached out to break off a sprig from the top of the grey-green shrub called Old Man or Lad's Love growing there and sniffed at it absent-mindedly.

'Baba – how many times must I tell you not to do that!'

Myfanwy looked gravely at him and ran off through the gate into the Dodds' next door. The two gardens formed the boundary of her world; he wondered what she would remember of it. He had thought so intensely in recent years about his own childhood, but he found that these thoughts would only take him so far. Some memories were too elusive for thought. This shrub, the scent of it, tantalised him with the mystery of what it was, what memory it was, that was eluding him.

The shrub was still only half the height of Myfanwy because of her habit of picking a stalk and sniffing it whenever she went in or out of the house. He'd written about it only a few weeks before in his notebook – he would look it up once the pear was pruned. The enigma of those contradictory names pleased him, but it was the elusiveness of memories that was the compelling interest of the subject for him. He had almost visionary memories of certain gardens he'd known as a child, when with your back to the house the garden path stretched on forever. He would mould those thoughts and notes into a poem, a long poem without too clear a structure, just as the scent led him to *Only an avenue, dark, nameless, without end.*

Next day another poem – it concerned that sense he had all his life, of not knowing which was the right direction to take in life, of feeling superfluous. There were times when his uncertainty was so overwhelming it had led to him thinking of death as the only route to peace. He had a good line: *The mouthful of earth that remedies all* – or should it be *A mouthful?* Should it be *to remedy all?* Yes.

He *was* that man in middle age, remembering himself at twenty, imagining himself at fifty and always wondering, where shall I go? Which way? Like a man standing helplessly baffled beside a signpost.

Was 'sixty' better?

He wrote in his notebook:

when I am fifty
what shall I wish?

A few days later he rushed to scribble down the words that came to him. He imagined a voice – a wise, ironic, enigmatic voice speaking. To be alive, it implied, only to be alive, would be enough. To be conscious, able to observe the world, the seasons, and to be glad of the freedom to make choices, to test things against his own experience:

> *To see what day or night can be,*
> *The sun and the frost, the land and the sea,*
> *Summer, autumn, winter, spring,*
> *With a poor man of any sort, down to a king,*
> *Standing upright out in the air*
> *Wondering where he shall journey, O where?*

Every morning he could hardly wait to get up to his study. Hardly wait to help Helen with the morning chores as he always did, bringing in the wood, clearing away the breakfast, while Helen went with Myfanwy to wave good-bye to the older two from the end of their lane. He would sprint up the hill, sometimes disappearing in the chilly mist that hung so long under the trees around his study. It was cold, but he could hardly wait long enough to light his fire before he began.

Early that autumn Eleanor's letters had told him about her brother's fortunes; Bertie was invalided out of the army and had unpleasant surgery in a fruitless effort to be declared fit again. Then miraculously Bertie's need to obliterate his sorrows in France disappeared. He was to marry the woman he loved after all; she had broken off her engagement with her fiancé.

Edward was delighted. Bertie Farjeon was his good friend.

Now their letters were about their writing again. Eleanor had sent some of her *Nursery Rhymes of London Town* for his opinion and was every day awaiting the post. As she stood in the Fellows Road hall slitting open the familiar envelope her heart was beating faster than it should.

Then she drew in her breath with surprise and pleasure.

'Thank you for the poetry. May I send you some in return?'

So – he was writing poetry at last. And sharing it with her.

Eight

He had a review to write and its subject was going to expose him to some of the worst poetry he could find: poetry about the war, not written by those who were a part of it, perhaps written too soon, too hastily. From the first week Robert Bridges was writing patriotic verse, soon joined by Kipling and Hardy. The recruitment drive was the main motive; after the retreat from Mons by the British Expeditionary Force recruitment was urgent. Britain relied on volunteers. So poets such as Begbie with his Fall In tried to shame young men into enlisting, and succeeded. Fall In was wildly popular, even set to music. Men said it had made them decide to enlist. They wanted to be part of a brotherhood perhaps, but they wanted to avoid opprobrium too.

The postman had brought two brown paper packages from Monro the day before, but Edward delayed the moment of opening them. Was this, he thought, what his war work was to be? Well, probably he would be able to do it better than he would do soldiering. But the poetry was even worse than he'd imagined: the war-mongering of self-proclaimed patriots hoping for a slice of profitability from the whole thing, or the ghastly hackneyed drivel of the sentimental. Even the reasonably competent among them, like Wheeler Wilcox, wrote only the commonplace sentiments you would hear in any grocery shop or at the hairdressers.

'The demand is for the crude, for what everybody is saying or thinking,' he wrote. He hoped that in time good poets would be ready for true poetry again. And when that happened their thoughts should appear as though they were not 'about' the war, but would be the poet's own response to it. These warmongering poets would not have any significance beyond the moment. *'No other class of poetry vanishes so rapidly, or has so little chosen*

from it for posterity.'

The marching songs of the men, songs such as 'Tipperary', were full of commonplace thoughts too, but somehow they became overlaid with the roughened, weary voices of experience. They were dirtied, bloodied, while these verses had all the mark of having seen nothing, experienced nothing. He was angry – but to be vehement was to run the risk of seeming to ridicule the war effort itself and he did not want to do that.

Gibson's work was better, so with relief he began to look at it more closely. Of course, the People's Poet was now the common soldier's poet. He took episodes from newspaper accounts and wrote, in the comfort of the Old Nailhouse, as though he were the combatant. They were done well – but he could not really see the point of them. Perhaps some took things further than the first thought; they showed some of the complexity of it all. He could temper his review with praise for those.

Hardy's poem, Men Who March Away, was pleasing – it was, he thought, about all wars. It could as well be about the Napoleonic as the present war, so it didn't have that taint of being written for the occasion that he disliked so much.

There would be work from Brooke in New Numbers before long, he believed. He knew Rupert well – in fact Rupert had been there in this study, reading out his poems at considerable length. He had enlisted straight away, Abercrombie said; as he stood on the Kent coast he felt the enormity of the idea that enemies could be on English soil. Edward had heard that the sights he'd seen in Belgium had swept away any last doubts he'd had about the cause. Where was he now, Edward wondered, how was he faring?

The last time they met their whole set had spent an evening at Gibson's in early summer. Robert and Elinor, he and Helen, Eleanor, the Gibsons of course and the Abercrombies and Rupert. Now Robert and Elinor were to leave, the rest were scattered and Brooke was – God knows where. Somehow New Numbers continued, even though Catherine was having another baby and was far from well. The next issue would arrive soon.

He turned back to the review.

Perhaps it was good that poets tried to move on from their

pre-war preoccupations and face up to life in wartime, if only as far as they, non-combatants, could know it. Some were perhaps moved by a sincere wish to make a contribution during such a difficult time. But how hard it was to do well. He opened another volume – more simplistic verse. Forced rhymes, hackneyed despicable imagery depicting the Germans. Some of it was so dreadful that it made him laugh, but the laugh was harsh.

He stared out of the window to where the terraces of the Luptons' garden sloped down to meet the trees of the beech hanger. A few plumes of mist still today, but he could see the distinct winter silhouettes of the trees emerging, sombre grey beech trunks and stark branches of ash and wild cherry, and among them the ancient yews, everlasting pools of deepest green, almost black.

What was the use of this work he was doing? It was becoming hard to stomach. All he could hope was that his articles and the *Anthology* would show England's worth without warmongering. As for poetry – he couldn't imagine the soldiers' lives, in spite of newspapers and their accounts. No one could know without experiencing that for himself. Gibson's attempts were essentially pointless.

The poems he had written were part of his familiar self. Nature's secrets, aspects of the country that are missed or overlooked, tiny details – the quality of mud, the white fragments of snail shells. Country people and situations, their pasts, and the loss of them. The quest for contentment. These were his themes and they were inexhaustible. Could he allow his poetry sometimes quietly to let in the war and what it meant here, in England, what it meant to have the country you loved attacked? He could rework something about the dead ploughman, perhaps. But he must not let himself be corrupted by sentimental, predictable responses. If he were to write about the war it could only be as a witness to what he had experienced as loss – flowers in a wood unpicked by lovers, a fallen tree hindering a plough because there were not enough men left on the farm to move it.

He'd had enough of the patriotic poets and their scribbling. It was time for his midday meal and he would hear Helen's signal to him soon.

He'd quickly write an overdue letter to Aunt Margaret, his mother's sister in Los Angeles. He always found her an interesting correspondent, and while the America idea was a possibility – a strong possibility – it was good to know that they had family contacts there. His mother had even said that she might come with them to America – though Edward was more aware than she was of the distance from the east to the west coast.

He wrote to Aunt Margaret about his northern journey and the men he had seen enlisting, and went on:

'I feel that is the only thing to do if a man is able-bodied and has nothing else to do. It is satisfying that so many men in a civilised age are capable of this kind of extravagant courage and endurance.'

He looked out, then, at the woods and the South Downs, where the morning mist had entirely cleared. Courage and endurance. Endurance he had; he had never minded the hardship of a cold bivouac, or a walk that was almost too much for him. Would soldiering make the same kind of use of mind and body as the work he enjoyed, like digging the garden, or carpentry, that fusion of thought and action? Or the planning and executing of a long journey? If that was so, he might enjoy the change and have something to offer. As for courage—? What was it and how could a man know whether he possessed it? In what way might it be tested, physical courage? He had not been given to fighting as a boy as many were. When his brothers scrapped he would look on with weary contempt, and if anyone tried to provoke him into a fight that contempt would be his deliverance. Other boys seemed to be born to fight, while others he had known would fight if they must, for their honour, or to protect a younger child. It seemed a difference in character, an innate difference, not something where you had a choice. Yet all those thousands of young men volunteering must believe they had courage enough. How could they know it and he did not?

But then, no doubt he was too old. He would be put to work at a desk – pamphlets, something of that kind.

These few crumbs of reviewing work, paying hardly anything, were stopping him from considering seriously what he should do, from facing fully the question of whether some worthwhile niche could be found for him.

Two threads of thought seemed to run independently of each other in his mind – the thought of going to America and the sense that he should be doing something for his country. First one, then the other, round and round in his head. If he succeeded in America, what a change it would be for them all, what an opportunity! Robert was good for him, he knew, made him believe in himself. And he was good for Robert – they were different but somehow not rivalrous, just able to confirm for each other what they were. But how could he believe in himself when he would know he was running away? And neither of these paths would he have considered in peacetime. What did either of them have to do with who he was?

Impatient with himself, he folded his aunt's letter for Helen to add to in the house, then damped down the fire with slack dust. He opened the door carefully so that the wind would not disturb his papers, and turned into the lane and through the combe to sprint off down the path towards home.

Nine

On Christmas Eve he began to write about walking in the first February sunshine down towards the glowing rose-coloured old bricks of Prior's Dean manor house. It was a modest seventeenth century house, three stories high, with diamond-paned windows. Its thatched farm buildings stood alongside. The winter sun brightened the mossy tiles and the windows sparkled; white doves perched on the roof enjoying the new warmth. The only sound was the gentle swish of tails from three carthorses leaning over a gate. As it was Sunday they were at rest.

The church was small, smaller than a barn, but beside it stood a great ancient yew tree, its complex trunk sculpted and hollowed into deep red caverns. The harmony of house, farm, church and tree, the lives of animals in that Sunday silence – the timelessness, the renewing of it all by the thaw – moved him immensely. The poem wrote itself quickly.

A tentative idea for another poem. He looked at his passages in *Pursuit* about the Other Man that Robert had liked. But what he wanted to express in a poem was more serious and compelling to him than that Other Man had been. He would have this Other Man move through a legendary landscape; the poem would take the form of a quest. He knew enough from his time as Baynes' 'Patient' that it concerned his darkest self, his unconscious, and perhaps his 'ideal' self – a man better liked, more at home in the world and with his future. There would be, there must be, fear, uncanny dread and an endless compulsion in the pursuit.

I wait his flight.
He goes: I follow: no release
Until he ceases. Then I also shall cease.

Sixteen poems before the end of the year. It would be worthwhile knowing what someone, someone more critical than Helen or Eleanor, would think of them and Harold Monro at the Poetry Bookshop was the obvious choice. He sent the poems to him, saying that they were the work of a friend. But Monro kept them for four days and then sent them back saying he didn't have time to read them.

What he really means, thought Edward, annoyed and disappointed, is that he doesn't have anyone to tell him what to think. I always do that.

He sent poems to Robert at The Gallows with a letter: *'I am in it and no mistake – I find myself engrossed and conscious of a possible perfection as I never was in prose.'* He thought Lesley might like to include one poem, The Combe, in The Bouquet.

Robert, he wrote, could consider himself 'the only begetter', if he chose.

So much taken from him, denied him, because of one unlucky step as he ran down the hill – his foot landed on a stone and twisted sideways. He fell headlong onto the short turf as the sheep scattered before him.

He was confined to bed, quite immobile. Helen had to do everything for him. A fine beginning to the New Year! A last visit to the Frosts at Ryton had to be cancelled; no one came to see him, not even Eleanor or his mother. The most he could do was crawl from his bed and sit in a deck-chair in the bedroom, where the east window looked out on the wintry garden. There he could at least write; he wrote about a ploughman he knew who'd been killed in France, and about the time last June when their train to Ledbury stopped at a station with an odd name – Adlestrop.

Memory must be his source – his memory and his field notebooks, which he had Helen fetch from the Cockshott Lane study. He had always kept a notebook everywhere he went, and the detail, the thoughts he'd had, the conversations with solitary strangers on the road, fed him with ideas. Sometimes he told himself that if he stopped using notebooks, if he only looked, allowed himself to experience passionately what he encountered, it would be better. It might free him from that sense he often had that he was nothing but a remote observer, a ghost invisible to other people. Perhaps, too, without a notebook he would remember only the poignant, vital aspects of what he encountered instead of risking losing that significance in a mass of detail. But he could not break the habit now – it was part of who he was.

He longed to be out of the house and further still, over the hills and far away, beyond the horizon. It was not enough simply remembering, as he often did. He was tired of the view from the window, tired of the cottage and his own limitation, and of Steep – he needed the sky over high hills, where he could look down on the last house, even on the last of the trees, from a plateau of gorse and furze. To be so tied down to the earth, even though he loved it – it was as though he were a fish confined to living among mud and the green streets of weeds.

Myfanwy would keep coming in to bother him. She thought it was a great novelty to have him there in bed. She did amuse him for a while with her made-up verses, especially her rhymes that had no sense but a good sound to her ear.

'Daddy, draw me something. I'm not feeling awfully well.' She was half-grizzling and did seem feverish.

'Oh come here then, you barrel of trouble – what shall I draw?'

'You choose.'

'Something from nursery rhymes?'

'Yes.'

'Here then. Wait a minute – mind my foot. There – what is it?'

'Let me see.'

He held out his notebook.

'I know – it's the three blind mice and the farmer's wife – what a nasty knife she's holding!' She laughed, then looked serious.

'I hope the mice do get away.'

'Mmmmh – do you think they will? What about the song?'

'Oh that's easy, I can change that – *She ran after them with a carving knife,*

Did you ever see such a thing in your life
As three blind mice?

You see, that doesn't say she caught them at all.'

'Right, I see – yes, that's clever – but now run along, Baba. Tell Mummy I want to sleep, will you?'

After two weeks he was able to be downstairs, but the ankle healed so slowly and he was more angry and miserable than ever. Late one afternoon, when Bronwen and Baba were ill with colds and hacking coughs, he hobbled into his cramped back room to be alone. Nothing and no one could please him. He was so sorry for himself that he could see little to live for. He plotted an epitaph for his tombstone:

'Here lies all that no one loved of him and that loved no one.'

But part of his mind was able to see his self-pity as contemptible; he became tired of this mood, this whim of his.

He could see from the window the meadow behind the house and to his right the place where the Lutcombe stream ran down to a little waterfall and the mill. The valley was becoming dim in the fading light and a slight mist was beginning to veil it. Watching the changes, he felt a part of him turning from his misery towards happiness, towards a place where he could find home and rest. He knew that beauty and its power to heal him was still alive in his heart.

He began the poem with his anger and self-contempt in short, harsh words; as it developed the words themselves transformed him from that self, neurotic and bitter, into something stronger. He made the lines swoop and glide to their conclusion as a dove slants down to a tree, to its home and love and its rest.

Ten

Half a kiss, half a tear

I was angry that Edwy had to wait so long to hear a proper response to his poems from Robert. A whole month and it seemed longer. There was a side of Robert, that side we saw at cricket and at quizzes and charades, which had to be the winner. Edward was different during that waiting time. He was usually writing to a commission, often with an advance; he was so business-like and reliable that publishers knew that what they asked for would be delivered, and delivered at the agreed time. His writing was always strong, as he knew, so waiting for a publisher's response on first reading meant little to him; at worst it would be some matter of the number of words.

But when he began writing poetry, and had twelve poems that he believed were ready to be seen, he was eager to have a response. He sent them to Harold Monro and that wretched man kept them for four days without, he said, having time read them, in spite of Edward being his own consultant and reviewer. He knew – he must know – how important this was to Edward. But then Edwy snapped at me that he hadn't told Monro that the poems were his own work. He was not going to declare himself as Edward Thomas.

Robert's letter did come, and Edwy smiled as he read, then quickly wrote back. And he included copies of more poems. Robert, he said, would be pleased to see the new one he called The Other. He was content then, until the accident.

How many times had he run down from the study without any mishap? How one moment's carelessness could have such a consequence! It was a dreadful sprain and so unlucky. For both of us. He sprawled between two chairs in the sitting room – miserably slumped to one side in his armchair, his sprained ankle on a cushion on one of the kitchen chairs. His long legs took up half our living room and blocked my way to the table, but he so hated being in bed that by nine or ten o'clock he would insist on coming downstairs. The sprain was making him shockingly irritable, and it might have been easier for me if he had agreed to keep to his room! It was so unlucky for Edward and I was low in spirits, too, because of his ill-temper.

And because the date of Merfyn's leaving us was so near.

At least Edward could read and write, although without being able to get up to the Cockshott Lane study he was frustrated at not having his books to hand. His tiny back-room study at Yew Tree held our household papers and only his most pressing business. I had to go up the hill for him to find what he needed. Edward was such an orderly person, so business-like about his work, that at least he knew where I would find what he wanted.

He did have a project to work on, one that was his own suggestion and just the right thing for him: an anthology. No one else would have the knowledge he had to compile it. A pocket-sized book that a soldier could keep with him, to be called *This England*. He was choosing prose and poetry to show the quality of England and English life, from centuries ago to the present day. Edward wanted people to understand their love for their country and why we had to defend our liberties and ourselves. But he had a horror of the sort of thing that was being purposefully written as 'patriotic'.

When he was not working on the anthology he was writing his own poetry. He wrote fast, and so many different kinds of poems. It was as if he enjoyed setting himself tasks, exercises even, to see what a range he could cover. Edwy was always most compelled to write whenever he was in pain, or when he was bored or confined, as in a railway carriage. Then the poetry would come.

To give him peace I would take Myfanwy, once she was over her cold, out on an errand somewhere or to call on our neighbours. Or I would walk along the lanes and pick what remained of the ruby-red haws and the plump rose hips and look for yellow hazel catkins. Then, when I took them home, Edward had some sense of the country outside. He missed so much not being able to walk freely. It was the worst thing that could happen to him, to lose the first signs of spring, and my offerings didn't bring much thanks.

The pity of it was that the Frosts were intending to come to stay, and Edward would have been so pleased if only he were well. He would have been able to show Robert a little more of our country, the woods, the cottages and farms of our corner of the South Country. Though heaven knows how we were to accommodate them, and I was not eager to see Elinor again. But then, perhaps I'd quite enjoy showing her how a family home should be run. And they were leaving for America, so it would be our last meeting.

As Edward said, though, they were 'rather incalculable' and I ought not to rely on them. And my darling Merfyn was going with them, to America. I was far from sure that they could be trusted to look after him properly. But what could we do?

Edward and I had begun to talk about the idea several months before. I was afraid for Merfyn for many reasons. Suppose England were to be invaded? And then – Merfyn couldn't please Edward. He wasn't especially clever at school, just keeping around the middle of the class. He was one of the kindest, friendliest boys you could meet; he was a lovely elder brother to both the girls. And he was becoming tall and strong. But I suppose he was undeveloped, untried, too inclined to take the lazy way through life and not really apply himself.

A friend of ours had left his teaching post at Bedales and moved to America. I wrote to him, explaining that we were worried for Merfyn's future; he offered to have him to stay with them. Mr Scott knew Merfyn, of course and thought that he might find his way better than if he continued living at home with his doting mother. Edward agreed. Of course they were right, but as the time came for him to go I was afraid for him. Ships were being torpedoed now. We had left it too late.

But the Frosts were determined to return home, so I wrote to Elinor at The Gallows, saying what a great kindness it would be at this difficult time if they would escort Merfyn to America. Edward told me that Robert had mentioned it as a possibility once before. He saw it as a prelude to Edward coming to America himself, no doubt.

My own thoughts about America were changing. It seemed to me that it might be worth our trying, if Edwy could continue writing and leading a country life, and if his mother really were interested in coming too. It need not be for ever – only for 'the duration', as everyone called it.

So Robert and possibly the whole family were visiting to make final arrangements. I went to ask at the school about the possibility of borrowing some camp beds. But when I came home there was a letter from Robert.

'You've wasted your time. They're not coming after all. Not even Robert.'

I could see how disappointed Edward was. They were travelling straight from Dymock station to Liverpool docks for the embarkation. Merfyn and I would have to join them there. I knew Edward would not be able to go, and that I would be coming home alone and sad, without my dear son. How could I be sure that I would ever see him again? Ships were torpedoed regularly. Merfyn, blown to pieces in a moment or slowly dying in an icy Atlantic. Why had I ever agreed to it? This was what war did to everyone – made us live with dread.

I thought of that blissful spring day fifteen years earlier, when I rejoiced to find that I was to have a child.

Edward was so doubtful and afraid; I'd had to comfort him. He could not believe that I was simply happy and unconcerned about the future. A baby coming, our baby, who would be born in 1900 – a new life for a new century. I thought of the day, the moment, when he must have been conceived and felt nothing but a surge of physical excitement and deep joy.

Edward had wanted to see me, but it was the summer term of his second year and he had to work, so I must come to Oxford. As the train drew in I knew he wouldn't wait for me to come through the barrier. He would buy a platform ticket and be ready to hold me. Yes, there he was, his lovely face, his fair hair longer than before, that slight troubled stoop to his shoulders. I was sorry that he looked so anxious and unhappy, so I ran to him and my look and my kiss calmed him. That's how it often was between us.

We wanted to be alone to talk, so he didn't take me into the city or to Lincoln College – instead we turned along a canal towpath. We watched narrowboats squeezing through the Isis lock, their rough horses waiting for them on the towpath, and followed them as far as the river and a great meadow.

'Helen, you are certain about this?' he asked me.

'Of course I am – somehow I almost knew what had happened even that day, but now there's no doubt about it.'

'And I know you write that you're happy. But really, isn't there the least trouble in your mind, or some reproach to me?'

'No Edwy, not at all. I'm so happy I could burst with happiness. We love each other and out of this love a child is coming. How can I not be happy?' Still he looked troubled and lost.

We rambled on by the river to where the ruins of an old abbey made a perfect place to eat the picnic he'd brought for us. Cowslips grew in the meadow and I picked some and buried my face in their freshness. Then we lay in each other's arms and I talked some more. At last he told me that he'd never loved me as much as he did at that moment. All our anxieties were gone and we talked happily about our baby. We knew we must be more together, though we could not really see how it was to be managed, or quite how we would live. I cared nothing for such things then. I had everything I wanted.

At the end of the afternoon we ambled slowly back and this time, across the Thames and a further strip of meadow, I could see the spires and domes of Edward's Oxford. My way lay back through the streets to the station and London, waiting eagerly for what was to come.

Robert did come to Steep after all. The Frost family had all had such a busy time, hurrying down to London to see certain officials, one concerning Merfyn, but Robert was kind: he sent a telegram and arrived from the station almost at the same time. Edwy was so pleased. With Robert's help he could reach the old

Harrow Inn. He was so keen that Robert should see it – its tiny room no bigger than our living room and Mr Coffin the landlord with his droll ways. So Edwy sat on his Humber and half scooted with his good ankle for the mile past the church, with Robert pushing on the saddle, both of them laughing like children. They stayed there most of the day until it was time for the train.

It was all arranged – Merfyn and I would come to Dymock by train on the fifteenth, meet them there, then take a train to Liverpool. And then I would have to come home without my son.

Edwy and Robert stood at our gate in the twilight, still talking. They stopped for a moment to marvel at our blackbird, still singing his heart out. Then they embraced and Robert was gone. The talk was all of how soon Edward would be following them to America. He limped back into the cottage with his eyes shining. I turned away so that he would not see my face and be angry with me for spoiling his mood.

Eleven

Bronwen was at school and Myfanwy playing outside with Tommy. He went painfully up to the girls' bedroom and looked out towards the hill, the familiar track to his study. Something had changed – all the hazels and willows around Ludcombe brook were cut down. He had never really noticed them – they were not much more than an overgrown hedge – but the hill looked bare without them. A bright newly cut stack of hazel logs stood there. It was possible to see, now the tangled willows were gone, the silver line of the little brook rising from a spring there.

Loss and gain.

Perhaps some good would come from Merfyn's absence. He wrote with pain about parting from him – how that parting seemed to suspend their troubled relationship in the past. He had an uneasy sense about Merfyn always.

He was too absorbed to notice that Tommy and Myfanwy had come in from the muddy garden with their boots on. Too absorbed to hear them going upstairs. Only when he was disturbed by a regular thumping sound and shrieks of laughter did he stop writing and listen. It was coming from the main bedroom.

'Baba – what on earth are you doing?' he shouted.

The thumping and laughter stopped suddenly.

He limped into the bedroom. On the bed, Tommy and Myfanwy stood looking anxious and still wearing their muddy boots. Their bouncing feet had churned the snow-white counterpane to light brown. Forgetting his ankle Edward grabbed them, one under each arm, carried them downstairs to the kitchen and smacked them both. He sent Tommy home and Myfanwy to her room. Then he fetched the counterpane and thrust it through into the outhouse. His ankle felt worse. Thank goodness Helen would soon be home from Liverpool – though he knew she would not be in good heart.

She at least knew what home was, he thought wistfully. He felt that he had never found the place that he could call 'Home'. He still used the term sometimes for his parents' house in Balfour Road. His leaving home had been unnaturally early because of Helen and her pregnancy; it had not been properly resolved, his growing up and leaving. At Oxford he thought of himself as a man – now he could see that he was still a boy, a clever boy. But he would not, even if he could, choose to turn back to his family home – if he did he knew he would soon be wanting Steep again, imperfect though it was. Sometimes it seemed that 'home' was always elsewhere.

Two years before he'd written about his childhood, as a way of trying to understand and resolve some of his unhappiness. When he thought of childhood, of children, the images that came were generally sad, morbid even. Weeping or drowning. Why? Had he been too much imbued with gloomy Victorian stories? He had a sense it was something that had always been with him: a look in his mother's face, perhaps, that only he could see, or that she showed only to him. He strained to search his memory but whatever it was – some damage he had suffered – it eluded him.

He had abandoned the memoir eventually but the thoughts stayed with him and he could meditate on the idea of 'home' in verse. A few days later the poem was finished and something new could begin. He must rely on his memory and his notebook again for ideas. That first hot day, last spring, May 23rd – a day when he was feeling well and cheerful, when the bluebells were as dense as seawater lapping at the trees in the copse. He'd met the old man who wandered wherever he wanted and who gave him cowslips from the hill and watercress from Oakshott rill in the green valley near Hawkley. To think of it, to read his notes, made him long to be well again and somehow he could turn the intensity into quiet words.

He found notes of a particular walk – it was when he was preparing *In Pursuit of Spring*. An owl's melancholy call had affected him. Hearing it, while he relished his own rest and comfort inside a welcoming inn, he'd thought of the poor and homeless. Now he wrote of:

'all who lay under the stars,
Soldiers and poor, unable to rejoice.'

After Robert left he wrote with a new intensity. Perhaps it was a way of keeping their brotherhood alive in spite of the unimaginable stretch of the cold Atlantic between them. He forgot the pain in his ankle, he forgot his old ways, his anxiety about money. He was between two lives now, the old writing life and the new. He was not thinking of counting words, of fulfilling deadlines. He could be in the absolute moment in some new way, all his faculties bent only on marking the page with the most exact expression of an experience he could achieve. The joy of finding the right word, the right rhyme! It was a kind of ecstasy that he had never known. The surprise when the exact words seemed to leap into his mind from nowhere, choosing themselves, almost.

He was writing a poem and making it the best he could.

Twelve

'Do you remember when we first met, Edward?' Eleanor asked.

He had written to Eleanor suggesting they meet at Shearns' vegetarian restaurant in Tottenham Court Road when he could manage to travel to London, as he must. It was rather a forbidding place even before the war, with treacly-varnished panels and mahogany furniture, but it was convenient for the publishing houses that both of them visited.

Eleanor took off her coat; the waitress put it on a curling hat-stand and led her to a table. She wore a dress of dark-blue wool, with panels of blue and green silk let into the yoke and at the cuffs. She had a soft-skinned, gentle look, an expression of warm sympathy, which she was ready to bestow on those she met – the waitress, two elderly ladies at the next table.

She saw Edward come in and as always her heart lurched. She waved and saw his quick smile. Then he was coming towards her, still limping badly.

It was after she had pulled out his chair, taken his coat, ordered and poured tea, that she asked her question.

'Our first meeting?' he said. 'Yes, it was at the Cottage Tearooms, wasn't it? With Godwin and Bertie – and you and Rosalind. You were even quieter than I was and more shy.'

'But we did manage to find out that we were both writers since we were in short frocks.'

'Yes, and then I found out that you'd a head-start on me by a year. Published at eighteen! It was simply too bad.'

'Ah yes, but you've more than caught up since,' Eleanor said. 'And I had my father's example and encouragement – while you—' She stopped.

'I had to make do with my future father-in-law.'

'Yes. Imagine – if you'd met *my* father— Well, he would have encouraged you too, I know he would. I do so miss him. And now Edward, another memory. Do you remember I asked you a year or so ago whether you had ever tried to write a poem.

'I believe I do – and what did I say? I can guess.'

'You said, "Me? I couldn't write a poem to save my life."'

They laughed again. Then Edward put a finger to his lips. 'But hush – it's a secret. No one must know.'

Eleanor couldn't hide her pleasure at what he had said. No-one must know: he meant, of course, no-one in her own circle, people like the Baxes. Of course Helen would know. But this was something she could claim for herself.

'Would you like me to type your fair copies for you? I'd love to do that.'

'Would you? – that would be marvellous. Thank you. As soon as I have a batch I'll send them to Fellows Road, if I may.'

Eleanor felt she was smiling idiotically. Edward poured her some more tea, smiling too.

There was something else Eleanor wanted to know. She had hesitated to ask, but now she felt as though she could say almost anything, except the forbidden thing.

'You don't see Godwin now, Edward?'

Godwin Baynes was a young doctor, specialising in nervous diseases. He was beginning to know and understand Carl Jung and he found Edward interesting and rewarding. He had taken Edward up. A mutual friend hoped that the extraordinary optimism of one would lighten the dire pessimism of the other.

Godwin's friends had wondered who the mysterious 'Patient' he talked of was. When they learned that it was Edward Thomas – everyone had heard of him – he was soon included in their circle of young, affluent, rather Bohemian people. Eleanor was part of one such circle through Bertie, and so she had met Edward.

'See Godwin? No, not since he left London.'

'But you travel everywhere, so lightly. It must be more than that that keeps you away.'

She looked shyly but seriously at him. Somehow he had never taken offence at her wanting to understand him.

145

'He – Godwin was good for me for at first. During the worst times, two years ago, he helped me. All that exercise and good food – fresh vegetables, no alcohol, no sugar '

He laughed and waved his plain Shearns' scone in the air. 'I needed it then. And to be away from home – those cricketing holidays – it all helped. And some of his ideas, too. He allowed me to see and understand some things about myself.'

He was quiet for a while. His finger drew a pattern through the crumbs on his plate.

'He helped me to see that my greatest problem was my extreme self-absorption, self-consciousness, so that I seemed to be nothing more than a self-considering brain. Thanks to Godwin, I know, intellectually, that I am more than that. Whether I will ever be able to feel and live it, I don't know. Only—'

'Yes?'

'Well, Eleanor, I think perhaps the poems help – I'm able to argue things out with myself through them. Sometimes it's almost as though Godwin and I were talking still. But the conversations are my own. Do you see?'

'Yes, I do. Actually, I've noticed that quite often they begin as if they were half answering a question. As if they are part of a conversation.'

They were silent for a time, then he smiled.

'Eleanor, do you still perform Godwin's cold sponge ritual? I gave it up this winter, finally.'

They both chanted together:

'Up with me, up with me, into the blue,
For thy song, lark, is strong.'

They laughed, but there was wistfulness in the laughter.

'I gave it up too,' she said.

'That ridiculous torture. The icy bath and icy water from a sponge down your spine! Oh dear – Godwin! No doubt he still performs it every morning, with the water like a great cataract and a voice like thunder.'

'I'm sure he does. And Rosalind too, although less noisily. Of course now Rosalind is Bertie's sister-in-law, so she's almost mine too. Edward, if you did want to see him, I know they'd be happy to have you come to Norwich.'

'No – Godwin can't help me any more. I'll find my own way ahead from now on. But look, Eleanor – it's my birthday next week. You must come to tea. I'll send you a note nearer the day.'

They parted with their usual friendly handshake.

Eleanor wandered the London streets for an hour without noticing where she was. Time with Edward was always the happiest time in her life. It wasn't what they talked about, what he said or did, what she said. It was simply to have been with him, alone with him, to have him near like that. Her love was stronger than ever and her longing for him intense. She found herself daydreaming about a life spent with him.

Oh, it was unnatural, unbearably unnatural, to have this blend of intense love and terrible unfulfilment.

When the note about his birthday came, Eleanor sprang up from the breakfast table, telling her mother that she must go and dress to catch the next train to Petersfield. But Mrs Farjeon, who was usually restrained in her comments, was dismayed to see her daughter's shining eyes, her eager excitement. She had the look of a woman who could not wait to meet her lover. Mrs Farjeon had to speak out.

Eleanor ran to her room and wept for a few minutes. Then she asked the maid to take a note to the telegraph exchange, sending her apologies. Her birthday gifts to Edward were posted some days before.

Much of the day she spent gazing into the fire, crying useless tears.

Sometimes she pictured him sitting opposite her in the chair on the other side of the fire, reading, smoking his pipe, while she read too; sometimes they'd smile at each other, or break off reading when they were compelled to share something the other would like. Then perhaps, she dreamed, he would say loving words to her. He would— But no, this was wrong, it was wrong to force him into an image that was not and never could be a true one:

> *'Forgive the words you have not spoken!*
> *Forgive the words I shall not speak to you!*
> *Forgive the broken silence, still unbroken,*
> *When strength and resolution are worn through.*
> *Forgive the looks you are strange to, oh forgive*
> *The embrace you will not offer while you live.'*

Was it too late? Could she change her mind, hurry to the station and be there in time for tea? No, she must not.

Thirteen

Half a kiss, half a tear

Edward complained that I treated everyone as though they were my children and my particular special concern and business and that many people did not like that. It was nonsense – I liked people, I was interested in people and I hoped that they would like me.

March the third – Edwy's birthday, and we were home together for it. He was himself again, his ankle healing and winter drawing to its end. Of course he was still a year behind me – in our letters I sometimes called myself 'your old woman'. I did picture myself, sometimes as an old woman with many children. That was what Edward meant I suppose.

Once his ankle was better Edward went to London to finish some work. I stayed away myself a few days at the Ransomes, near Salisbury with Ivy, Arthur being away, reporting in Russia. Edward was not at all impressed by his exploits – he said that Arthur was playing at being superman. He was a friend of Arthur's, but we both preferred Ivy; I thought Arthur had abandoned her shamefully. Edward always worked away a great deal, because he needed to, but we kept our closeness through our letters. Arthur and Ivy did not.

Their little girl Tabitha was Myfanwy's age, so we fitted nicely together in the house.

Ivy was a Bohemian of the kind I used to be, when I was young and living amongst people who liked me as I did them. In those days Edward did not approve of my friends and he was stiff and awkward with them. He was quite a Puritan.

Well, as Edwy had predicted, Ivy and I drank champagne together and smoked shag tobacco! She dressed wonderfully in full skirts and peasant blouses with great hoop earrings and high-laced boots, and we drove about over the downs in a donkey cart like gypsies. She was tremendously freethinking, perhaps too free-living even for me to approve of her entirely. She hinted that she had had lovers when Arthur was still with her. I think she enjoyed being shocking.

I could never be unfaithful, because no other man could interest me. But I did my best not to judge others; we did not have the attitudes of our parents' generation. And there were times in Edward's absences when my body longed so much for love that I could understand Ivy's temptations.

As for Edward, he would write or talk to me about lovely young women he'd seen. There was the schoolgirl, Hope, in Norfolk. He told me all about her – her beauty and eagerness, her lively ideas. It pained me terribly – but I kept that to myself and just asked him to think about what was happening. I told him that he should be careful not to break her heart. Edward – perhaps many men are like this – had daydreams about such girls. I thought and hoped that they were unreal, a girl who did not exist. But I could never be quite sure.

I had seen a woman, a real woman – Eleanor Farjeon – fall in love and remain in love with Edward.

I didn't write everything about our stay at Ledbury. Eleanor came to stay in another house nearby, a house called Glyn Iddens, while we were just along the lane. One night her landlady entertained us all, rather formally, to dinner.

Eleanor was with us – with Edward and me – so much, always generous with the children, always clever and interesting. She was part of our family. She was fond of me too.

He met Eleanor, her brother and their friends so often in London that I'd asked Edward to bring her to stay at Wick Green. It was a time when he was being dreadfully critical of me. I saw at once that she was in love with him and that the only way forward was to make her *my* close friend.

Eleanor was younger than me – but she was not beautiful. She was small and like me she wore glasses that sat on a rather large nose. So she would never do as one of Edwy's perfect girls. That was at least some relief.

But they became such close friends and he confided in her in the same way he did with Robert. I didn't mind that so much, but she had friends who wanted Edward's company and took him away from home. I was rarely invited – or they chose times when they knew I would not be able to come because of school. He moved amongst these people, admired and liked, smiling and clever, while I stayed at home – as if I was not his wife but his housekeeper or nurse.

Eleanor knew, I'm sure, that she must never tell Edwy how she felt about him. It was unspoken between them, but not between Eleanor and myself. I left her in no doubt that I knew exactly how she felt.

The first time she came to Steep to visit us, I said something trivial and silly, and Edwy behaved so harshly to me that she was astonished. Of course he was soon sorry, but she had certainly seen an aspect of him that was new to her.

They'd written to each other regularly since they met. Now he sent his poems to her to type. Her typing was better than mine and Eleanor had a great deal of time on her hands. She would be happier doing unpaid work for Edward than anything else. He began using her address as a return address for poems he sent out anonymously. Some went out to Blackwood's and some to Monro again. No success.

I wanted him to succeed with his poetry of course, selfishly perhaps, because it was making him more content with our lives here. At times he seemed truly happy, full of energy, wanting to make love too, which I was eager for. He was thoughtful, 'miles away' at other times, but still more content. It was a new Edward, unfamiliar to me. There was, though, the problem of an income.

He decided on a pseudonym – Edward Eastaway. It was a family name, connected to the Thomases. I liked it – it suited him. If only a letter would come with an offer to publish! But after those first few weeks' eagerness to hear from Robert, Edward was unperturbed. I think he knew that what he did was good and that eventually it would be recognised.

So it was his birthday and we were all back in Yew Tree again. It was a warm spring, primroses along the stream, celandines, and the wild garlic leaves carpeting the verges and running into the woods. Edwy had invited Eleanor to come, but she hadn't been able to. So we were a little family of only four at the table, but at least a wire came, telling us that Merfyn's ship had arrived safely in New York.

A few days later, though, we heard that Merfyn had been held at a place called Ellis Island, in Detention of all things, while the Frosts of course disembarked quite merrily. It seemed that as he was under sixteen he ought to have been with a legal guardian. Robert's letter painted a terrible picture of this Ellis Island. A man shot himself rather than be sent back where he came from. America – the Land of the Free! I was horrified to think what scenes Merfyn had endured.

But some days later another letter came from Elinor saying that Merfyn was released and quite settled with the Scotts. And Mrs Scott – actually I believe they may not be married, but we don't mind that – wrote too. Merfyn was happily sweeping snow from their pond so that they could all go skating, she said. But how far away he was! I hoped he would be able to go to see the Frosts soon, when they had found themselves a proper home. Elinor was vague about that, but then, that was Elinor, of course.

Fourteen

It was a terrible voyage for the Frosts; they were afraid of being torpedoed and at night they lay fully dressed on their bunks wearing their lifejackets. The Atlantic was rough and the children and Elinor were sick constantly, but at last the Saint Paul and its companion the Lusitania docked safely. Then there was a problem about Merfyn.

'That damn-fool embassy man got it wrong, Ellie – it's not my fault. We'll be able to sort it out tomorrow.'

Merfyn was to be detained at Ellis Island, a boy of fifteen along with some very doubtful characters.

'I'll wire Scott and get him to come and collect him. Merfyn'll be fine.'

'Well, we do have to be sure to book ourselves into a hotel – yes, Mr Scott will have to come tomorrow and fetch him.'

They left the docks, searching for a cab to transport the six of them and their luggage, the children excited to be in their own country again, and Elinor smiling more than she had done for many months. She noticed that people in their fashionable winter clothes looked much more prosperous than the English.

Robert stopped to buy a paper. He chose the New Republic and turned to the critics' pages.

'My God Ellie, Lesley, look at this!' Robert's face was flushed and his jade-blue eyes shone.

'Look – Amy Lowell of all people – she's reviewed *North of Boston*. Looks like a mighty favourable review! Oh my stars! Ellie – can you believe it? I think we're going to be fine, just fine. My, it's good to be home.'

He hugged Elinor and Lesley to him, then he hugged the other children.

'This is a new start for the Frost family and our adventure in poetry!'

Something in American culture had changed in his absence: poetry was all the rage. Poetry magazines and books abounded and his name was already known. Within a few days of returning Robert was being asked to speak at literary lunches and to give readings of his work for the Poetry Society. He had fun teasing Sedgwick, the editor of the Atlantic Monthly who had rejected his work two years before.

Elinor and the children went to stay as paying guests with a family they knew while Robert tried to locate a farm for them to buy and make their home. He was walking one June day over Ore Hill, near Franconia in New Hampshire, when he saw a little white farmhouse that he wanted at once. It had views across to the la Fayette Mountain and the White Mountain ranges and it was high enough for him to evade the hay fever that dogged him each summer. The small town of Franconia was near enough for them to be useful without being part of it.

The farmer watched him as he approached.

'No, it's not for sale,' he said to Robert's question. Robert tried him again next day and as the farmer thought of extra land he needed and would be able to afford by selling the little house, he agreed.

'One thousand dollars and it's yours.'

They shook hands. But some weeks later the farmer began to see Robert Frost's picture in the papers and he thought that this well-known man could pay more. Two hundred dollars more. Robert agreed without much argument and the house was theirs. Some of the money was borrowed, some was from his grandfather's legacy.

He had wanted mountains. He'd found mountains and wrote excitedly to Edward about the nearness of the five high ranges one behind the other, and the Haystack and Liberty peaks. Their hill sloped steeply down before the house to the Horn River. Indoors they lacked plumbing and a furnace for heating, but there was pasture, a spring uphill for water, a wood store and a barn. Robert's letter was full of enthusiasm about his farm, and his plans for a summer school and a joint collection of poetry. He did not believe, though, that Edward should send work himself to men he'd known for years. He should use an agent.

'You are a poet or you are nothing. I told you and I keep telling you. But as long as your courage holds out you may as well go right ahead making a fool of yourself. All brave men are fools.'

He wrote again when he received Edward's equivocal answer about the summer school.

'You begin to talk as if you weren't coming to America to farm. We have gone too far into the wilds for you or something. But listen: this farm is intended for the lecture camp. We will not make it our winter home for a couple of year.' Later he wrote... *'What's mine is yours. I say that from the heart, dear man.'*

He wrote too about Edward's troubled response to a draft of a new poem, The Road Not Taken; choice, Edward implied, was a fantasy, hence two roads are much the same and chance determined most things.

Edward had completely missed the point, Robert said, and had taken the poem too seriously. It was not at all, as Edward seemed to think, a comment on choice, on will. Edward himself was the inspiration if not the subject of the poem, it was true, but simply his habit of never being content with whichever route they took on their walks because of what they missed by not taking another. It was the last thing Robert himself would do – he believed that once you had put your hand to the plough, then you must never look back. No, the poem was about Edward, his manner, his style. It was his way of showing that he understood his friend. So, he implied, Edward might just as well opt for coming to America and joining him on Ore Hill, even though he would then, no doubt, sigh and worry as to whether he had done the right thing.

In July the Frosts moved in to the farm. Robert and Elinor were ready to meet the removers who brought their long-stored goods on a wagon. All their old possessions from the Derry farm piled higgledy-piggledy in the kitchen, and the men clumping about heavily upstairs, could not spoil their elation. Elinor did become thoughtful as she looked out of the kitchen window: how well she would come to know that view, those tall weeds where the kitchen water was thrown out, over the years ahead. Many years maybe, even though they were not so young and all their long past years were piled up there, in the chaos of the kitchen at her back.

'My, am I glad to have a home of my own again,' Elinor said.

'Yes, and such freedom – our own birch woods. No one to tell us what we can and can't do, where we can and can't go. I couldn't have taken that one moment longer. But we had some good times in England, didn't we, Ellie?'

'Well, some, I guess.'

'And it's turned out for the best, you must admit that.'

'I know.'

A few days later they moved in with the children, the younger three running off together to the Hyla brook. Lesley climbed Ore Hill and after a while ran down towards them.

'I've found a great crop of blueberries all round the wood over there – do come see.'

So they picked blueberries, they fixed up the house and swam in the brook that hot summer. Robert and the children went back to playing baseball, though Robert always claimed the highest score, which would make Carol sullen. It was Carol, at fourteen, who was to work the farm: Robert believed that a son must earn his father's love but his mother's is rightly there for free.

Robert himself began to be busy with writing, organising his work and with Poetry Society matters. The little post-office at Franconia, where their mail was retained for them, had never known such mail as arrived daily for Mr Robert Frost.

But Elinor was not wholly content for long.

Robert would sit out on the white-painted porch, gazing into the autumn morning. He liked to see the mist clear and the mountains take up their true shapes while the last shreds of mist remained only in the deepest valleys.

'He's watching the dragon come out of the Notch,' the

children said. It was the Franconia Notch, the saddle of the mountain facing them. He had always believed that you could not get too much winter in winter, something he'd missed in England. He was beginning to wonder, though. Would they pay for their mountain view with too harsh and bitter weather? Would his plan for orchards fail? One late frost would kill the early blossom.

One morning he was thinking about a reading he was to do the following week; he wondered if it might be intriguing to read some work in progress and discuss it a little with the audience. But Elinor broke into his thoughts. She came out onto the porch with a flier for the reading in her hand and sat on the rickety basket chair, her head high. She looked at Robert defiantly.

'You know Rob, I do so hate these public performances of yours,' she told him. 'Your mesmerising of the audience, your made-up personality. It's all so false.'

'False? I don't see that at all. Elinor – you're never content. You've no interest in my reputation. Don't you want me to earn decent money for once? What is the matter with that, for God's sake?'

'The whole thing, the way you reveal our private matters to those poetry ignoramuses and how they do lap it up! That's what they want you for, for this character you've created, this Yankee hayseed farmer character and you so educated. I hate it. Your work was pure, but these performances – they only degrade it.'

'Oh really! And the money – does that degrade us too?'

'I don't care about the money. I was much happier at the old Derry farm, when your poetry began as a *private* thing, between the two of us, not letting everyone in like this. All these intruders.'

'Ellie, listen. This poetry business – it is a business, and more than that. It's a war. At the moment it's between me and Sandburg, neck and neck, or equally matched, however you want to put it. Words are weapons, subtle but lethal weapons to play the game with and I damned well intend to win. So you had better get used to it. I'm not about to quit. You want a life that goes just – oh, poetically. To be a poet is a condition, not a profession, I know that, but to be known, to sell and resell and make a good living, that takes a business mind. It can't be all simple living and hardship and nothing to do with the world outside. I've had enough of that now and if I have to playact the sage farmer I will. You had better just get used to it.'

She looked so troubled that he suddenly softened towards her.

'Darling Ellie, come here, here, sit on my knee, my love. It will be all right, you know. It's still only the two of us – it really is and it always will be. You're tired, my flower, my own wife. You're just tired. That's all.'

She came to him.

Fifteen

Edward's poems were impatient to be born. He limped up to the study under a pale blue sky as the last frosts melted. He wrote about sowing and the scents of digging, of bonfire, of earth. He wrote about this time of transition when it was not yet spring. Spring was not a simple thing; its progress was slow and halting with many set-backs and reversals, a mirror for him of his own way of emerging from melancholy to the beginnings of a brighter mood. He meditated on beauty and on ambition, on his old grim discontents and on the power of the natural world against them.

They were all meditations of a kind. He aimed to write quite short poems in many different forms, according to their subjects; his literary knowledge came into its own. Not often did he use what he called the Frosty form of long dialogue poems. Quatrains, he found, could be so varied. He wrote about subtle changes he noticed in the country because of the war.

> *The flowers left thick at nightfall in the wood*
> *This Eastertide call into mind the men,*
> *Now far from home, who, with their sweethearts, should*
> *Have gathered them and will do never again.*

In a long poem he wanted to set all his sense of England and its past, of change and continuity, of places, names, legends and tales. It was a poem he felt he had to write. It wouldn't be an obscure learned literary poem. It would draw on traditional tales, proverbs and children's stories. He wanted to show a kind of archetype, one going back as far as Herne the Hunter, and the veteran of centuries of wars. Yeats was much too free with his 'dreams', but the imagery was an example of what he wanted, using Irish folk symbols in a natural way, so that they emerged as instinctive and right, not as invented. He would try to do the same with the English tradition.

Lob would be an old travelling man, one with no land of his own, met on the road and sought out again. *Everyone has met one such man as he, English as this gate, these flowers, this mire.* He brought to it his favourite 'most English' poem, from Shakespeare:

> *This is tall Tom that bore*
> *The logs in, and with Shakespeare in the hall*
> *Once talked, when icicles hung by the wall.*

Wild flowers and wild places, their names passed on for centuries. Perhaps a hobgoblin or Puck. He was more than any one man, and indestructible:

> *Do you believe Jack dead before his hour?*
> *The man you saw —Lob lie-by-the-fire, Jack Cade*
> *Jack Smith, Jack Moon, poor jack-of-every trade*
> *Old Jack, young Jack, he never will be dead*
> *Till millers cease to grind men's bones for bread.*
> *Jack-in-the-hedge, or Robin-run-by-the-wall,*
> *Robin Hood, Ragged Robin, lazy Bob,*
> *One of the lords of No Man's Land, good Lob,—*
> *Although he was seen dying at Waterloo,*
> *Hastings, Agincourt, and Sedgemoor too,—*
> *Lives yet. He never will admit that he is dead*
> *Till millers cease to grind men's bones for bread...*

It drew on what he loved about his country in the same way that Chaucer and Shakespeare had used folklore and folk-songs. It would be about the mystery of the past, of the generations linked through centuries by these traditions. Not one monarch or politician would mar it.

'*Look at all these poems!*' Never had he enjoyed writing so much. It was what he had been waiting for so long, and he simply hadn't known it. But he was having no success in having his poems published.

'I am sure the one thing is to try and keep myself for the moods most likely to crystallise all my familiar and unfamiliar material,' he wrote to Robert. *'I hope experience and honesty will lead me to a better way if there is one for me.'*

'Hhhm, in Bottomley's opinion, Helen, I'm still "too bound by the structure of prose". He finds them uncomfortable to the ear. But I think he's wrong – I want to loosen those old over-regular rhythms and break free from them.'

Harold Monro looked at his work, this time knowing that they were his, and said that he was not able to publish them. He found something rather 'unfinished' about them – exactly the effect that Edward valued most, the sense that perfect expression of experience was not possible.

Edward was not prepared to defend himself to Gordon or Harold. Better to go out, to walk among the tall stems of bluebells, their bent heads showing a touch of colour like a hint of sky under the bright new birch leaves. Only Robert's opinion counted with him.

But nothing solved the problem of earning a living. He could only contemplate doing work he could believe in now. Perhaps finding his voice in poetry had made him less fit for earning a living in his former way even if there were commissions to be had. Luckily the new anthology he was working on was something he could believe in. He wrote in its introduction:

'I wished to make a book as full of English character and country as an egg is of meat. If I have reminded others, as I did myself continually, of some of the echoes called up by the name of England, I am satisfied.'

He had decided not to include Shakespeare's 'this England' speech in spite of the anthology's title. Monarchs were not the essence of England; her people defined her. So 'When icicles hang by the wall' was of course included, with Dick the shepherd, log-bearing Tom and greasy Joan. And Falstaff, Jack Falstaff, praising the virtues of ale. He favoured Falstaff's warmth and earthy humour over the cold ruthless reformed Henry absolutely.

He must include Henry V on St Crispin's Day, but he was unwilling to give the king the last word. Should he include the words Shakespeare gave a common soldier on the night before battle?

'But if the cause be not good, the king himself hath a heavy reckoning to make, when all those legs and arms and heads, chopped off in a battle, shall join together at the latter day.' He would. How dishonest it would be to deny that stark reality when he was making the anthology for today's soldiers!

The biography of the Duke of Marlborough just qualified as worthwhile work too, with English troops fighting in Flanders again. He was reluctant to begin it, though, because he would need to spend weeks indoors in the British Museum. Nevertheless, it had to be done for the money was badly needed.

So he stayed with his parents and worked for two months in the Round Reading Room. The great dome soared above his head, a splendid extravagance of iron built for its beauty alone. Below it was the giddying round of windows. His early start saw the eastern morning light through them, his late finish the reddening of the western sky. He was on the steps among the pigeons before the Room opened, one of those who had a favourite seat and claimed it every day.

April and May were passing, so much of his favourite months missed as he saw the noon sun only through the struts of the cupola, sharp and bright as a gold coin.

Sometimes he stretched up from his books and notes, and looked around at the other readers – many more women than he had seen before, and far fewer young men. As he wrote about the old wars he thought of the new and of the deaths of men so much younger than himself, their lives cut short when they were hardly begun.

He arranged to meet Eleanor for lunch one day. She was typing Lob and had a suggestion to make – a line that she felt was lacking. He agreed with her.

Eleanor told him that she had spent time with friends in Sussex; two of these friends were the Lawrences.

'Tell me about him,' Edward said. 'I did admire *The White*

Peacock. His writing about nature is quite extraordinary. I envy it.'

'It is impossible,' she said, 'to convey what Lawrence is like, but I'll try.' She hesitated.

'He – he doesn't hold anything back, delight, irritability, nothing. You have to take him all-of-a-piece or not at all. He doesn't care a jot what embarrassment he causes. Neither does Frieda. He's somehow the opposite of you – constantly expressing himself where you're suppressing and yet—'

'Yes?'

'Well, in one way you're the same – what you do give of yourself is true, never any sham or pretence. And you expect the truth in return.'

Eleanor herself didn't tell Edward the truth on this occasion. She had shown Lawrence some of the sonnets she'd written about her love for Edward, though they were the less intimate ones. Of course she had not explained but somehow he had seen the truth. What he had said in response had shaken her; she had fine poetry in her, he said, but she would never fight things out to the last issue. There was a littleness, a cowardice in her.

Later he had sent her his comments more fully in a letter.

'Never the last dregs of bitterness will you drink, never face the last embrace of fire.'

And he was indignant at the promotion of resignation and self-denial he read in her sonnets.

'It is not true. We can by the strength of our desires compel our destinies. "Destiny is the strength of our desires." Let that be your line.'

So she turned the subject away from Lawrence and Frieda as soon as she could. The way they had shaped their destinies out of their own desires, the ruined lives of Frieda's three motherless children, she could only deplore. Was it cowardice on her part, not even to try to have Edward for herself? Lawrence would surely say so.

In Yew Tree Cottage Helen had been spring-cleaning so that when he did come home to Steep one April afternoon the cottage gleamed. New gingham curtains were at the kitchen window, the chair covers were cleaned and the big round peg rug washed. Jugs of wild flowers stood on the windowsills.

Myfanwy and Bronwen had plenty to tell him as they sat around the tea-table, the ubiquitous damson jam spooned onto their bread, tea served in the pretty service. Myfanwy insisted on bringing her doll's pram up to the table so that her doll could watch proceedings. Bronwen had a new skirt and blouse to show him, which she had cut out and sewed herself. He relished for that afternoon this world of women and their gentle concerns, their love for him and for each other. After tea Baba brought out her *Reading Without Tears*, a solemn-looking book bound in bible-black. Its title amused him, but he was impressed to find that, yes, she had learned to master words on a page for herself.

He went for a walk in the misty stillness of evening. Something in the birds' songs, the single spirit of their singing together, and the calm after London, was like a welcome. He had a sense that he and the birds of Steep were one, that his needs and pleasures were at one with theirs and that he was home. A labourer walked with a slow heavy tread and turned into the thatched wood-shed beside his white cottage. Soon afterward a rhythmic sound of sawing came from the man's shed and the birds had fallen silent. He was home, among country people and thrushes and chaffinches and the oaks and elms that were their homes.

In the bedroom the white bedspread was bleached as good as new. He threw himself wearily onto it and Helen came and lay in his arms in their favourite way, like two spoons. They listened as a roll of thunder rumbled far off, and nearer. Then came an hour of welcome rain.

Early next day he walked through still moist air up the hill. The first two hours of the day he gave to his verses. Then he worked on *Marlborough,* writing for seven hours, reading and checking for three hours more. At the end of the day he was almost too tired to enjoy the variety of fresh greens in the woods. He looked down at Steep, seeing the coils of smoke rising from chimney-stacks where the evening meals were being prepared and wished himself already at home. But the walk in the half-light of the wood, watching the wrens chase about the whitebeam twigs, revived him. As he reached the back garden and heard a thrush's urgent evening song he felt almost reluctant to be indoors before it had ended. He would be even more reluctant to return next day to the Museum, but it must be faced.

By June both the *Anthology* and *Marlborough* were done. He had no other commissions.

With nothing to absorb him he soon found his old troubled thoughts returning and a terrible loneliness that he knew was of his own making. A friend had written to him accusing him of having 'an air of superiority' – how mistakenly! It was his cover, his shell hardened by years of habit to hide his terrible self-consciousness. Nothing he could do would break it; it needed some external thing, an accident or monumental change. Like landing in New York almost penniless, perhaps. That might do the trick.

Sixteen

In the house in Franconia it seemed that winter would never end. Carol was failing on the farm; as they had feared, little of the fruit blossom had survived the frosts. The days were still short and cold, each morning beginning in a haze that lasted until mid-afternoon. The whole family suffered from colds.

But Robert was hatching a plan. He was avidly writing and was now so well known as a reader and lecturer that he was asked to speak at the University of Pennsylvania. At Harvard too he'd been invited to read as the Phi Beta Kappa poet. He and Elinor had a fine time there, leaving the children behind for once.

The poems he was working on would make a new volume that he planned to call *Mountain Interval,* for by now he knew it was to be only that, an interval. Some of the poems were first drafted in the Derry farm, others in Gloucestershire, a few since they came home. His reputation was growing all the time. The time was right for a new departure.

He was annoyed with Edward – why did he keep equivocating instead of packing his bags and coming to them, especially as he was getting nowhere with publishing his poems, whereas Robert had such influence and could pull strings in America? It was no good sending off his poems to people who knew him, like de la Mare and Garnett. It was not the way to do things; he'd told him this before and he was telling him again. And he wrote telling Edward that he could have the farm all to himself, or for his family, as they intended to move lower down the mountain where he would be able to travel more easily and become a regular teacher. Edward could keep an eye on the place for them.

In Steep Edward's mind was partly on Robert's promises, partly on his current poem.

'I'm off now, Helen – bye.' He was starting out to the study.

'But Edwy, what are you going to do up there? I thought you were going to go to London again today.'

'Oh, what's the use? I hate going round editors *begging* them for work. If they want me they know where I am. And the agency's looking around for me anyway. Can't you see how it is for me? There *is* no work. Don't you understand that?'

He heaved the back door open too hard and it crashed into the wall. Helen cringed. 'Well, I do hope something turns up soon or—' Her voice trailed off. 'Oh, I know it's not your fault – it's this dreadful war.' She came to him and put her arms round him, meaning to be consoling but she made matters worse. He pulled away.

'You make me feel worthless, Helen. I'm going.'

He went each morning to the study although he had no paid work to do. It was wretched to be willing to work, to know what he was capable of doing and how little he needed direction once he had a commission, yet to have nothing, to be earning nothing. But he could work on his poems if only he was in the right frame of mind.

He came back for his midday meals and the arguments went on.

One June day they faced each other across the dirty plates and the breadcrumbs scattered on the tablecloth. Helen had a cold and was feeling miserably lethargic, so she hadn't whipped away the plates and cloth as she usually did.

'What do you want me to do? Go to America and stay with Robert? I'd have to be away at least six months for it to be worth the fare. And no guarantee of earning anything there.'

'Oh, I would miss you so much. But – then you could come back with Merfyn, in time for Christmas perhaps.'

'I could – or I could send for you all – but only if things were going well for Frost and me. He's so sure that I can change my spots and become like him.'

'What! – I hope you wouldn't do that.'

'I mean become more "extrovert", as Baynes would say. More outgoing and confident and as loquacious as Rob himself.

Perhaps he's right.'

'But you talk beautifully and cleverly. Robert talks so much it's hard to break in.'

'Well, I can talk among my friends, but I suppose I could try teaching at that school in Coventry, as a kind of practice for lecturing at this summer school of Robert's.'

Helen was thinking and surprised him with what she said.

'Well, now I think I agree – it might be right for you to go to America. I think it would be best. Anything would be better than this, with you so tormented.'

He was surprised and pleased. For a moment he was excited— a way forward, a new world, Robert and he together again, and with his new confidence in poetry.

'But you realise it would take all our savings simply to get me to America.'

'Oh dear, would it really? What could we do about Bronnie's school fees then?'

'She could go to a cheaper school.'

'Oh dear. Take her away from Margaret and her school?' Bronwen stayed with her aunt and cousin in London during the week and she loved her school there. The fees were already almost beyond their reach.

'Yes, Helen, of course. And when Merfyn does come home we'll need some savings to invest in his future, whatever that might be. Perhaps he'll expect us to buy him a working motor garage. Well why not?'

'Oh Edward, please don't. Oh dear, America does seem difficult then. But – are you sure there is nobody you know – with all your knowledge of publishers and publications – have you really tried everyone?'

Edward jumped to his feet and banged his fist on the table.

'Damn it Helen, of course I have. Do you take me for a fool? Look, I can stand no more of you rubbing in my failure. If I had any work it would be impossible in this atmosphere. I'm going to the study. And the sooner I can make plans to get away from here and go to America if I can, or go anywhere, the better it will be.'

He stormed across the meadow and kept on up the hill, hot

and angry in the afternoon sun. Instead of going straight to his study he walked along the ridge for an hour before turning back.

Once he was in the Bee House he felt calmer. But Helen wanted so much from him. She talked of wanting a simple life but the truth was that she wanted a style of life not so different from that in which they had both been brought up, with a good income and a housemaid at the very least. A writer's life couldn't be expected always to provide that kind of security.

He leaned his arms on the desk and rested his head on them. He wanted to weep. He had worked so hard – those many thousands upon thousands of words, that long row of his books. Twenty-five of them on the shelf above his desk, from the decorative green cover of *The Woodland Life* that he was so pleased with when he was only nineteen, to the last two, new and untouched: his 'fiction' that he had hoped would make money but hadn't. And the proof of *Proverbs,* children's stories written years before, when the two older ones were small. A few fresh additions had made it publishable. Eleanor and Clifford Bax had pushed it for him. But would it sell? He doubted it.

Infinitely more words, uncountable words, a million words, in the hundreds of articles and reviews that were ground out of him over the years.

Somehow Robert appeared to get along without hard work at all. He even joked about his idleness, his liking for a leisurely life. Perhaps if he were in America, with or without Helen and the children, he would find he could do the same. But no, he suspected that Robert did work hard, and had some private income too. And Elinor really did not seem to mind their poverty.

Suppose he were to fail in America. It was true, people saw him as having an attitude that was easily mistaken for cold superiority, an aloofness, which he was afraid would damn him there. The truth was quite different; he simply dreaded people in advance of meeting them. Sometimes people irritated him, it was true. But he suffered more from too much humility and faintheartedness than from superiority.

That aloofness, it was as if over the years he'd built a house of glass all around him, keeping people out. He didn't want it – he

169

wished someone would break through it. Robert almost had. And above all, Eleanor, gently and timidly, with her instinctive way of understanding him.

Helen simply behaved as though it weren't there, he thought, and sometimes for her it was not. No one else would ever know him so well in one sense, but when his house of glass was in place she behaved as though she couldn't see it or feel it, like a silly bird that dashed against a window. Then she would be stunned and hurt. Yet she was never broken. She would never give up her hopes of him, he knew, her hopes for that happy, ideal marriage. And she would never, ever, let him alone.

He wanted solitude again. Always he had this need for solitude followed by the need for company. For moving on, then for coming home. Now the need to be away from Helen, from the children, was strong. America would give him that. Who could tell what he might become? He *would* go, and find out.

Could he really change his nature, be warm and approachable, give lectures, and learn to like Americans? He found it impossible to make a decision without seeing the objections to it.

But no, he could see only one chance – to go to America. He must stop simply waiting for something to turn up. He would begin to decide how many days to give to New York and how many to Boston. Robert could give him some introductions, being well on his way with a book in a third edition already.

What if he should fail, and have to come home a failure?

Well, Robert would tell me not to go in on myself like this, he thought. It's unwise to look at yourself in the glass except to shave – that was one of Robert's sayings. He couldn't help it sometimes, but he could help dwelling in the inner recesses of his mind for days on end in the way he used to.

America then, as soon as it could be arranged.

But there was that question, or that resolve, was it, under the new moon in Gloucestershire. That sense that England was not his unless he was willing and prepared to do something, perhaps even to die, for her. Hardly a day passed without him thinking that what he ought to do was to enlist.

This pattern of thinking was so well-worn for him, from

sleepless nights and daytime dreams. It was a labyrinth of familiar paths that he kept treading, making no progress.

He came in late for supper, knowing this irked her. Then he was quiet and grim. Helen's cold was worse.

'Why don't you go to bed? I'll see to Baba's bath – it's not exactly pleasant having you look the way you do and hearing your sniffling.'

Miserably Helen said goodnight and went upstairs as though her feet were dragging chains.

He always enjoyed bathing Myfanwy in front of the fire in the tin hip-bath. She had her repertoire of songs and rhymes – nonsense mostly, but always with her sense of rhythm. Then, as she sat quietly, wrapped in a towel on his knee, he sang to her in Welsh, her eyes gazing vaguely at him, until they closed and she was asleep. He carried her up to bed.

Oh, how could he provide for them all? Wouldn't the Army be at least some kind of security, a regular income? Wasn't that a more certain prospect than America?

But what kind of a soldier would he make? He had never even worked for anyone. All his adult life he'd made his own way. He was his own disciplinarian, and a very stern one. To be given orders by someone else – surely it would be intolerable.

How could he resolve these questions? It seemed impossible. He despised his indecision, his Hamlet-like character. What would Robert think, with his 'go all out for your goals' approach, of the way he was now?

He went into the kitchen corner and put a pan of milk on the range to make Helen a cup of cocoa.

Seventeen

In July he wrote to a friend.

'I am going to cycle and think of man and nature and human life and decide between enlisting, or going to America before I enlist. Those are the alternatives unless something comes up out of the dark.'

Jack Haines was a solicitor who lived near Dymock, a fanatical amateur botanist who had become friendly with Robert and Edward during their Leddington and Ryton days. After Robert left, Edward and he wrote regularly to each other and in late June Edward and the Humber took a Great Western train to Gloucester to stay with him. They were planning to cycle around Gloucester for a few days. Then he would travel on to Coventry to enquire about that teaching post.

It was a chance to pay another visit to May Hill, where he'd been more than once with both Robert and Jack together. Its separateness, its individuality, standing there apart, pleased him.

A coppery sun was just rising as they pedalled up through slopes of bracken and foxgloves, the bundled shapes of sheep emerging grey-white on the lower slopes. They talked about Robert as they went, remembering how he would sometimes find their walks over-long, good-humouredly complaining, and how he'd laughed at Edward's indecision when two paths diverged. Tears came, to his surprise, and he blinked them away.

Some old firs and a beech tree were all that was left of a wood that had once clothed the slopes, Jack told him. As the gradient flattened, the hill became a broad common topped by a square plantation of young Scots firs. It was a clear bright day, one of the days when you could identify twelve counties from the west side of the hill, it was said. He recognised the deep green of the Forest of Dean and the dip in its contours that was the Wye. Far beyond were the dark hills of Monmouthshire and further still the cloudy mass of the Black Mountains. Turn east and you were looking towards the Severn and the Cotswold Hills.

Jack spent his time closely observing the plants through his round glasses, often taking out his magnifying glass to see better. Once Edward heard him mutter, 'Veronica Officinalis – the heath speedwell – good.'

Edward looked towards Wales. That inheritance would always be part of him, but without doubt he was mostly an Englishman. To claim that he was Welsh was something of a sham, and he loathed sham and deception above anything. He valued Wales, that beautiful country, its lyrical language and its people, but he must admit to being a visitor, an admiring visitor whose roots gave him a small claim.

Sitting down with his back to a fir, facing the English counties, he began to write a draft of a poem in his notebook. It was about English words, names, villages and hills. He would include Wales. And himself and what, most passionately, he wanted. He thought of all his prose writing, the millions of words he'd written. Poetry was different; sometimes it was as if the words chose him, not the other way. He wanted to celebrate the history and the ever-changing, ever-renewing quality of words. They were old and yet worn new again and again, like ancient streams, always young, especially after rain. Words, and names, and things – real, exact concrete things – these he could celebrate. And the poem needed to be upright, standing tall like the hill itself.

He wrote feverishly on May Hill, composing a kind of prayer – a prayer to words, ending:

Let me sometimes dance
With you,
Or climb
Or stand perchance
In ecstasy,
Fixed and free

In a rhyme,
As poets do.

Eighteen

Half a kiss, half a tear

He was home again, tanned and golden-haired, fit from his cycling, and he said very breezily, 'Well, nothing's come of Bablake School – no definite work, too temporary an arrangement – it was no good to me. I don't really know why he wanted me to consider it at all. A complete waste of time, except for the Merfyn business. But I did write something I like.'

I'd had enough. Something in me – my patience – snapped. No certainty of any money beyond the next few months. Already we were relying on my sister to keep Bronnie with her at weekends as well as in the week, and I missed her terribly. And yet Edward came home looking so well and cheerful.

'Yes – well, at least Merfyn'll have something to occupy *him* when he comes home.' I stared out of the window, not looking at him.

'This again – look, what do you want me to do? I can't insist on being given work. You imagine I don't care about earning no more than a hundred and fifty a year. I loathe going around publishers' houses begging like a pauper.'

I started to suggest something I'd thought of, but he cut me off.

'Oh I'm so tired of this. Just leave me to find my own way without your hints and suggestions. You may well find I take another way out entirely.'

I didn't know what he meant. Was it a threat of suicide again? I thought that was in the past. But I always knew the thought was there in him, even though he didn't talk about it anymore. I felt sick, and then I felt angry. It wasn't fair.

'Oh I see that again is it? The coward's way.'

'That was not what I meant, in fact. But do you imagine I want

175

to be in this intolerable situation, with you making it a thousand times worse?'

'Then get out of it – do something, anything, to bring this to an end – you and your wretched Hamlet maunderings. I can't bear it any more. I know we're nothing to you – I'm nothing.'

I started to cry, but then I was angry with myself for that.

Standing next to the sink with the breakfast dishes piled unwashed in it I suddenly grabbed a dish and hurled it across the room at him. He ducked, but the dish broke the stave of our Windsor chair near to where he was standing, so great was my force. The fragments of white pottery lay where they fell on the quarry tiles. Edward stared at me and then went out saying nothing.

Eventually I fetched a dustpan and brush and began to clear up, crying. The ugly broken stave. Our ugly faces. So this was my home, this was my life. My marriage. Was this me, cheerful happy Helen?

When he came back in the evening we laughed awkwardly about it and Edward said I had a rotten aim and it served me right for never taking any interest in cricket. He glued the chair. But really, we were both shocked.

Nineteen

Next day the proof of the Anthology came in the post and he went up to the study to correct it. He was pleased to find remarkably few errors, but there were two blank pages left to be filled – two blank white pages. Could he perhaps fill them himself, with his own poems?

The verses he wrote in the winter about the Prior's Dean Farm were as 'English' as anything in the work. It was linked in his mind with that other farm at Dymock, a pink-washed house crouched at the foot of a great tree and the timelessness of that haymaking. Haymaking and The Manor Farm; they were both about the seemingly unchangeable that he wanted to record, one for summer, one for winter, and they would fill those blank pages. They seemed to make a plea for less destructive times.

So his namesake, the poet 'Edward Eastaway', would at least have two poems in print. It was as much as he could hope for while the war lasted. He laughed: how easy it had been, after all, making a new identity for himself, simply changing six letters for eight new ones, it seemed.

No other work was to be had. He had made enquiries about a post with the Ministry of Information but that came to nothing. Friends he had helped in the past, petitioning for grants and bursaries, were doing nothing for him in return.

America was the answer – it had to be. He was fit and strong and Robert seemed to think that he could 'farm' as well as write and lecture. If Helen and the children came later they would be free from all the shortages and problems the war was bringing. He could see Scott, and take some advice and contacts from him as well as from Robert. He could collect Merfyn to come with him to Franconia. When the Frosts moved lower down the mountain, the two of them would have a home of sorts; it certainly wouldn't hurt Merfyn to do some land-work and perhaps he and the boy would at last begin to appreciate each other.

But it surprised and troubled him that Americans appeared to care nothing for England or her fate. They said that it was not their quarrel, even though so many Americans had their roots in England, Scotland or Wales. Woodrow Wilson claimed that it was idealism that kept them on the path of peace. Had Wilson heard nothing of the suffering of Belgium and France? It was simply self-interest and greed masquerading as idealism, he thought. How could he be at ease in such a country? Should he not be putting the plight of his own country first by trying to enlist as a soldier?

But perhaps he had to put himself first and then his family. Grand scenery, somewhere he'd never been, a land he'd never known. He would welcome that and probably find it an inspiration – he always had. Or was that only true because the new landscapes he'd explored were part of his own land, another of its half-familiar treasures to be discovered? Places that came to life through knowing their traditions, history and especially their writers?

What was he to do? How could he know what was right? It was extraordinary, the way other people seemed able to make decisions without difficulty. How could they not see the impossible complexity, the near-equal balance of good and bad, in almost every choice?

He wrote to Robert about Rupert Brooke's sonnets. They were published in New Numbers simultaneously with the news of Rupert's death.

'The whole nation is mourning him,' he wrote. The country was in love with Brooke and his noble sacrifice, his passion for England. His beautiful, romantic appearance and his poetry helped to bring in a flood of new recruits. His last sonnet, If I should die, was read in a Westminster Abbey sermon and printed in all the national papers.

This cult of self-sacrifice and the use of poetry in the service of propaganda made Edward uncomfortable. But he felt unable to criticise a false note, he added, when he himself had not enlisted *'or fought the gamekeeper'.*

So perhaps Robert was prepared when Edward wrote again to tell him why he would not be coming to New Hampshire after all.

He travelled up to London by train and walked fast to Albemarle Street, hunting for a brass nameplate – 'The Artists' Rifles'. A printed poster was pinned to a sandwich board on the pavement, announcing 'Recruiting Office'. The regimental symbol printed at the head showed Mars and Minerva intertwined. He looked up at the sky for a moment, then turned, breathed deeply and walked through the open door.

He was attested fit by the Medical Officer the following day. He had passed the first test that he'd set himself.

Book Three

One

Half a kiss, half a tear

The day life changed was the day Edwy went to London, telling me he was planning to call on a publisher he knew, looking for work. I was in the kitchen when the telegram came saying that he had enlisted in the Artists' Rifles. My legs began to collapse under me.

'No, no, no – not that!' was all I could say. Scenes of gory battle ran through my mind, with Edward dead, mangled among cannon-balls and blood. I had no idea then about modern warfare, trenches, heavy guns, shells, mud, tin helmets. But the blood stays the same, blood is always the end of war.

Why had he done it? Married, with three children. He did not have any obligation to enlist. And without telling me! It was humiliating, to be left out like that, as if it didn't concern me. How dare he? Was it too late, could he withdraw?

My son gone, Edward going. Why hadn't I encouraged him more in the American venture? So stay-at-home, so homey, so narrow in my thinking, fussing about Bronwen's school! I'd thought I could at least keep us all safe at home. Now see where that had led!

I had complained too often about his Hamlet maunderings. It was my fault.

He would be coming home a soldier and it would be my job, so the posters told me, to welcome, support and encourage him. It was too late, I knew, for anything else.

So the next day I smartened up the house and myself and went to meet him from the train. His hair – so dreadfully short! His face very lean and hard-looking because of it. Instead of his old loose tweeds he was in stiff khaki. When he kissed me he didn't smell the same – that peaty, tweedy tobacco-y smell that always excited me had gone. Khaki has an unpleasant smell that seems to take all the individual character of a man away. I was almost repelled by the look and smell of the man I'd always adored with all my senses.

But I had to try to be proud of him, of course. In an odd way, I was.

The girls were fascinated by their Daddy the soldier, interested in all the buckles and badges, wanting to help polish them, as they'd heard a soldier must do. His Artists' Rifles badge – of Mars and Minerva appropriately – was a particularly attractive one. Edward told me what he knew about the Company and it did sound as though it would suit him as well as anything in the Army could. At least *he* seemed satisfied that he'd made the right decision.

Only three days before he was to go away! We knew that it could be a long absence and Edwy had to sort his papers in the study, help me with the garden and even chop some wood for the autumn ahead. But we had to find time for a walk together.

'I've asked Mrs Dodds to have Myfanwy and give her some lunch. We can go for the whole morning,' I said.

Edward put on his old clothes and was back to being his old self, apart from that shorn hair that I hated.

'Well at least you'll have a regular income from my pay,' he said. We talked about how I would manage practically. His pay would be quite small, but he believed he would still be able to do some occasional writing work. And I was planning to teach English to some foreign ladies.

'Do you think you'll be able to manage the garden?' he asked. I saw myself suddenly, all through the summer, after the children had gone to bed, sitting alone in the little porch, perhaps hearing the nightingale which once came to sing in our damson hedge. Edward not there. I tried not to, but I cried.

'Dearest, don't cry. It will be all right – there will be leave, I'll be able to come home often, I'm sure. At least while I'm still in England—'

'Don't! Edward, please don't say that. You can't mean to contemplate that. You simply can't—'

'At any rate the whole thing will be over in a few months, I believe. Now I've enlisted I feel keen to get started. At least I'll know that I was prepared to do something, even if it wasn't much.'

Was it not enough? I decided then to act as if I took it absolutely for granted that Edward would be taking a non-combat role in the Army, some paperwork, a desk job, with his education and at his age. It would be harder for him then to think of doing anything else.

Sometimes on that walk we were silent together in the old comfortable way, looking, remembering what we both loved in the Steep countryside we'd known for so long. If only we could go on walking on a summer day like this forever, with no cares or fears, I thought. But I couldn't forget for a moment that this was a farewell walk.

I had to keep telling myself that Edward had enlisted because he loved his family, his country and his country's freedom and he wasn't content to leave their protection to other men. He was such a fine man and I loved him with all my heart: I would try to *make* myself see it that way, I would tell everyone that was how I felt. I would keep our home extra welcoming and warm for him, so that he would feel that nothing had changed there at least. But underneath I knew that I had lost to a force too strong for me, Edward's sheer decency, his scrupulous honour, which was what the rest of the world knew of him. Only I knew how cruel he could be, and in a way this was more cruelty. I would have to live with my failure to hold him near me and this time I was afraid that my usual appetite for life was gone.

Two

He had written to Eleanor that he would be coming up to town again and would like to meet her at Shearns' tea-rooms as usual. But she felt that she could not bear the idea of meeting him in that rather intimidating public place and asked him in a telegram to come to her house.

The maid showed him into the drawing room and she stood up. His hair was brutally shorn but he was still in his usual clothes and he had a happier expression than she had seen for some time. As he came towards her he bent his head and kissed her cheek. This had never happened before and her heart pounded. She held both his hands and looked up at him.

'Well, I've joined up.'

'I don't know why, but I am glad.'

'I am glad too,' he told her, 'and I don't know why either.'

They looked at each other, smiling.

'Do you think you will still be able to write?'

Edward thought he would write no more poetry for a while; he expected to find that his life was entirely occupied with the Army.

'I do have a few last things for typing, if you don't mind. Don't worry if you're too busy. Well, I won't say they'll be the last – but there's going to be a long break – longer even than I had to have because of the Duke.'

She felt he was different and soon realised what it was. The agony of indecision had gone. So long as he stayed safe, in England – and at his age surely he would – she could be happy with his decision.

She thought, too, that it was possible he would be closer to London and would perhaps look more and more to her for her sympathy and understanding. That was what men always did with Eleanor. She found that she was always a source of warm sympathy for men she knew. Perhaps only Lawrence had seen that it was not enough for her, not all she wanted. But yes, on the whole Edward's move had made Eleanor glad.

As soon as he had enlisted Edward wrote to Robert, explaining, almost apologising. Robert was not angry – he wrote, *'I am within a hair of being precisely as sorry and as glad as you are.'* He didn't want Edward to be killed but he was glad to think that he could be. He had made the right choice. Since he knew of all the twists and turns Edward had endured, he appreciated how seriously his decision had been made: *'Only the very bravest could come to the sacrifice in this way.'* The sinking of the Lusitania in May, killing neutral American men women and children, was changing his thinking about the war as it had for many Americans. That summer he felt a restless, almost reckless need to do something with his anger over it.

In his next letter to Robert Edward wrote that the practice he was getting, lecturing and managing officer cadets, would make him much better fitted to lecture in America after the war; it was simply a postponement of their plans. Edward gave Robert his first impressions of being a soldier:

'It is all like being somebody else, or like being in a dream of school. Am I indulging in the pleasure of being somebody else?'

He was aware that he looked like a different man in his immaculate khaki with polished buttons. It seemed that you had to act a part as a soldier and a future officer. Just by acting the part well enough you would get by. Still he felt that he was an undigested lump among the other recruits, not really fitting in. He didn't mind that, in fact he wanted to be sure that he did not lose too much of his true self. But then, with the new energy and near-certainty he felt – was that old melancholy self so precious? Was it, in fact, his true self at all? Not entirely, perhaps.

Nobody persuaded me into this, not even myself, he thought. It was as he had imagined, a kind of instinctive leap, beyond the reach of reasoning, going to London that day. It was where all his thoughts and moods and indecision were leading since the war began. He could not foresee what would happen in his life now, but then it was his belief that rarely could events be foreseen.

Billeted at his parents' London house while he waited for training to begin, he had time to do some additions to *Marlborough*. As he worked he found his feelings towards the subject had changed. The great scale of the Duke's wars and this new identity of his began to cohere together a little. He felt a sense of inevitability about his enlisting; war is a constant in history and history shows that it is cyclical. Now war was a part of him, he himself was a small piece of this latest manifestation of history. Perhaps his minute part in the cycle of history could still include writing, to show other truths about war, the sheer sadness of it all and the complexity.

He finished work and went out to smoke in the garden, still thinking about the old wars. Digging with his heel in a flower-bed to bury a scrap of clay pipe from his pocket, he imagined the shards of two pipes:

The one I smoked, the other a soldier
Of Blenheim, Ramillies, and Malplaquet
Perhaps. The dead man's immortality
Lies represented lightly with my own.

He found himself thinking of a scrap of verse he wrote in January when he was sprawled across two chairs in their living-room. It was about an itinerant farm-worker, a man he'd met often in The Drovers. He was presumed to have been killed in France but his body had not been found. There was a problem with the first line: *'The labouring man here lying slept out of doors.'*

The rhythm was clumsy.

'This ploughman dead in battle slept out of doors.' He remembered the man's cheery defiance as he said he always slept for free at 'Mrs Greenland's Hawthorn Bush' and how no one knew where he meant. Mrs Greenland – such a homely-sounding, motherly sort of deity.

And where now at last he sleeps
More sound in France – that, too, he secret keeps.

That night, in the bedroom he'd had as a child, Edward dreamt that he and Robert were walking together – he was sure it was near the river Leadon – when a dark stream burst through into daylight, ran above ground for a time and then disappeared into a cavern in the ground again. What struck him most in the dream was that in following the flowing waters he forgot his friend – somehow in the way of dreams Robert was no longer there. He knew enough from Baynes to guess at the sense of the dream – he had found his own voice in his poetry. And perhaps in his life. Robert was no longer always necessary as an influence.

But as the dream was ending he'd remembered Robert and Gloucestershire and said to himself, 'Some day I will be here again.' That was something he would hold on to, a dear memory and a prospect.

Hampstead Heath was the site of map-reading training. A monstrous gun, the pivotal point of their exercises, stood incongruously in the middle of the Heath declaring the state of war.

Of course he knew much more than the instructor did about maps. He enjoyed and excelled at the long route marches and was terribly bored and frustrated by guard duty. A powerful inoculation made him ill for a few days, but once he was well he urgently wanted action and to be given his new orders.

The day came: inevitably his ability with maps had been noticed. 'Private Thomas, you'll be going to Romford shortly, to be a map-reading instructor. Starting first at High Beech until the new camp is ready.'

He was to be sent to the Artists' Rifles new training camp in Epping Forest, to help turn the new recruits into competent officers in only thirteen weeks. The army needed two hundred and fifty more officers a month, it was said. He was pleased. It was an intelligent use of his abilities and he felt sure it would be valuable work. But he was anxious at the thought of teaching.

It was said, though, that the war might well be over by October.

Three

From Liverpool Street station the train took him east through gentle, orderly countryside to Romford and on to Gidea Park halt. November trees were black and bare against the horizon.

Hare Hall camp was built in the grounds of a Georgian mansion. Tall elms and horse-chestnuts at the entrance, instead of the barren wire he expected, declared its past as a country estate. There were guard boxes certainly, but a pretty eighteenth-century lodge too. Planted all over the gracious parkland between some great oaks were new white bell tents. A line of wooden barrack huts stood at the centre of the camp.

His first impression of a great house and park soon faded as he was drawn into the changed life of Hare Hall. Exercises, parades, routines, the new way of passing time. Much of his life was spent in lecture huts, the canteen, the reading room and the mess. Hut Number 3, a sound wooden hut sleeping twenty-five men, was home. The park became a site for compass exercises, and the great Georgian house was the remote home of the most senior officers, of whom he was in awe.

Lieutenant-Colonel Shirley was the inspiration behind Hare Hall. Edward heard his lectures to the new batches of recruits several times but he was always moved by the good sense and moral nature of the man. He watched as the Colonel took his place on the dais and surveyed the young fresh recruits who'd volunteered to fight. It was clear that he felt concern, real protective concern, for them.

'Never think of yourselves as avenging the wrong but as championing the right,' he said. 'There is no courage or value in rash self-sacrifice but in continuing to live for your country, rather than taking the easier route of dying for it.'

He stressed that the officer's first duty was to the welfare of the men he commanded, always putting their welfare above his own.

'You must know and understand your men; always check that they're receiving their mail and their provisions. And – most important – it will be your job to check the state of their feet and their boots. Nothing is more vital. It is comradeship that is the saving grace of the British Army, comradeship that is the key to keeping up morale and so it is the key to victory. Our men, like yourselves, are volunteers, but the Germans, and also the French I'm afraid, are almost wholly conscripted.'

He would end his lecture by again discouraging rash acts of heroism.

'Individual glory is not the finest thing a soldier can achieve. The finest thing is the knowledge that you have done your duty by your company.'

The Colonel's expectations were high and everyone worked to his standards. Discipline was firm but rational and Edward did not complain. He reflected on the strange unfamiliarity to him of thinking collectively. At school he had loathed the emphasis on teams and on joining in, not thinking of yourself. Here it made more sense to him.

His work was to take charge of a new batch of ten or twelve officer trainees for five days on end. One of those trainees was Wilfred Owen, a regular visitor to Monro's Poetry Bookshop in London and just about to interest Monro in his poems. He would have known the name of the critic Edward Thomas, but not the name of Lance-Corporal PE Thomas and certainly not of Edward Eastaway, the name under which Edward had tried to have Monro publish his poems, without success.

'I am lance-corporal now instead of private. This means a schoolmasterish life,' he wrote to Robert. *'Every officer is supposed to be able to read and make a map in quick time. It's important for tactics and manoeuvres. I have lectured on making maps and on the use of compass and protractor. Once a week I've had night operations to get used to the sound and sight of troops in the dark. I feel I could be useful in this way, if*

people would not think less of me.'

But people did think less of those that stayed at home, however usefully. He thought less of them himself. His thoughts were turning already to France.

'I really hope my turn will come and that I shall see what it is and come out with my head and most of my limbs. Then I may go to America and this time will not have been wasted.'

To see *what it is*. To experience the thing itself.

His letters to Robert always included his new poems. Robert read and admired them and their author; he wrote to Abercrombie that the war *'has made a new man and a poet out of Edward Thomas.'*

To Edward he wrote that he himself tried not to be troubled by the war, but he thought it was half of what ailed him, an ill-at-ease sense that began that August day. He had that sense of recklessness but nothing to do with it. What could he do about it all from America? Nothing. Well at least, he said, he would try to help the publication of Edward's poetry there.

'A rainy Sunday, everybody is in the hut playing cards,' he wrote to Robert. Imagine him in so much company! His friend John was hanging pictures, trying out positions, in preparation for an exhibition that the Artists' Rifles were mounting. That was life at Hare Hall on a wet winter Sunday.

Last week, he told Robert, he lectured to thirty men and it hadn't worried him at all. *'It all helps.'* When the war was over he would be ready for their summer school.

'I've never been so well or in so balanced a mood. Slightly out of things, perhaps, but no one makes me feel that.' When he wanted to be alone in the evenings he could be and when he wanted to join in things he did.

'I never thought I should notice the inconvenience and uncongenial society so little. I fitted in not perfectly but passably, and have made one real friend.'

John Wheatley was constantly drawing and he took Edward as a model – Edward would look up from notes he was writing to find John sketching him. It was embarrassing and flattering together. He learned to laugh and then to ignore him.

Another man, another artist he liked, was Paul. He recognised in him some of his own struggles, without anything being spelled out. They both had an air of detachment, he supposed. They did not talk about their deepest feelings, but Edward's dry ironies were met with the same kind of humour. And Paul Nash liked the same aspects of England as he did, those ancient, mystical Wiltshire landscapes – the enigmas of Avebury and Stonehenge and an iron-age fortress they both knew near Oxford, Wittenham Clumps.

'I can understand your fascination with them, Paul, the history and legends, but most of all the way we can escape the earth a little. Even if you stay at the foot you know that you could climb, that the possibility is there, you could climb to the lofty sky. I know another hill that resembles them but it's a singleton, a lonely one, a pre-cursor of the Malverns – May Hill, near Gloucester. I wonder what you would make of it.'

It was interesting to think about conveying the spirit of a place visually, as Paul did, to use no words.

There was another artist nearby who had been at the Slade too, like these new friends. Someone Edward once knew well but hadn't seen for many years. At Hare Hall Camp he was living less than five miles away from Great House, Upminster, the home of Edna Clarke-Hall.

Four

He looked up at the sweeping hipped-roof of the fine sixteenth century house, its silvery timbers set in mellowed walls. William, Edna's husband, was a very successful barrister. He could imagine Edna in such a house, enjoying its venerable romance. Would he be welcome, he wondered.

He tugged the iron pull and heard the bell deep inside the house, then footsteps coming to the door. He knew suddenly how eager he was to see Edna again and to watch her surprise, and, he hoped, pleasure at seeing him. But Edna was in London that day, the servant who answered the door told him.

After a moment they recognised each other. She remembered Edward from the old days.

'The mistress has two boys now, Mr Thomas – Justin and Denis. How is your little boy?'

'Not so little. He's fifteen and staying away from all this—' He gestured at his uniform. 'In America at the moment. But I have daughters too, one just thirteen, the other only five. Well, I'll look forward to meeting Mr and Mrs Clarke-Hall soon. My apologies to them for arriving with no notice.'

When Edna came home that evening Martha was bursting to tell her the news, knowing how much it would please her.

'Guess who called today? Your old friend Edward Thomas! In uniform too – really smart. Very different, but I still knew him. He's only over at Gidea Park, so he says he can call again soon.'

'Edward a soldier! I would never have believed he could do that. That's dreadful.' She was dismayed, because she was wholly opposed to the war. But still Edna was delighted at the thought of seeing him again. As the days passed she found herself impatient for his visit, and she kept glancing along the gravelled sweep of her drive to where it turned out of sight under an avenue of lime trees.

It was a week before Edward came again. Edna was pleased that Willie was in London, where he often stayed during the week. She and Edward could talk more freely than they had in the old days, when they were both newly married and at the start of their adult lives.

Edna – slender, extraordinarily beautiful, with a mass of chestnut hair and expressive eyes, was so talented an artist that she was accepted at the Slade at fourteen. She didn't need to attend drawing class – there was nothing she needed to learn – so she developed her own way as a painter, especially as a water-colourist.

It was William Clarke-Hall, a lawyer friend of her father's, who had persuaded her parents to send her to the Slade. In her mind Willie was of their generation, twice her age. She was grateful to him but she'd never regarded him as a lover. When he proposed marriage she was too young to know herself, her feelings, and his nature. The marriage was unhappy from the beginning. Edna was nineteen, Willie thirty-two, she was open, honest and forthright with her feelings, he was reserved and formal, but he had been, for a time, overwhelmed by Edna's beauty.

Edward had been in his last year at Oxford, already a father at twenty-one and married, though not yet living with Helen. A close friend of his, a law student, knew William and liked to talk about legal matters with him. Edward went on these visits, but spent the time talking to Edna. It was 'them and us', as Edward said – the lawyers and the artists.

Edna was glad to have someone who understood her, because already her new husband constantly criticised her behaviour and indeed her thoughts; he blamed her for her introspection or what he called self-absorption. Worse, she was young and wild, wanting to sleep out under the stars and climb the high elms around their house. She went out barefoot in simple cotton dresses and Willie said she looked like a gypsy.

Along with her wildness was the problem, for Willie, of the

informality and spontaneity of her painting. Her art suffered; she managed to exhibit once in a group with some old Slade friends, but nothing more. All her promise seemed to have disappeared. She found what inspiration she could in *Wuthering Heights*, identifying herself with Catherine and her yearning for passionate love, something that she felt was cruelly denied her. She'd said a little, even at that early time, to Edward to hint at her unhappiness but she'd restrained herself from too much complaint then.

After Oxford and a year in London the Thomases' life took them away into the country, to Kent and Hampshire, and the friendship faded. Fifteen years passed. Edna had two children. Her old teacher from the Slade persuaded her to exhibit in a one-woman show early in 1914, and in the Saturday Review she was described as a sensitive and expressive draughtswoman. Her sense of colour, the reviewer said, was individual and instinctive.

None of this altered Willie's attitude towards his wife.

She hasn't changed much from her twenty-year old self, Edward thought. What an extraordinarily beautiful woman she is! Such perfect features and such eloquent eyes. Her expression was so sensitive and intelligent. Possibly the sadness in her face cast its shadow in a way that made her look more intensely beautiful to him than ever.

She'd so looked forward to his coming, she said, taking his hand in hers once the maid had left the room. She led him, still holding his hand, to a window-seat and sat there with him. She did not want to hear about his Army life at all. He accepted that; to him she was like no other woman – he couldn't expect her to respond to the ugly necessity of the world as Helen had to. But he found that Edna did have strong views: 'The thought of one nation hating another is terrible,' she said.

'Of course, I agree with you. I don't hate the German people in the least.'

'But so many do – the war makes people hateful. I have a German governess, Carola, for my boys. My neighbours all say she should be dismissed and they glare at her whenever they see her. Yet she's been with us for years. Monstrous! War is simply evil – what are its consequences? Nothing but blood and famine. It makes me desolate. Almost the only things I've painted since it began have been two pictures of those horrors – Blood and Famine. Two terrible faces.'

'I understand that, Edna. But – I do believe that we have to defend ourselves – we didn't want this war, but it's come and we have to respond.'

Edna shook her head.

'Well, let us talk about something else,' Edward said. She didn't have the solidity of women like Helen or Eleanor, he thought, even though she was a married woman and a mother. She was too like a lovely creature in a fairy story, almost an illusion.

What Edna wanted to talk about was her marriage. She hadn't meant to, perhaps, but soon she began and couldn't stop.

'Willie simply put me on a pedestal when we married and then forgot me. And he despises my work. He thinks the only valuable paintings are those vast canvases of half a century ago – mythological subjects, allegories, classical themes. What I paint is the everyday world – to capture the beauty of the world about me, the things and the people, especially the children, spontaneously.'

She showed him a painting of a woman, some trees and a goat. Edward loved it.

'Why do you like it so much?'

'Because it is so true,' he answered. 'It is truthful and not at all sentimental. You must have more like these, haven't you?'

'Not really – I haven't been painting much at all. The children, always being responsible – I lost the habit of being absent-minded enough for painting. And then, Willie thinks so little of it. And the war saddens me so much. I have been trying to write poetry.'

The next time he called they walked in the copse beside the house, collecting some firewood, then went indoors and pulled their armchairs up to the December fire.

The room was a curious one, reflecting the two personalities who lived in Great House. Willie, in his mid-forties, had the taste of an older generation, a Victorian taste, with crowded furniture, superfluous small tables and plant stands. But near the fireplace Edna had created for herself a calm and yet a colourful space, with a rug made by a friend, two simple statuettes on the mantelshelf, a woven shawl in greys and blues thrown over her chair, a modern green reading lamp. In that setting she was like a pre-Raphaelite heroine with always that slight wildness about her that he loved.

The firelight lit her face as she looked at him.

'I did have an exhibition last year. Did you know?'

'Yes. I wish I'd been able to go. I must have been away.'

'It was a success, as they say. But I've done hardly any painting since. I want to, I really do, but Edward, I know you don't want to hear this from me again. But seeing you has made me – oh, I am simply too unhappy to paint. I have the boys, but theirs is the only love I have.

'When you and I knew each other all those years ago, it was still such a surprise to me – Willie's coldness, his constant disapproval of the person I was. I hoped it would change, but it hasn't. It never will change. Why did he want to marry me if everything about me is an anathema to him? I believe, you see, I was made for love, but it's denied to me. He says he chides me because he loves me, but if that is love why does it look like hate? If I run, he makes me walk. If I laugh I'm looked at coldly.'

She holds nothing back, Edward thought. What was it she wanted from him? Understanding, or more than that? They looked into the fire. He cleared his throat.

'Edna—'

'Edward, don't say anything. I know there's nothing to be done.'

'But I think there is. Keep on painting if you can, as well as writing. Get away from here – that's what I do. Can't you go and stay with friends for a while?'

'No – you don't understand. Willie would never allow that. I always have to put him first – and I have put him first for all these years, playing the hostess for him. And if I left against his will, I would lose everything – the children, my home. I love my boys; they are all the love I have. He's a lawyer – what chance would I have against him?'

'Then you must try to paint again here, at home, whenever you can. Set your sights on a definite goal and work towards that. *This* is what matters – your work. Don't let him stop you – don't let him. You have servants, money, you do have the time you need, so don't be so downhearted that it stops you working. Look, what do you think of first when you imagine picking up your brushes?'

'Of *Wuthering Heights*, I suppose. My obsession. And sometimes of something I've seen Denis and Justin doing. And colour in everyday things – like the blue in this shawl, that earthenware jug and its marigolds. The brown cupboard door.'

'That's good. Those everyday things you speak of are life itself. You can capture them – not many people can. And obsession is good. Don't mock yourself. An obsession means passion, individuality, originality.'

He hesitated for a moment.

'Look, I have to leave now, Edna, but I should be able to call on you again next week. Try to have something new for me to see, why don't you?'

Edna put her hand tentatively on his arm as if to detain him. How glad she was that he'd come to her again, that he understood her. She felt sure that she understood him too, and that his soldiering mask could very soon be torn away and the young man she'd liked so much found again.

Walking back to Hare Hall he thought of the two of them, fifteen years before, both so young and still full of hope. How *pleased* with each other they were then, with so much to say, so much in accord. Perhaps they hadn't even recognised how much they liked each other, how happy they were in the few moments they had alone together. He knew that he'd hidden it instinctively from Willie, from his friend Haynes as they were returning to Oxford, and from himself.

She made him feel so alive. It was like walking in a shower of welcome warm rain, the touch of it on your skin, your hair and eyes. You wanted to laugh and sing. He remembered his youth and almost felt young again.

Five

The routine of life at Hare Hall was not too irksome. He was up at six o'clock for the trainees' physical exercises. Then seven hours of practical training followed. It meant walking miles into the country, teaching map-reading and making panoramic sketches. He did not make the men march once they were beyond the boundary of the camp.

'Walk at a good pace, but let the terrain determine it. Try to find a rhythm and pace that you know you can sustain.' On occasion he would set the task of traversing the wintry ground as silently as possible, or of using the cover of hedges and ditches, while he listened or watched to judge how skilled they'd been.

The part he still found difficult, in spite of what he'd told Robert, was the lecture he had to give before the practical exercises began. At first he had skimped on words, simply wanting to get it over with, doubting whether he could hold their attention. But that was no help, because then he was met with puzzled faces and questions. Gradually he learned the skill of making a better lecture – outlining what he was to say, saying it and summarising afterwards. In fact, it was the same principle as an essay, he realised. And it was certainly excellent practice for lecturing with Robert when the war ended.

An Annual of New Poetry was to be published and Lascelles Abercrombie was one of the editors; he wanted some of the 'Edward Eastaway' poems included, some of the earliest – Old Man, After Rain, and A Private. Edward heard with pleasure that Abercrombie appreciated and understood the poems and was too generous to bear a grudge for his criticism.

He worked on new verses – a poem on beauty he began in January, another on sedge warblers, and one about a cuckoo. Birds had enormous significance, a kind of holy importance for him. He felt that their place in nature was always as it should be, not like man's place, so often destructive, or false, or discontented, and that they were users of a language too as he was. He could not remember being so content and invigorated. He was making a good enough job of soldiering, the prospect of having a few poems published, and there was Edna and her lovely house to charm him each week or so.

A weekend's leave at Steep, with an hour or two in his study, brought back memories of living in the new Wick Green house and his wretchedness there. He'd often met casual strollers who admired the house, who saw it as a romantic and charming place. Sometimes he'd even found himself admiring it too in a distant way, as though it was not his own home. He would put both perceptions into a poem, have himself tell a stranger the reality of it: the mists he welcomed at first but which became too much, too unvarying, and the wind, his grey misery on the day Myfanwy was born, the back-breaking stony untilled soil of the raw new plot.

As he wrote a further idea came. He'd changed since his enlistment and he knew that, in fact, he could cope better with the problems of the house now, could even have enjoyed what it offered for him and for Helen and the children. Given the chance, he would act differently. He would like to try the house again, '*As I should like to try being young again.*' To try to put down roots there, if he could.

So many days of his life had been to no purpose, wrapped up in his own pain, almost loving it, always obsessed with it. He had seen his unhappiness, his neurasthenia as Baynes and the other doctors called it, as the essence of himself. He'd been half convinced that if his depression were cured he would lose his life's most intense experiences. Now he saw that he'd wasted so many of the pleasures of life, as if the sun had shone in vain for him. Nothing had pleased him, so he'd punished those who were dearest to him and the guilt of that always made his depression worse.

He remembered the day when he had, on an impulse, taken

up his shotgun with the real intention of killing himself. Bronwen was little then, a merry, lively, noisy child. That day she'd irritated him beyond bearing with a game she was playing. He shouted at her and saw her merriment vanish and her little mouth form a square as she wailed in shock and dismay. He was utterly sickened by himself; they would all be better off without him.

He knew that Helen realised his intention as he left the house with his gun and that she waited in agony. He came back in the end, ashamed and wretched, and still his bitterness towards Helen and the children went on for months afterwards.

But he had begun to change, even in the months before the war. Meeting Robert had been a great part of it. He would never go back to being what he was. If the war ended soon – and people were saying this might happen by October – he would go to America and start afresh.

Six

In New Hampshire Robert continued to be successful and Elinor continued to struggle with his success.

She saw him open his mail and gleefully pin up above his desk fresh invitations for readings. Her mouth curled a little with silent contempt. Some days she found fault with him constantly. He was exasperated and almost frightened.

'Elinor,' he said, 'you must cease pointing out to me all my short-comings. It's going to drive me crazy.' It was his old fear.

Their lives were still hard, even with the money Robert was bringing in. Carol, at fourteen, was barely old enough to run the livestock smallholding and as winter drew on he grumbled that it was too much along with his schoolwork. He and Robert built a hen-house together, but they argued. Then Robert's cold was turned into a chest cold by the rain. Something had to change.

On the way home from a reading some miles away Robert called at Amherst College and when he arrived home at Ore Hill he had news he hoped would please Elinor. He knew that she respected the academic world.

'Ellie – listen – I'm going to teach at Amherst. I want to teach again. They want me to give only two classes a week, so I can write but the pay will be enough for us to live on. The kids can go to a better school. We'll just keep this place on as a summer home, because they're going to let us rent a professor's house. OK?'

'But Robert, we can't simply leave – I'm not sure I want to. I do like the privacy here, if we could only have a furnace and a bathroom. You always get started on something and then you're off on another before it's finished. I know you are a good teacher, but—'

'Well, I'm taking the job, if needs be I'll travel there and back, until you make up your mind and see sense. But I know you'll come.'

There were the usual quarrels about these decisions, less explosive between them than they were. By the time the autumn came Elinor was pregnant again and she became too ill to move.

In November Robert wrote to Edward that no letter would take the place of seeing him, and that he was kicking and thrashing with resentment against everything.

'I like nothing, neither being here with you there and so hard to talk to nor being so ineffectual at my years to help myself or anyone else.'

He hadn't succeeded in getting Holt to publish Edward's children's book, *Four and Twenty Blackbirds*.

'And you know how it is with us: Elinor is so sick day and night as to affect the judgement of both of us: we can't see anything hopefully though we know from experience that even the worst nine months must come to an end. The devil says "One way or another." And that's what Elinor says this time too. There is really cause for anxiety. We are not now the strength we were.'

Seven

Half a kiss, half a tear

Merfyn was to come home for Christmas! He enjoyed his time in America and learned a good deal – about American motorcars! But he was homesick and his letters were all concerned with ships that could bring him to England.

We wanted him home. His absence was an extra sorrow for me, added to Edward's. After Christmas Merfyn would go to school in Coventry, taking mathematics and mechanics, until the time came for him to take up an apprenticeship with Edwy's brother Theo at his motor-works.

What a family were the Thomases! So different, only the youngest, Julian, at all like Edward in his ways. Edward resembled his mother in looks, blue-eyed and fair-haired, while the other five were dark, stocky and Welsh – Grandpa Thomas's boys.

One day when I was in town and visiting the Thomases, Julian told me what kind of reception Edward's father had given his poems. 'Pure piffle,' he'd said. In his opinion no one would publish them. When I heard this I hated Edward's father and that was not really my way. He was, I suppose, simply an unimaginative man, and a man of the old century – but how could anyone dismiss his own child like that?

I would never tell Edward and I knew I could trust Julian not to. His father's opinion counted for nothing at all. Edward was beginning to find that his work was valued by those who knew their business, by people of modern letters like himself.

So Merfyn was coming home. He had visited the Frosts at Franconia, a brief visit as Elinor was unwell. Robert had told *us* the nature of Elinor's illness. Another baby was coming. But late in November another letter came: there was to be no baby after all. I tried not to think too much about this.

No new baby would come for us. Month after month the blood show, the dragging discomfort, the disappointment. Edward was disappointed too, because at last, with his regular salary, he'd agreed that we could have another child. Perhaps that was some recompense, one consequence of his enlisting, at least, that I could be thankful for. We stopped using preventatives, but our lovemaking was so rare now, because of his short leaves, that I had not conceived. It was cruel. I began to be afraid that we'd left it too late. I was not so young, no longer that girl pulling him down into me on the moss of Richmond Common, a baby made so readily and joyfully as we moved together and our need for each other was satisfied.

How easy it was too, with Bronwen! Too easy. Poor darling Bronnie, not wanted, not at all, a disaster where Edward was concerned. My pregnancy with her was one of the most unhappy times of my life. And then, lo and behold, as she grew she turned into his greatest delight! The Merry One.

Merfyn did come home for Christmas 1915. There was the usual muddle that somehow always followed in his wake. We waited all through the morning of the 20th of December for his train to arrive, but he had missed it. Edward had to go back to camp and so his first sight of his returning boy was on Christmas Eve, when Merfyn went to meet his father at Petersfield Station. Edwy told me that he hardly knew him and it was true that he was much taller and had filled out. What surprised us most was that he was more English than ever, with hardly a trace of an American accent. Merfyn had certainly not taken root in America and I doubted whether Edwy or any of us ever would.

He and Edward were both more patient and content with each other and Christmas passed happily. But at New Year there was a dreadful quarrel with Edwy's father. Grandpa Thomas had never understood Edward and standing as a Liberal candidate, it seemed, gave the right to dictate to others what they ought to think. The Thomas fathers and sons, it seemed to me, found it hard to love each other.

Eight

1916

It was the contempt that enraged him and put him out of sorts for days. He knew how often he'd treated Helen with contempt. It pained him to know now how that felt.

'Do you really believe that a German soldier is less brave than an English Tommy?' Edward asked his father. 'That's sheer nonsense, stupid jingoism.'

Edward hated his father's attitude, his bigotry and ignorance. Worse, even now that he was in uniform he felt his father treat him as though he were still an awkward schoolboy. Years of reproach – for his second-class degree at Oxford, for Merfyn's conception and the early marriage, above all for choosing to be a writer instead of a civil servant, he knew they were all there in his father's lack of respect for him.

No matter that he had supported and educated his children by his own arduous efforts, nor that he was a respected critic, he thought. And now he was a soldier, a junior officer, his father still seemed to feel he had the right to lecture him for a lack of patriotism. It was unforgivable. Nothing was good enough for him.

This so-called patriotism – Edna was right, it made people hateful. Only a fool would condemn the German people, who were led by events even more than the English were. As the formally declared enemy of England, of course he would fight and kill German soldiers – but it was for love of England, not for his hatred of Germans. But his father was a man of certainties, a City man, unimaginative and unsubtle, a Positivist, foolishly believing that all was progress. Edward would never forgive him. If it weren't for his mother, who was worried enough, having two sons in the Army, he would never see his father again, he thought.

Edward expected to be promoted in January, with an increased salary.

He spoiled his chances.

He was in charge of a hut of twenty men, responsible for upholding discipline, and when one man failed to return from leave Edward should have acted at once. Ten o'clock on a Sunday – it was hard to see why it mattered. He'd wait another hour before reporting the chap AWOL. It was probably not his fault at all, but a delayed train or something like that.

He gave him the benefit of the doubt again at eleven, then fell asleep. By the time of the six o'clock parade next day Edward was in trouble. The man finally arrived at seven and they were both called in to the Major.

Not only was he not promoted, for a time he was demoted. He felt no resentment at the treatment he received, only contemptuous self-disgust. He'd had a 'dressing-down' by a man younger than himself, at his age – and well deserved. Of course he should have reported the matter.

I'm no good at soldiering, he thought, unpicking one stripe from his sleeve. I'm much older than the other officers, yet these almost-boys follow the rules and do what's required of them, even if it makes them unpopular. For days he fell into his old wretchedness. The 'dressing down' compounded the contempt he'd felt from his father the month before. To tell Helen was to face her sympathy and her defending him; he felt sick at the thought. The drabness of the camp, the absence of beauty, the sweat, and worse, of so many men, made him sick.

So much was going wrong; the war was not going well, and the whole country was weary of it. The early appetite for fighting had quite gone and conscription would be necessary. It wasn't possible to find out from news reports what was happening as the press was silenced, but he knew that the trenches stretched south and east from the Channel all the way to the frontier, and that the armies on both sides were deadlocked, the losses unimaginably high.

Yet he was not encountering danger and not even managing these home front responsibilities well. Was it only by going to France that he would feel worthwhile? What if he should be killed? Well, he would know nothing about it and it would put an end to all such questions. 'A mouthful of soil to remedy all.' Death itself had no terror for him – at times like these he was still drawn towards it.

Awake one night at midnight in the hut with the other men sleeping, he lay listening to rain and was conscious of such intense loneliness that he felt his own annihilation would be welcome. Lying awake, listening to rain. He had known that mood in the past, and had thought then how utterly blessed it would be, to be dead, emptied, washed clean and without pain.

He wrote:

> Like a cold water among broken reeds,
> Myriads of broken reeds all still and stiff,
> Like me who have no love which this wild rain
> Has not dissolved except the love of death,
> If love it be towards what is perfect and
> Cannot, the tempest tells me, disappoint.

It snowed and one snowy day Edward, John Wheatley and Paul Nash were sent on an expedition together. The soft snow lay deep over the Essex countryside, hiding anything that was modern or ugly, turning the scene to one of timeless beauty. They set out early, so the lanes ahead of them, enclosed by black hedges, were untouched until their own footprints marked the snow. The creak of it under their boots, the untried purity of it, exhilarated them. They were boys again for a while, boys in khaki, scooping up handfuls of the powdery snow, squeezing it lightly into a ball, aiming and throwing, running for cover and retaliating, all the while laughing.

Then they fell into a line of three and marched, faster and faster. Edward started up a song and Paul and John joined in. The other two were more than ten years younger but he was at least as fit as them, fitter in fact than the youngest, John; at twenty-four he was quite plump and somehow soft, with a perpetual gentle smile. He was soon too out of breath to sing, but he kept up the pace. Paul absorbed the scene as he went, the angles and the muted colours of fields and buildings, the sky as it stopped snowing and the white disc of sun.

They had their sandwiches, but to be indoors was a more attractive idea. To take off their boots and leave them by a fireside while they had a tankard of ale. The landlord, seeing their uniforms, insisted on giving them their first drink free; and he didn't mind them eating their own 'snap'.

After they'd eaten, John took out his sketch pad and started to draw Edward, who lit his pipe and looked down, a little self-conscious, as John worked. To distract himself he asked Paul what he made of the snow-covered landscape as a subject. It was the first time they'd talked very much to each other about their lives outside the Rifles and he felt rather constrained.

'I like it – I think I'm best at these winter colours, the white and grey, that greenish glow to the snow. Such a strange light.' He went to the window. 'You know, I wonder why Palmer never painted a scene of snow. He would have made a great work with it, I'm sure. I can envisage this as a Palmer – those sheep huddled against the tree.'

'Yes, I see what you mean. How utterly English it is, this winter light. Spring and autumn are good for me in writing, the misty seasons – but winter too, rain and mud, the thaw, that half-and-half state when the snow's not quite gone. March, when I was born; it suits my vacillating nature, no doubt, and my gloom.'

'Really?'

'Oh yes, my old moods were usually distinctly wintry, gloomy. Wavering and watery too!'

'Well, we're alike in that, Edward. I've been "half in love with easeful death" since I was a child. I'm better than I was – being married has made that difference. But winter can still bring back those moods intensely. But you – I know, I'd heard from Bottomley that you could be melancholy. Yet you seem always humorous, always interested and interesting – I found it hard to believe.'

'I'm glad to say that I've both changed and not changed. In the right company I think the humour was always there. And I suppose the war, and maybe not having to grind out books I didn't want to write, has put an end to my gloom to some degree. After all, it's no great hardship for us, this life, is it? Sitting by a fire at an inn with a fine pint, and a good walk in the afternoon. What could be better? Except that – don't you sometimes feel that it's all wrong? Our life here? Thinking of the men in France.'

'I do. Sooner or later I think I'll have to go out.'

'I wonder – if we get to France, when, or if, we're faced with the reality of death what will that be like? I've been absorbed with the idea of possible death, the mystery – sometimes even wanting it, but—'

'Do you think like that now?'

Edward didn't answer at once.

'No, now I want to live.'

They were quiet then; only the sound of the crackling fire and John's pencil.

'More snow,' Edward exclaimed. He smiled at a sudden memory as he watched the great flakes floating slowly past the window.

'I find it a sad thing – the awful silence of snow, and the strange light, as you say, as though there is gloom and yet at the same time this glaring white. I remember when my little girl first saw snow I told her that somebody up in the sky was plucking a great goose and the flakes were feathers. She was three, but she knew it was only a story and she laughed at me. I made a poem out of it, but I couldn't have her laughing – oh no, she had to be weeping in my poem.'

They left the inn and went on, tramping through the untrodden snow into a north wind, faster and faster, although they had a grim billet at the end of their day and only the camp to come 'home' to after that.

The walk itself, the tramping, the striding and singing, made them happy. But then John, panting at the too-fast pace, said,

'How quick will the beaten horse run home!'

'Home!' Paul exclaimed. 'Is *that* what you call it? Some home!' They laughed. There they were, from Hampshire, London, Wales – yet they had all three to call the camp 'home'.

It was that idea that Edward brooded on afterwards. It had always been such an enigmatic word for him. He somehow always saw the word in parenthesis. And 'homesick' – what did that mean? What did such words mean?

But the desolation had passed; death would steal from him the things that sometimes brought him happiness – even, briefly, ecstasy. And then, even the knowledge of having died – you would always be cheated of that! But was the best he could hope for the repetitive ritual of camp life?

He wanted more.

Nine

Since November he'd visited Edna every week or so. She responded to his encouragement and his understanding, filling her journals with descriptions of him, his blue eyes, his gentle smile. She had persuaded him to lend her copies of his poems which she copied out into her journal. They talked of painting and spent time in her barn studio. He slipped easily into the mentor role; he always had, even at Oxford, without really being aware of it. Perhaps it was something to do with being the eldest of six brothers, however much he'd tried to evade it.

She had a favourite way to be with him; it was something she showed often in her paintings: a couple near a great hearth, a good fire, the man in a chair, the woman sitting on the floor at his feet, leaning her head of tumbling hair against his arm. *Young Couple resting, Young Couple talking* – always this same position, one that for her symbolised trust, intimacy and perhaps the prelude to lovemaking.

Usually the couple were Cathy and Heathcliff, her obsession, as she called it. They were washed in brown over black pencil drawings. In her day-to-day pictures, mostly of the boys, she used more colour, but sparingly.

Edward returned to the camp after a visit to her; he was full of chivalrous notions about her that he wanted to work into a formal, metaphysical poem. She, or rather her extraordinary physical beauty, he would liken to a silver cloud drifting across his darker self.

And even so now, light one!
Beautiful, swift and bright one!
You let fall on a heart that was dark,
Unillumined, a deeper mark.

It was, he knew, a conceit, and he kept it to himself.

In February she had shown Edward a painting of her son Julian holding a large black-and-white cat. She caught exactly the way the child held it, so that the poor cat was clutched a little too tightly and lovingly around its middle while its rear legs and tail curved, unsupported and silently protesting.

She captured the moment before the cat wriggled out and jumped down.

'That's exactly right, Edna. I love the bend of Julian's head and the cat's expression. And the way you've kept the colour so limited. Just that dash of blue and the gold of his hair, the rest subdued. What are you going to call the picture?'

'Oh, just *Boy with a Cat*, I should think.'

'Well, why not – I like that. They're each as important as the other in your picture. Anything else to show me?'

'Not now, Edward. Or rather, I have something I want to show you, but it's not a picture. It's a letter – from you!'

She went across to her bookshelves and pulled out a book of prints. It opened easily at the place where some papers were hidden. She produced three pages of yellowed notepaper covered in his own handwriting and handed it to him. Then she sat down in her usual way at his feet, smiling, her bright chestnut-brown hair touching his hand as he held the letter.

'Oh my, from Atheldene Road – that awful hole. Good heavens, Edna, have you kept this all that time? Since when – Merfyn was a baby there, so it would have been 1900. Just like me then not to have bothered with a date.'

'That's right, it would have been then. More than fifteen years ago – we were still at Thames Ditton, of course. Oh Edward – I don't know – we were younger, but I believe we were somehow not young. We were both trying to be grown-up before we were ready. I certainly was. Newly married to Willie, not knowing what I was doing, what I was committing myself to. Condemning myself to, I could say. The strange thing is, I feel younger now than I did then.'

'I do know what you mean. But let me read this elegant

epistle. *"The approach of our next pilgrimage to Thames Ditton."* Rather pretentious – that was my style then, I suppose.'

'Read on.'

'My wife has indeed become one of your admirers tho I will swear I have not done you justice in my descriptions, and she would relish a visit from you as much as the return of the swallows.'

'Mmmh. I never did visit.'

'No – but that was because of the dreadful flat, as it says. It is a *trifle* exaggerated – this *"misty hollow, this dismal street."* Good Lord! I suppose after Oxford and Lincoln quad it was outrageously grim. Helen, though, was quite content – she had Merfyn. But it was almost too much for me.'

'It sounds as though it were. And then you go on with these trees that never existed.'

'What a lot of nonsense I wrote – *"living in the shade of imaginary poplars"*, indeed.'

'I wonder what you meant.'

'Oh I know well enough – I was disheartened, frightened even. I lived in a kind of mystic rural fantasy at that time, desperately wanting to make a living writing and to live in the country – it was what I needed.'

'Edward, why do you think you wrote to me then?'

'Well, because, I suppose once I'd left Oxford and not seeing Edmund who introduced us, I was afraid it would be all too easy to lose touch with you. And those visits to you – they were a kind of lifeline thrown to me among my troubles. And I needed one to be thrown to Atheldene Road – I really did.'

He read on, smiling.

'Oh look at this. *"Of course I live – if living it may be called – by my writing, 'literature' we call it in Fleet St – a litter of pigs – he made an awful litter."* Ha ha – an attempt at humour.'

'I thought it was quite amusing,' Edna said. 'And then you lecture me about Shelley, but you needn't have worried – I loved Shelley and I still do.'

'Good. Oh back to the poverty line – bone soup—'

'I felt for Helen when I read that. Were you really so poor?'

'We certainly were.'

'Read the rest. It's the part I like best.'

"'I am selfish enough to wish I could ask you to come and see" – it's crossed out – *"see my wife and me.'"*

'You wrote, *"See me"*, first, look.'

'True. This description of the flat – why did I think you would be interested?'

'Read it out. I love it – I can picture it exactly.'

He began to read as though it were a salesroom catalogue.

'(1) a study with walls of French grey, softer than sleep
(2) some copies of pictures by Leonardo, Andrea del Canto, Rossetti and Burne-Jones, and a dear old photo of Tintern that was the last thing I looked at when I went to bed at 6 and lived in short frocks
(3) between 900 & 1000 books
(4) a green armchair from Wm Morris, 2 or 3 others, all so comfortable that in them I can laugh at poverty even on an empty stomach
(5) a drinking cup (an unconventional "christening" cup for our baby, Philip Merfyn) inscribed with mottoes by all my friends
(6) a blazing fire
(7) me.'

His voice changed as he read the last lines.

'Will you write to me?
Ever sincerely yours
Edward Thomas.

'Yes, I remember it all. What I was feeling as I wrote – I had to laugh at myself, make myself amusing to you. It did me good to write that letter, as if I were watching from outside, and could laugh at my predicament. Yet showing you that I did need to see you still. I was absolutely longing for my friends, desperate to escape that flat.'

'And you did visit me for a time. Then you stopped.'

'I know.'

'I minded terribly. And now, Edward, I would be wretched if I were not to see you, to share my thoughts with you. How much I could give up to see you more! To be with you, sometimes at least, as though we were—'

'Edna, please, you know that's not possible. And I do doubt whether it's really what you want.'

'But I know my own mind. Only— Oh, if only we'd met earlier! If only Edmund had brought you to visit us before you were so utterly tied to your wife.'

'Edna—'

'I know after that it was too late – but I could have left Willie, lived with you in a cottage, or the grimmest of flats in London and we would have been happy. I could have worked so much more, achieved so much, and you too. You would have brought me some laughter again. If we'd been together you would have accomplished even more than you have, I know. Because I free you from your dolefulness— Oh I don't know how exactly – but you know it's true. Now, I've lost my youth and my beauty, I suppose.'

She'd reached a slim arm up to his face her fingers lightly stroking his cheek. Then she took his hand and brought it up to her mouth, all the time gazing at him with her eyes full of longing, then of tears. Edward looked back at her – he was very disturbed and moved. Lost her beauty? No, to him her beauty was almost unbearable. He looked away before he could speak.

'Edna, it would not have been as you say. There is a difference – I don't know – something in the way we see the world. We are on different planes, you and I. And you don't know how I can be, how I am, you see only one aspect of me. I'm no Heathcliff to your Cathy. You speak of Willie's cruelty – I know you would have found mine equal to it, or a good deal worse.'

'No, Edward – impossible. We are of an age, and both artists—'

'I live with the pain of being – you don't know – only Helen knows a little – I think I am a man who cannot love.'

*

'Thinking of her made me sad.'

No – 'saddened me at first', he wrote. That old letter from his boyish self, her words and her need of him disturbed him immensely, aroused him. He was distracted at his work, and angry with himself for having allowed this to come about. To write about it might be one way – might clarify his thoughts, help him to think the matter through to some sort of conclusion.

> *...the creature with bright eye*
> *That I had thought never to see, once lost.*
> *She found the celandines of February*
> *Always before us all. Her nature and her name*
> *Were like those flowers*
> *Bending to them as in and out she trod*
> *And laughed, with locks sweeping the mossy sod.*

He got up and paced about the room, then looked again at what he'd written. The romantic maiden, the *'in and out she trod'* – again it was a picture from a golden age, chivalric and unreal. Only the celandines and their scent were real. He would have to put an end to this vision of her. He wrote:

> *...remembering she was no more,*
> *Gone like a never perfectly remembered air.*

But he still could not stop thinking about her, the passionate way she talked and gestured.

She was so beautiful – he could have her! Could he be unfaithful to Helen? – it would mean lying and dissembling and he doubted that he was capable of that.

Helen could exasperate him; she was so overwhelming, so insistent. He wished himself unmarried often, but somehow he was a man who simply couldn't consider that way out of his marriage. Part of him knew, too, that it was the mystery of the unattainable, untouched, untamed beauty that drew him, a desire for the impossible that could be transformed into poetry.

He must try to make Edna a memory, simply a memory. Now that she'd hinted at her feelings so nakedly, so passionately, it was all he could do. Once he left Romford, he resolved, he would never call on her again. But until then – well, he would see.

Edward was made a full corporal. And six poems were to be published by his friend Jimmie Guthrie's press. Two more were published in a journal: Lob, and Words, the poem he wrote on May Hill. To read it there was different from reading his old works. He felt an unfamiliar, exalted pleasure, almost pride.

So March should have been a good month, but conditions in camp became difficult. He returned from leave to find his hut bare and reeking of carbolic soap. Measles: there was an epidemic at Hare Hall and in adult men measles was a serious matter. They were to be quarantined, virtually confined to barracks, other than within a small area of uninhabited countryside. All leave was cancelled. Upminster was out of bounds. Confinement was a torment to him; he liked to work hard and then have his liberty. He needed to be free to stride away from camp for a few miles, to be alone, never to be a captive.

But he resolved to bear things cheerfully if he could. He and the men who were fit marched about within bounds, singing, experimenting with finding tunes that you could march to successfully. 'John Blunt' was good. 'As I was walking down Paradise Street' was a good song but impossible to march to, with all the slow Blow the Man Downs.

On a wet Saturday Edward sat in the hut listening to the babble around him. Someone was playing a gramophone, a card game involved sudden shouts of triumph, and everyone was talking. So, this was now home, since he could be nowhere else.

He had time to write about the walk with Paul and John in the snow and the way the word 'home' raised an ironic smile for all three. They hadn't talked about it then or since, what each of them really felt. For himself, that evening as he thought of home, of Steep, he was surprised to find that he was looking westward into a sunset blurred with his own tears. This close companionship the Army enforced on him – he was afraid that it would threaten him in the end, that he'd lose his own identity, his individuality. Paul and John – yes, he was lucky to know men here who were a little like him, but they were not real friends like his old friends. They were all just thrown together by circumstance. He was a prisoner, longing to be elsewhere, anywhere, his restlessness at times feeling like a fire inside him.

It was unbearable to think that his own home was barred from him. Yet how often he had been sick of his home, always planning how he could make an escape, to friends, or to be on the road again. Home. He wrote:

No more. If I should ever more admit
Than the mere word I could not endure it
For a day longer: this captivity
Must somehow come to an end, else I should be
Another man, as often now I seem,
Or this life be only an evil dream.

Ten

Eleanor decided that she would go to Flansham.

Flansham was the Sussex home of Jimmie Guthrie, Edward's close friend, and of Jimmie's Pear Tree Press. She had never met him, but Edward assured her that she would be welcome. He wasn't free to go himself to witness the production of his first volume of poetry; she would act as his amanuensis. The thought of being the first friend to see his works in print – apart from Jimmie himself – filled her with a glow of happiness. She had an investment in the poems as she'd typed them, commenting on things that she thought were unclear, and Edward had sometimes made small changes because of her comments. But that wasn't important – she simply wanted to hold in her hands something that she knew would make him happy. So when she was next in Sussex she would go, although she would have to overcome her old shyness about meeting strangers.

She prepared for a long walk from her rented cottage in Felpham, taking her haversack and the reliable ash walking-stick she took on all her walks. Eleanor was a city child and it wasn't until she knew Edward that she became a good walker. A stick, cut and prepared by yourself, was essential for him and so it was for her.

She turned inland, reading her map, something else she learned from him. Navigating her way along little lanes, she came to the hamlet of Flansham and the White House. It was a low-eaved Sussex farmhouse, simply and prettily pargeted. She looked for the pear tree of the Press's name and although it was leafless, still she thought she recognised it from the upswept branches to the right of the studded door.

A plump man opened the door and held it back for her, smiling amiably.

'My name is Eleanor – I do hope you don't mind—

'Come in, come in.'

She tried to explain her unannounced visit but it wasn't necessary – he was instantly welcoming. He introduced her to his wife Marion and then took her upstairs to the Press itself.

What an extraordinary room – a long attic that stretched the length of the house. It was crammed with wide tables stacked with paper of all sizes, textures and colours. There were two bulky machines, which she knew were presses. In drawers alongside them were lines of type. He showed her the intaglio blocks – copper, steel, and his latest invention, plaster. She smelled printer's ink, woodblocks, oil and paper. Jimmie had a dozen projects underway, some just started, some near completion. He was eager to show her everything, leading her from one table to the next, and thrusting pages in front of her so rapidly that she was almost dazed. It was all finely done, with exquisite care, she could see. The paper – she never saw such paper before.

'Where does it come from?' she asked.

'It's hand-made – some of it's hand-coloured too, or dyed with natural dyes. Some is what we call Jap Vellum. All horribly expensive but there's no satisfaction in using anything else for engraved work. It has to be the best. And most of what I print is sold to subscribers, no more than a hundred or so copies. Now, for Edward's – I will show you what I have in mind.'

He stopped by a table containing sheaves of papers in subtle colours – creams, a dusty blue, a delicate pink.

'I'm thinking of two colours in each volume, but none quite the same in their arrangement, so no two copies will be exactly alike'

'That would be marvellous – but—

'Yes – tell me what you're thinking.'

'I always associate Edward with green. Do you have some green, very light of course, like, well, like a slice of an unripe apple?'

'Yes – I do have the very thing. I think you're right.'

'And will there be an engraving on the frontispiece – Edward mentioned it?'

'I've sent him a sketch of what I've done, but I couldn't tell from his letter whether he liked it or not – he said it looked like a cross between Christ and Walt Whitman.'

They laughed.

'I think that means he liked it.'

'I've discussed the order of the poems with him too. But he found it hard to decide. The question for me is whether to number the pages. If not, he can delay the decision about the ordering. You know which poems he has chosen, don't you?'

'Yes – Beauty, probably my favourite, and Sedge-Warblers, Aspens, and then the three that, I suppose, echo the war, No petty right or wrong, A Private and Cock-Crow. That's another favourite – I know it by heart. It would illustrate wonderfully, don't you think?'

'Say it to me.'

So, shyly, in her rather high and piping voice, she did.

'Out of the wood of thoughts that grows by night
To be cut down by the sharp axe of light—
Out of the night, two cocks together crow,
Cleaving the darkness with a silver blow:
And bright before my eyes twin trumpeters stand,
Heralds of splendour, one at either hand,
Each facing each as in a coat of arms:
The milkers lace their boots up on the farms.'

Jimmie took up a scrap of paper as she spoke and when she finished he made a quick sketch.

'Yes, I can work on that. It's perfect – two perfect images. Wonderful. Now this question of his name, the Edward Eastaway instead of Thomas. He's still determined on that?'

'Oh yes, Jimmie, he won't consider anything else. Although of course his friends know, but he wants to be judged on the merits of the poems alone.'

'And he will be. Well – it will be an excellent introduction, and I'll do my absolute best for him. But of course, this is only a beginning. I know that.'

'I know it too,' Eleanor said.

Eleven

Half a kiss, half a tear

His leave cancelled, even on his birthday, which we always spent either at the Thomases in London together, or at Steep. I was finding his absence ever harder to bear, but at least there had been his leave at home, or we would stay at his parents for the weekend if he hadn't the time to come home. We were lovers as always, but no baby came. Every month I bled, every month I cried. Then the quarantine kept him away entirely.

Loneliness and unhappiness were changing me. I seemed to be swallowed up in a dull fog, my real nature beaten down.

After all, home was just a cheap dull house with a tiny kitchen and no bathroom. My energy was gone, my joy in keeping Yew Tree Cottage pretty and homey was gone. I could not make myself happy anymore by a whirlwind of housework. I'd found over the years that it worked for me, but it didn't help me now. When we were first married Edward blamed me for *not* keeping the house clean and ordered. He expected me to run a home as well as his mother and mine, but they had plenty of help. Only with practice and effort did I learn to please him and now I was letting it all go.

After I'd taken Myfanwy to school and washed the breakfast things I found myself slumping on the window-seat just staring out of the window. Or I'd begin a task half-heartedly, knowing even as I started that I wouldn't complete it, or would do it badly.

The windows were smeared where Myfanwy would press her face to the glass to look down our narrow front path to the road. The floor always needed cleaning. I would feel impatient with myself and that would give me a burst of activity, but not for long. The dreadful listlessness would take over again. I would pull myself upstairs to make my bed as though heavy weights were dragging me down, and sometimes I'd fall onto the bed and simply lie there staring at the ceiling – in the middle of the morning. What did it matter? Who cared what I did now that Edward was never at home?

Spring here, without Edward to enjoy it with me. I tried, for Myfanwy's sake, but I couldn't pretend to be happy.

The Somme, months and months of battles, went on and on and we began to hear of the terrible losses. In the village there were widows and bereaved parents, blinds drawn down, the sound of weeping heard where a cottage door stood open and visitors came with their respects and to tell their sadness. At the post office stores in our lane so many customers wore black armbands.

It was dreadful of me, but sometimes in flashes I would find myself imagining the telegram arriving, the news, myself in black mourning clothes, the children – thinking of how I would tell them. I seemed to be going mad – this was not me. Edward was safe in Essex! It was, I suppose, the mind's way of trying to protect itself, by rehearsing the worst that could happen. I hated it because I began to feel that it was inevitable, drawing nearer all the time. Morbid thoughts haunted me. To see someone simply draw their blinds in the evening would bring me to tears.

If he sent me copies of his poems, his wanting my opinion did please me and bring back a little of our old life together. Edward would never be like Robert, eager for Elinor's approval, but he did like to know that I understood his work. Certain poems, though, distressed me too much.

I became convinced that Edward was in love with another woman. Those poems – about celandines, about the touch of rain. I wasn't that woman. I always thought that Edward would find a woman cleverer and prettier than me and I would have to make myself accept it, rather than lose him entirely.

One miserable rainy day, not long after our dear old Rags died, I looked around the room – dirty windows, breakfast dishes not done. I knew that a pile of washing lay muddily on the wash-house floor and the stupid copper's fire was out. I thought suddenly that I was no better than Elinor Frost and I understood how Elinor must have felt – her indifference to it all, having no energy or interest in it. What was the point, anyway, of gleaming windows and tidy children, of meals that took half a day to prepare and were quickly eaten and forgotten? What did it matter? What good had it done me, all my efforts, when it hadn't kept Edward's love for me safe?

And that was the day Edward chose to arrive in the evening without warning, expecting, of course, that I would be overjoyed to see him. His face was glowing from the exhilaration of walking in the rain, hurrying up Bell Hill from the station. But my face, my dress, my hair – all unprepared, dirty, soured with self-pity and fear.

I flustered around trying to put the house straight and of course his mood changed then because his surprise was spoiled. He said he wished he hadn't troubled to come and I said I wished he hadn't. Then I broke down crying and I told him that most of my wretchedness was because of my jealous thoughts.

'Fancy you thinking those poems were about a love affair. It takes two to make a love affair and as you know I am incapable of it.'

'But Edward, the verses speak of memories, real things that happened.'

'That's how poets work, Helen. An incident, any little thing, even a thought, you build on that.'

'I wouldn't blame you.'

'Look, I've only ever responded to you, Helen. You know that the one thing I can claim is that I've never deceived you. I haven't loved as you would want me to, it isn't my way, you know that. But there is no affair.'

I cried with relief, because I knew he was speaking the truth.

'And if you were to respond to some other man I don't know what I'd do. So let's have no more of this nonsense. Come out and look at the moon with me – the rain's stopped, I think.'

We went out into the garden; yes, the sky had cleared and the rain stopped. I put my arms round him, but he was still annoyed.

'Helen, I rely on you not to allow this state of affairs to go on.

It's so unlike you. I rely on you to keep things running in your old familiar way. "Keep the home fires burning", you know.'

I remembered what he said and I tried. I knew the Ivor Novello song of course, everyone did. *'No Englishman is silent to the sacred call of "Friend"'*, was a line I liked. And the chorus was something I found myself singing as I struggled to light the fire, something Edward had always done so easily. That night we sang it together, tongue-in-cheek at first, then half-laughing, half-crying:

Keep the home fires burning
While your hearts are yearning,
Though your lads are far away
They dream of home.
There's a silver lining
Through the dark clouds shining.
Turn the dark clouds inside out
Till the boys come home.

He left the next day and again I felt that most of my old strong spirit was gone. All my striving to please Edward – would I have been a better wife, really a more helpful wife, if I was more – if I'd not let him mould me so much as he liked? Or if I minded less how he behaved to me? Perhaps I loved too well, too absolutely. But I knew I couldn't change.

Just sometimes, if the sun shone, or if a friend paid a visit, I would find my old cheerful spirit again, and a little bit of defiance, or independence. I would say in my mind to Edward, I doubt if you're even thinking about me at all, so why am I always thinking of you?

Twelve

Robert had not written, not replied to his letters or responded to his poems. Three months passed and when he did write he complained of being very busy, and downhearted, troubled by the war. He sent a sad and thoughtful poem about a wounded soldier's wife which showed that his sadness was real, and that he thought of Edward, and perhaps of Helen, more than it might seem. After that he wrote more regularly again.

Edward knew that Helen was lonely and in an agony of apprehension about the future. He wrote to Robert:

'Helen has had enough of solitude and wants the war over.' And perhaps it would be over soon – he began to think so himself. *'If I can and if nothing unexpected turns up I shall come straight out to you after the war. I'm able now to see myself lecturing.'*

He was aware, though, while he was writing, of a voice in his head questioning how likely it was that there would be such an outcome. The past was more real to him. *'But Leddington, my dear Robert, in April, in June, in August...'*

The first lines of a poem came to him easily:

The sun used to shine while we two walked
Slowly together, paused and started
Again, and sometimes mused, sometimes talked
As either pleased, and cheerfully parted
Each night.

Some of this he'd written in his article in those early months of the war. That article ended with the moment when he knew that somehow he must pledge himself to England. Now, without forgetting that moment, he could remember and reflect on their friendship – on the way the sun shone all that Gloucestershire summer on their walks and conversations.

It seemed to him, looking back, that those were his last carefree days when the war had barely touched them all. That shared enterprise, hammering out their theories on the craft of poetry. The country itself so new to him – so different from the high downs and the expanse of sky he had at home. He remembered small orchards carefully nurtured and protected, dense with fruit and full of rich ripe scent. And he remembered the swell of excitement when he allowed himself to take seriously the possibility that he might be ready to be a poet. The surge of ecstasy he'd felt, too, on May Hill the following summer.

Darkness fell as he took a train home on leave from Gidea Park station. He thought more about Leddington and how he might never see it again. It was a place he always thought of with such gentle affection – a kind place, with its neatly laid hedges, its small river, cattle in the valley meadows, and the orchards. It had been full of the promise of a new beginning for him. He remembered a morning when he'd sensed the possibility of using language as pure as that of the birds, without striving or struggle, and the thought that there might be readers who understood him, readers who knew that not everything could be adequately expressed and spelled out. That sometimes his language would be like whispers that only some would hear.

Yet that August 1914, a kind of Eden for him, also contained the beginning of the terrible reality of war. He needed to write all that, remembering and commemorating it. Accompanied by the gentle rocking of the train he wrote in his black notebook and by the time he reached Petersfield the poem was done. But it was 'other men' who walked together at the poem's ending.

He wanted to give something to each member of his family: a poem. A gift, or a bequest.

The first was to his favourite, to Bronwen, his daughter who'd never been much troubled by his black moods; she was blithe and full of life, as Helen had surely been when they first met. She prided herself on knowing all the wild flower names as well as he did himself, so he based the poem on that.

And then another, for Merfyn, born when he was hardly more than a boy himself, and now starting his apprenticeship in Essex – out in the world already, a world as unlike his father's as could be imagined. Their difference meant that things were never easy between them. But Merfyn was his heir; and the poem reflected that: '*he should have the house, not I*'.

Once it had seemed that his children would be there always, always his responsibility. Now he could see that they would one day make their own way in the world. Merfyn would be a man unlike himself, at greater ease in the world than he would ever be. And kinder, probably one day a loving husband and father. What will he tell his children about me, he wondered?

He worked hard to get Myfanwy's poem right. He thought of her playing with Teeka the kitten, bubble-blowing with Tommy Dodds using a bowl of soap-suds and two new cheap clay pipes. Pushing her doll in her doll's pram, Eleanor's present, wrapped in a worn old shawl, dressed as 'a lady.' The way, as children were, she was soon discontented with her playthings.

> *What shall I give my daughter the younger*
> *More than will keep her from cold and hunger?*

Well, he'd done that at least. And he knew her well enough to know what she did not need. It was simply Steep, her own little world there, which he would leave her, if he could.

The other men in the hut were quietly reading or playing cards. He sat staring into the coals of the stove. He needed to write a poem for Helen. He knew what she wanted most – himself, his whole heart and his love. He would be willing to give it to her, for all her faith in him, for what she had endured with him, if there was a true 'self' to be found. But that was hidden still, even from himself.

Some things he could wish for her – more children, as many as she would wish, better sight, and a better heart to bear whatever troubles might be coming to her. He stared sadly into

233

the flames. Helen had lost so much of her optimism, she'd become thin and dispirited and yet he could still calm and cheer her, if he was inclined to cheer her, that was.

The war showed no sign of being over and by the late spring of 1916 he was becoming painfully bored and restless. Paul and John and some of his fellow map-instructors were transferred and had not been replaced.

The work was so familiar, so repetitive, that it presented no challenge. The battalion had a new regime and a higher status; bugle calls woke them and sent them to their beds. But the pettiness of new regulations irritated him. So much bull – far too much nonsense about smartness rather than concentrating on efficiency and common-sense, so many rules. The aim seemed to be to keep everyone living and thinking in exactly the same way.

After breakfast there was an hour of sitting around waiting for inspection, which would extend to half the morning. He felt that his days were idled away for lack of organisation and he hated nothing more than idling. It was not real leisure, in profitable solitude or good company, yet it was not useful work.

He shared his new hut with twenty men and as the NCO he was not supposed to do any menial 'housekeeping' work. But after a few mornings of watching the day's orderly make a hash of lighting the round black stove he'd had enough.

'Here, let me,' he said, stuffing his feet into his boots and crossing the floor. I'm good at fires.' He took out the mound of damp slack with a shovel and started the fire again, building a neat pyramid of kindling wood and waiting till it was well alight before adding a little of the coal.

'Look,' he said to the men when they were all about to go across for breakfast parade, 'I've always been an early riser – I'll be happy to light the stove every day if you like. I do it at home – what's the difference? I'll put this enamel jug on top and we'll have hot shaving water.'

So one rule, only one, he broke every day. It was one frustration dealt with, but only one.

*

Granted a day's leave in May, too brief to travel to Steep and being disinclined to visit his parents, he planned a day-long walk into the countryside west of the camp. Once he was out of the suburbs he began to feel his old self coming back to him – his Walking Tom self, as his friends called him, striding along, looking, thinking, and solitary again. He needed it, solitude after company. Then he could enjoy company again.

He had no plan, so he followed his favourite method, taking a series of left turns every few miles, so that he would be likely to find himself having walked a circle and discovered some lovely, unknown and unexpected sights on the way.

By noon he was hungry and looking for somewhere to sit and eat his lunch. He might find an inn later in the day for a drink.

A stile led out of a wood to a field being ploughed. In the corner near the stile was a fallen elm tree, its branches invading the field. He sat comfortably on the trunk and looked back at the wood – on the path he had just taken were a couple who were clearly lovers. They suddenly left the track and went into the dense undergrowth. He turned away and watched the ploughman and his team of horses making the remaining square of charlock shrink with each round they made. The bright brasses decorating the horses' heads flashed as they turned into the sun at the corner and began to approach him. For one moment he imagined them treading him down.

At each round the ploughman paused briefly to talk. It was a strange conversation – a minute's stop, then the ten minutes it took for the team and the ploughman to come round again. First they talked about the day's weather, then about the blizzard that had brought down the tree where he sat.

'When will they carry it away?' Edward asked.

'When the war's over.' The war had taken a good many men from the district and a good many of them were lost.

'One of my mates is dead. The second day in France they killed him. It was early in March, the blizzard night. Now if he'd stayed here we should've cleared this tree.'

235

'Well, it would have been a different world. Everything would have been different.'

'Ay, and a better world,' the ploughman answered, 'although if we could know everything it might be for the best.'

Then the man asked, seeing Edward's uniform, if he had himself been out. He shook his head.

'Nor d'you want to, I suppose?'

The conversation felt suddenly constrained. Then Edward answered lightly, 'I could cope with losing an arm, but not a leg, and if I lost my head, well, I shouldn't want for anything.'

The ploughing was almost finished and the ploughman bade him good-bye. Edward watched as the ploughshare twisted and clods fell inwards behind, the sliced earth shining down the deep furrow.

Later, over a pint of mild at a crossroads inn, he began some lines. He had a sense of something vanishing, that he and those horses and the ploughman were not destined to stay peacefully in these English fields. Only the lovers, in one form or another, would endure. Troubled, he stopped writing for a time, his fingers tracing the line of a deep grain in the table where his notebook lay.

That same March blizzard brought down all the seven elm trees in the garden at the Gallows that had troubled Robert so much. The Abercrombies weren't there, in Gloucestershire, any more. Lascelles was supervising a munitions factory in the north by then. And as Robert had foreseen he was not there:

Some day when they are in voice
And tossing so as to scare
The white clouds over them on,
I shall have less to say,
But I shall be gone.

Edna was waiting for him in the grounds of Great House, in the dappled light of a lime tree, her dark hair shining a rosy chestnut haze. Her two fair-haired boys and the German governess were at the far end of a long lawn at the side of the house.

'Willie is at home, Edward.'

'Oh. Then I had better go indoors and wish him good afternoon.

'No, don't go yet; he doesn't want to be disturbed, I'm sure. Please, sit down with me.'

Edward looked uneasily at the house.

'Well, for a moment, Edna, but you know I must at least present myself.'

'Stay with me now. Please.'

When he was sitting beside her Edna lay back and gazed at him, her eyes shining. He looked back quizzically, then looked away. Her desire for him was very clear. His eyes met hers and held her gaze. Then he turned away again and began to stand up. He spoke with his voice trembling.

'Edna, d'you know perhaps it would be best if I left?'

'No—'

'I'll write to you. Make some excuse for me to Willie. If I come here again—'

'No – don't say "if" in that way, Edward!'

It was in the train going home to Steep next day that he wrote, but he wrote a poem, not a letter.

After you speak
And what you meant
Is plain,
My eyes
Meet yours that mean—
With your cheeks and hair—
Something more wise,
More dark,
And far different.
Even so the lark
Loves dust
And nestles in it
The minute

Before he must
Soar in lone flight
So far,
Like a black star
He seems—
A mote
Of singing dust
Afloat
Above,
That dreams
And sheds no light.
I know your lust
Is love.

Thirteen

Half a kiss, half a tear

We were going to leave Steep, and Hampshire, our dear county with the high downs and views as far as the sea.

Ten years before we'd come to Berryfield, our first Steep home. We chose Steep so that the children could go to Bedales School – and yet now Bedales was part of the cause of our leaving. The smug pacifism of the Bedales' folk, even in the face of villagers who were suffering so much as they lost their menfolk, disgusted us. When I told one teacher that Edward had enlisted his reply was, 'That's the last thing I would have expected him to do.' This with a look of condescension that infuriated me. The more so because it was what I'd thought myself, of course.

And then the distance Edward must travel for leave was too great. Bronwen was at school in London. Merfyn would start at the motor-works at Walthamstow when he finished at Coventry. Myfanwy would be happy anywhere with me and with her Daddy whenever he could get home. So it was better that we move nearer to London and to the northern edge, for all of us.

We might not have decided to leave, though, because Steep had been our home for so long. I felt some safety in that; there were people who knew me and who cared about us. The village post office and stores were so close at hand, and the letters we sent to friends and businesses about Edward's work always went from there. Our neighbours on either side – one grand, one simple – well, although they were not friends they could be relied on.

But the last straw was Mrs Lupton. She demanded that Edward give up his study on the Hill, even though Geoffrey Lupton said that it was Edward's as long as he wanted it. I wrote to her reminding her of this – Geoffrey was fighting in France – and I told her how essential it was for Edward to be able to keep his work there, his library of books and papers, and to pick up some work if only for a few hours when he was home. But the woman was as hard as nails, and cowardly, sending her man to demand in the rudest way that we empty the study forthwith. I nearly hit him! Without his study, even were the war to end, Edward would want to leave.

I felt powerless to stop our world being destroyed bit by bit. Our old life was disappearing. I couldn't believe that I would never again call 'coo-ee' and wave from the bottom of the hill, and see Edward come sprinting down to eat with us. But it was decided for us.

At the end of June Edward had a long leave and he made a start on clearing the study. He was up early, taking his usual cold bath and drinking hot tea, with a mug of milky tea for Myfanwy and tea for me; I could see that his face was set with resolve. As he left to climb the hill I offered to come too but he shook his head. I saw the great fire he lit as he burned swathes of old papers and letters. It was a beacon telling me, telling everyone, that his writing life at Steep was almost over.

In September we were able to leave Baba with friends and walk together for a few days, visiting other friends and thinking about our life together at Steep, about our children and our hopes for more children to come. We even went into a wood and made love on the mossy ground just as we used to do so many years before. In Froxfield lane we picked blackberries, then sat looking at the hills we loved, the flowers on the gorse, the perfect blue of hare-bells, the bracken beginning to turn gold. If only we could have gone on together, walking on a cloudless day in this country where we knew every corner, every tree, and where we were sometimes happy.

It was hard for me to read, later, that he felt then that *just hope has gone for ever*. I think he meant that there, in Steep, this was true. Or perhaps that at our age, we've learned not to expect too much.

But there was something he was moving towards, I knew that. He wrote:

...the future and the maps
Hide something I was waiting for.

Those were his words. What was it that he was waiting for and what were the maps? I didn't ask. My own hope was becoming even harder to sustain. I'd learned what the war in France was really like. No one could imagine such horrors as we saw on the cinema screens – those newsreels of the battles of the Somme.

The Petersfield cinema was full. Those films were a great draw. When I came out into the street I could still hear in my head the rattle of machine guns and the scream of shells. Mrs Dodds had taken care of Myfanwy during the matinee so I had Tommy to tea in return. As I sat him on my knee to wipe jam from his face after tea, I felt a dreadful grief overtake me. This little chubby boy, his dirty knees and stocky little legs against my skirt, filled me with a horrifying vision of him broken and bleeding. I felt more anguish, more real horror at what war meant, then, than I had as I watched the film. The thought of all those poor men, and their mothers who bore them only to have them torn to pieces, rotting in No Man's Land in the lashing rain.

We women had been blind and weak. We knew so much more than men do about the life force. Why had we let the men overrule all our instinctive care for life? Why had we not, mothers on both sides, opposed it with our last breath? Instead we'd waved them off singing. *'We don't want to lose you but we think we ought to go.'* We betrayed them, I thought, and we betrayed ourselves and our old wisdom.

I had been deaf and blind. The war must end! We must plead with those in power to bring it to an end. The murderous blighting of everything I saw on the cinema screen – land, homes, trees and above all, young men! We read sickening things in the Daily Mail about the barbarous Germans; they said that the Germans boiled down the bodies of our dead soldiers for fat. Edward said this was nonsense, but how could he be sure? Men would become beasts in that Hell of war.

Edward, of course, could stay safely at Hare Hall. He could be on the permanent staff as a sergeant and an instructor and remain in England. He was doing a valuable job there, better, no doubt, than anyone else could.

I was becoming terrified that he might not make that choice – he would not be content with it and would feel compelled to offer more of himself. He seemed impatient, restless again as he always used to be before the war. He reminded me of a swallow readying itself for its autumn migration, preparing for its flight. He would not be happy without testing himself to the full. What could I do? What influence did I have over him? I would not give up. I'd show him how much I needed him, how the children needed him, and how worthwhile the work he was doing was, training younger men to keep themselves safe. I would speak as if it was *inconceivable* to me that he could choose anything else, that he could make me so desolate.

Fourteen

'*A new step I have taken makes a good moment for writing. I offered myself for Artillery and today I was accepted, which means I shall go soon to an Artillery school and be out in France or who knows where in a few months. After months of panic and uncertainty I feel much happier again. I am rather impatient to go out and be shot at... to be made to run risks, to be put through it. My mother is not happy over my new chance of going out as an officer. Nor is Helen. She is not often happy now. She is tired and anxious.*'

Robert read Edward's letter out to Elinor.

'Poor Helen. But he is splendid, don't you think. This war has made such a poet and a soldier out of him. He still writes of "panic and uncertainty" of course, but do you remember how he used to be? Uncertain about everything – his work, his wife, his family, his future.'

'Yes. And you did him a great deal of good, Rob, I'll say that for you.'

'I think so. But he did good to me, Ellie, let's not forget. Oh, I'm glad he dares to go out and risk getting shot at, but I don't want him killed. He's the best friend I'll ever have – a brother to me. D'you know, I think that business with the gamekeeper lies behind it. There's something reckless in the way he writes. Now I read it again I don't feel too happy with it.'

'Oh, nonsense. You give yourself too much importance, Rob, as always. I think he feels that if a man is able-bodied he must do his duty. But poor Helen, I do feel sorry for her. She is not bearing it well any more than I would in her place. I will write to her.'

Robert had a poem that Edward hadn't seen. It was about a man steeling himself for war. He would send it to Edward with a letter: *'You rather shut me up. Talk is too cheap when your friends are facing bullets.'* He told Edward not to be reckless, not to keep pushing himself too far; he should just be content with being useful, not heroic.

'You know Ellie, I don't reckon I've felt entirely right in my mind since the war began. Sometimes, you know, I even imagine myself in uniform.'

'Huh – I can't see that.'

'But it's true. Only, I'm a father of four, and first and foremost an American. And I'm not as young as I was.'

He had tried not to let the war trouble him overmuch, like most Americans. President Wilson was right, he believed – America was the only peaceable nation in the world and the only idealist nation. It was not their quarrel, though the torpedoing of the Lusitania had made a difference. The monstrous treatment of the Irish rebels after the Easter rebellion shocked all the Irish-Americans. They would never want to be allied with the British. Neither would people of German descent.

But then, he'd had his first success in England, he had English friends, Edward especially, and he'd witnessed the quiet determination of people like the Chandlers not to be bullied by Germany. That quiet good humoured self-control and strength was not something he had, or could emulate – it made him uncomfortable, humbled, almost.

Edward went to Great House to tell Edna.

'What? How could you? To kill— You, to be part of the Artillery, to kill and no doubt be killed in your turn. The hideous ugliness of it! This war is monstrous, worse than any before. Terrible suffering for no purpose. I don't understand you. You have turned into someone I don't know. And you'll be going away – I can't bear it.'

Edna had come to rely on him, even though what she had of him was so much less than she wanted. She hadn't lost the hope of having more, yet she could honour his capacity to be so entirely his own self. He was like no other man she knew; he resisted her longing for passion but they hadn't become distant or angry at one another. She believed that she did not really count for him while the war lasted; but perhaps afterwards it would be different. For her it hardly mattered who won the war so long as it ended and the killing stopped. What was victory? Something that lasted a moment, while the devastation of war lasted for lifetimes?

Her blindness to what must be done, her simplistic pacifism, surprised him. But he knew the loss that his leaving would mean to her. He struggled to find the words to tell her again who he was. 'I can't love, Edna, and haven't for years, even where I should, with Helen, as I've told her often enough. I want you to think of me as I am, a man trying to see what he's capable of and often failing. Nothing more.'

'No – I see a man whose qualities are what I need and want, a life which might have merged with mine to strengthen us both.'

'No Edna. This is just extravagant talk. You know it.'

'I know myself well enough to know that I shan't be able to bear it if you're killed. I will want to die – to remember you, and to think of all we said and did together, and what we might have done one day. Or if you were to be injured, and I to have no right to know. I may never see you again, never hear your voice, never touch you again.'

The thought of parting was so agonizing that she hurried towards it, losing the last few hours she might have with him.

'I'm beginning to hate this between us. The wretched pain of it. I want you to go. Go now. Please.'

He stood at the door, uncertain, and reached out his hand to her. Behind him a glaring red sun was setting and he was silhouetted against it. She turned away, weeping, and he left.

Those two words 'Go now' stayed with him. It was as if they closed a door between himself and Edna, and the intoxicating beauty and inspiration that had been Edna's gift. He'd never felt cut off from her before, even during the years when they never met, but now he knew that a door had closed between them.

Edna foresaw quite clearly what would happen to her – a long blackness, a hopelessness, which would continue for years, when she could not paint, only try to express her grief in poetry.

Her recovery, and her long and fruitful life, she could not foresee.

Edward wrote to Eleanor, arranging that she should visit when he was on leave that July. She was always ready to visit Steep.

Eleanor's first encounter with Edward's wife had been a letter in Helen's terrible scrawl. Eleanor had made it out and found it a sad letter, humble and apologetic, telling her not to expect a clever, sophisticated person. Helen always presented herself as the simple dedicated homemaker. When they had met, all her domestic skills were on show – the baking, the substantial dishes made up out of next to nothing. The gardening, preserving, the sewing. She had a favourite word – 'homey' – which grated even on kind Eleanor.

They'd established her position concerning Edward early on.

'You know I love him, don't you, Helen?'

'Yes, Eleanor, I do.'

'If it hurts you or him I would have to go away and keep out of your lives. I will.'

'No, you mustn't – that would be terrible. You must never go. If having you would make him happier I would give him to you at once. But it would not.'

Eleanor didn't believe her claim to such unselfishness; it was Helen's exaggerated way of talking. And it left Eleanor somehow powerless. But she didn't blame Helen; she was fond of her and thought she understood her. When Edward was absent they would sit up talking past midnight because Helen so badly wanted company. She knew how lonely Helen was now and how isolated she felt in the country without Edward, where she had no real close friends. So Eleanor often came to stay with Helen even when Edward was not there. She knew that Helen did have a kind of natural capacity for happiness and still was sometimes happy, simply by spending the day with some company and through the satisfactions of good weather, the garden and Myfanwy.

When he did come home on leave, he often invited Eleanor to visit for a day.

So they were all together that July Saturday walking up the Shoulder of Mutton hill. It was cloudy and the grass was damp from recent showers. As they came back down the hanger path they stopped for the children to look for fragments of china at the crossroads by the ruined cottage.

'It's too hard at this time of the year with the long grass,' Edward said. 'Come on.' But Bronwen found a piece, so Myfanwy had to keep looking. Mostly they were bits of blue-and-white, but Eleanor saw a dark green piece and surreptitiously dropped it into Baba's view. Then they could go on.

Edward talked about France, the fighting there, and about the young officers he was training. He worried that the training might not be sufficient to be effective.

'It's as thorough as we can make it. But how can we imagine that we can create anything like the conditions that they'll find in France, in English parkland? How can I know what they need?'

He fell silent and thoughtful.

'Edward, do you know what you are fighting for?' Eleanor asked him.

He stood quietly, looking down the slope towards the village. Then he stooped and picked up a pinch of the chalky earth. Crumbling it between his finger and thumb he said, 'Literally, for this.'

Fifteen

Helen decided to go on a walking holiday with her sister, who was recently widowed and needed a companion. He felt that she was leaving everything to him without much thought. It was not like her.

The house was only partly cleared. There were beds and enough kitchen-ware for meals. The cream dresser was stripped of the tea-service he'd bought Helen to make up for losing the big Wick Green house. Bronwen's framed wild-flower paintings were gone, leaving an unfaded mark on the sitting room walls.

Up in the study he still had a great deal to clear. What should he do with his favourite poster, the one he always relied on to make him smile? It was an advertisement for an indigestion mixture, with the lugubrious slogan *'Spring is coming – bringing debility.'* He crumpled it up – it had lost its power for him.

There was a painting Lesley made that summer in Leddington. He packed it away.

After a morning's work he decided that instead of going back to Yew Tree he would go to the inn at Hawkley; it was hardly a greater distance, but in the other direction. From Old Litten Lane he followed the north-side hanger, passing the great excavations of badgers whose destruction someone had overlooked. Tiny chips of white snail shell glinted in the russet-brown earth.

Beyond the cropped flinty sheep-fields lay the lushness of Oakshott stream valley. Its green bowl was surrounded by high hills, with Cheesecombe Farm lying comfortably at the base. Watercress grew all along the stream and under the plank bridge. It hadn't been gathered this year. He thought that the old man, who he always thought of as Jack Noman, must be dead; 'Jack' had last appeared with watercress on a lovely May day more than two years before. Edward reached down and dipping his hand into a cluster of the streaming leaves, he snapped off some stalks, bringing them up to his face. The water cooled him and the tang of the cress filled him with memories.

With bread, cheese, cress and ale he sat facing the sun outside Hawkley Inn. He was suddenly sad. At the cottage he had only been fretful at the disruption and nuisance of moving, but now, after this walk, he felt what Steep and Hampshire meant to him and what it was to leave. It was a landscape which had often made his life bearable, had helped him to find something of himself, just by walking, feeling the earth under his feet or his whole body when he lay down to rest. He had come near to wanting to root there, to do no more roaming.

The climb back up to Wheatham Hill from the valley bottom was strenuous, a steep path through the woods. Down its centre was a cleft, a miniature canyon of creamy chalk where rain formed a stream-bed in wet weather. Once at the top, he went a little lower down the Shoulder of Mutton to where the trees were thinner and he could see over six English counties at a glance. His eyes followed the long white road away towards the downs and the distant estuaries of the south coast.

He sensed that there was some knowledge that he was not quite allowing himself; that this was more, perhaps, than leaving Steep. Was it because of what they meant to him, those counties – his Hampshire, and Wiltshire, Berkshire and the rest – that he must leave them? He believed that for him, now, all roads must lead to France.

His view from the hill was blurred with tears. The thought of parting from everything he knew brought for a moment a sense of dread. It was this loss, rather than what he was going towards, that he felt and feared.

He had after all, found a home, and it was at Steep.

Sixteen

In Trowbridge he was back in the schoolroom and not enjoying it at all. When he could he ran on the downs, determined to be as fit as it was possible to be.

His last weeks in England were, quite by chance, almost a farewell tour, a last visit to places he'd known since he was a boy. He was based at first in London, then in his other favourite county, Wiltshire. Impossible to be in Wiltshire and not think of Richard Jefferies, and of old 'Dad Uzzell' who'd taught him, a London boy on holiday, so much about the country. They were both part of what had formed him, his true foundation stones. The Uzzells were still living in their terraced house near Swindon, and one Saturday he managed to call on them.

Trowbridge had changed since *In Pursuit of Spring*. That quiet sleepy gentleness was gone; the place was full of soldiers and he was one of them. He must learn to be a gunnery officer, grasping the mathematics and physics of explosives and of distances, and at the same time there was regular officers' work, supervising men on guard duty and fatigues.

'Will I ever grasp these theories? I'm too old to learn, I suspect. How are you getting on?' he said to the young officer he was paired with for training. They were in the dimly lit, brown-panelled classroom in the evening. Neither of them enjoyed the formal dinners in the Royal Artillery Officers' mess, when you were compelled to wear white gloves and spur chains, in spite of the fact that you were living in a tent. They both avoided them when they could.

His companion was a schoolmaster from Winchester, a short, slight man with a boyish figure and a rather nervous face. They discovered that at Oxford they had both been at Lincoln College. Now he was a Latin master. 'Mathematics was definitely not my strength at school,' he said. 'But what is it that you're finding difficult? I'll help if I can.'

'School – anything *I* learned at school I forgot more than twenty years ago!'

The young man's diffidence reminded him rather of Merfyn. 'Yes, if you would show me, I'd be grateful – it's this Statics course.'

During free days he went to Steep to help with the final move away from Yew Tree Cottage.

'I'm not sure who you are anymore,' Helen said. They were in their Yew Tree bedroom for almost the last time, in the bright eastern light of the morning. He dressed and saw himself in the full-length mirror. For weeks he'd seen only his face when he was shaving, in a cracked bit of mirror in their dark barrack room.

His tall figure was less stooped, broader in the chest and shoulders than he used to be, but with a haggard face. He had grown a moustache, something that most officers, certainly all those over twenty-one, did.

'Good Lord – I didn't know myself. What's become of me? I look – I'm in disguise, Helen.'

'I told you, that's how it seems to me.'

'No, I'm still what I was, Helen. It's just the old tweeds are put away. But, you know, in other ways – well, perhaps I hope I'm not the same person.'

'You do see what I see though, don't you,' she said. 'You've become a soldier, a professional soldier. That uniform doesn't look strange on you anymore – it's natural to you now.'

'Well, I mean to be a soldier and see what I'm good for, it's true, but I don't let go of anything, Helen. I have work that still matters to me, typescripts I must collect together, revisions to do – and all in our last days here. Nothing is finished, you know. Nothing. Do you want to come up to the study with me? I'm going to pack up the last books and have them collected by Johnsons from Winchester, to sell, I've decided.'

'No, I don't think I will. It will make me too sad and furious all over again with the Luptons. And I've *still* some last packing and

251

cleaning to do here.'

She sighed in the disheartened way she had.

'Oh stop it Helen. This is how it has to be.'

'If you had just been content—'

'When did you know me content for long? Helen, what surprises me, you've withstood so much discouragement in the past, so much hurt that I inflicted on you at times with my discontent. Yet you were never broken or really low and downhearted then. Now, when I'm at last sure of myself and of what I'm doing—'

'At least then I could believe in our being together, in having a future, seeing the children grow up together. Now—'

'We must hope for the best. I'm not easily destroyed, you know. It's worse for women I know. Mother is suffering badly too. But as for me, I'm even surer about my writing and about our marriage. Does that help?'

'It helps a little, I suppose.'

He started out for the meadow, walking through the hanger where the beech leaves were beginning their transformation into bright gold. He must put together all his poems and send the ones he'd selected for a possible edition to Robert. It was to be an American imprint of the Selwyn and Blount edition that Roger Ingpen was printing: a whole selection of poems, as many as sixty.

He would be 'Edward Eastaway', of course. Another camouflage. When he'd looked in the mirror that morning it had been a shock. It wasn't his real self, or at least, not his whole self. It was a persona, as Baynes would have called it, a necessary front to present to the world. His truest self was still here, selecting and ordering his poems for a publisher, and putting titles to them.

As his work was to be published in war-time, he would put a soldierly poem first. It was written a few days before, in response to the trumpet call that woke them. He was not really happy with it. When he sent it to Eleanor to be typed he explained why it was written in continuous lines like prose, with just a capital letter to mark each new line. It was because he wrote surrounded by men, new acquaintances. He hadn't wanted them to know that he was writing poetry. More camouflage, he thought wryly. They see me as a straight-forward contented warrior, not a dreamy poet at all.

If he should go to France, and that was still by no means certain, what would it do for his poetry? It could not fail to change him. Could he explore those changes in his poetry, perhaps when the war was over, or sooner? Sometimes he'd refused experience: Edna's passionate talk, fighting the gamekeeper, going to America. But the soldiering experience he was eager to embrace, to use his will, to act and then let fate determine his future. The other options, working on Coastal Defence, or continuing to be an instructor, would not satisfy him now, he knew. If he could get to France.

Back at Trowbridge he lay on his bunk, hearing the two long notes of the trumpet playing Lights Out.

Sleep, the act of falling asleep, was always a pleasure to him. So was dreaming. He would dream of losing himself in a towering forest, or while barely awake he'd evoke an image of strange lofty white substances, cloud-like, surrounding and enfolding him. Sleep, and not knowing what the future held for him, merged. That loss of consciousness, and that image of being alone, lost in a forest, came together in a poem.

There is not any book
Or face of dearest look
That I would not turn from now
To go into the unknown
I must enter and leave alone,
I know not how.

The tall forest towers;
Its cloudy foliage lowers
Ahead, shelf above shelf;
Its silence I hear and obey
That I may lose my way
And myself.

Seventeen

Half a kiss, half a tear

In October we moved to High Beech, a part of Epping Forest –
Edward found the house for us. He had been there briefly on a
training camp and liked the open commons and miles of ancient
forest. It was convenient for London, for Walthamstow where
Merfyn was working, and we heard that quite a colony of artists
and writers was beginning to live in the area.

Ours was the abandoned cottage of a nurseryman who was
away at the front, so we had good well-tilled soil, and a hen-run,
important because of the shortages – I managed to buy some
Leghorn pullets. In late September, with the beech leaves turning
russet and the sun still slanting warmly through the trees it
looked quite hospitable. Silver birches, always a favourite of
mine, swayed delicately together at the end of the garden.
Edward and I put up wire-netting to protect the vegetables
against rabbits.

He took Bronwen and Baba walking in the forest, showing
them the strange old trees once pollarded for firewood and grown
into curious shapes. They found secret ponds, places where we
might go to catch a glimpse of fallow deer coming to drink.
Bronnie, who was such an expert on wild flowers, would have to
learn about mushrooms and toadstools. Edward showed the girls
how to leave a trail of white pebbles as they went, like Hansel and
Gretel, so that they would not be lost.

This was somewhere perhaps for us to make a new start after
the war, close to many of our friends and to London, but still as
rural as we could wish. Merfyn could bicycle to his work; he was
earning fifteen shillings a week so we were better off in that way.
Bronnie would have to go a cheaper school in Loughton, the
Girls' High School, though for a time she'd stay on with my sister

Mary and her cousin Margaret.

Edward was on his Officer training in Wiltshire – so near to Steep! It was a long slow train journey for him to come to us. I longed for him to be with us, there on the edge of the forest. We were like woodcutters in a fairy tale, our only neighbours deer and badgers. Myfanwy would have no playmates and before long I would have to find her a school. I was doing my best, making the most of things.

But by November, with the dark coming early, I felt differently about the house and the Forest. The lovely canopy of summer and autumn had turned to nothing but a brown muddy mulch underfoot. It rained and rained, the house was cold and the dreadful little paraffin stove instead of a proper range was a great nuisance.

Still Edward liked the little house, the deer, the starlight, lamplight on the trees by the window. He liked the way darkness rushed in when the lamp was turned out. He would walk into the deepest, darkest part of the forest and come home very late. No white pebbles for him. This was habitual with him. It seemed as though he *chose* to lose himself whenever he found a forest that would serve. But I was afraid of what he was thinking while he walked alone so long.

Then the terrible day he took the final step; after one such leave with us at High Beech he volunteered for overseas service. From that day on, I lived with constant dread. I felt as if I were no longer alive, just existing. Ten times worse than even those dreary days in Steep, when loneliness was my only cause for complaint. Then Edward was perfectly safe! Now those old morbid thoughts became a constant refrain, over and over in my mind until I wanted to scream. It was as if no *compromise* was possible for him. He had to push himself, face the final challenge. Because there were other positions that he could have taken, Coastal Defence for one. But no, he wanted France and the front line, to be willing to risk his life. He wanted to be sure of seeing some fighting, he said, before peace came and found him still safe in England. Why?

Slowly, dimly, intermittently, I realised something about

Edward and about our marriage. Maybe all marriages. That he was not the same as me. Perhaps other people always knew that about themselves, but somehow I had not really known it. That we were different absolutely and wanted different things.

I had never been able to stop his suffering, yet this war had given him a zest for life and a purpose, and taken them from me.

That was what I thought. What I felt I cannot express.

Christmas, and Edward not granted leave to spend it with us. I tried to make preparations for the sake of the children, together at last after we were such a splintered, scattered family. But without Edward – it was as if we had to accustom ourselves to being without him always.

Then the day before Christmas Eve, a letter came: *'My dearest, my draft leave will include Christmas after all!'*

I knew I must live in the present, that we could at least be together like doomed lovers, doubting that they would have a future and making the most of their time. So I told the children and we danced all around the house, singing, 'He's coming home for Christmas' to the tune of 'For he's a jolly good fellow'. And in the same post came a cheque for twenty pounds, a gift from a private fund for writers. Twenty pounds – so much money! I hurried up to London and bought the best Jaeger sleeping bag, thick gloves and a volume of Shakespeare's sonnets for Edward, more presents for the children and a red dress for myself – Edward loved to see me in red. And I bought fruit, sweets, and other luxuries, even some wine.

The children collected fir, ivy and holly from the forest. We dug up a little Christmas tree from the garden and made it dance with sparkling decorations and candles ready to light.

Our Christmas Day was perfect. We woke to hear the children, Baba especially, exclaiming over presents in the lumpy stockings. Edward had crept in as usual and filled them while they slept. We always put exciting little things in them; bigger presents waited until later. Edward went down to make tea, his army greatcoat over his pyjamas, and then we all five squeezed into our big bed. Merfyn did still have a stocking, but we acknowledged his grown-up status with shaving soap, cigarettes and a new mouth-organ, and Bronwen's with the grown-up things she liked, scent, ribbons and a lacy handkerchief, as well as a new sketch-book and crayons. Merfyn played, 'It's a long long way' on the mouth-organ while Edward wound up a grey clockwork mouse I'd bought Baba. It scuttled over the floorboards and to please her Bronwen and I duly screamed in the way women must.

As usual, Eleanor was too generous, with a great parcel of presents, each one gorgeously wrapped. Edward was happy to have the sumptuous warm Jaeger sleeping bag from me and straight away marked the name tape – PE Thomas.

The day passed happily. As soon as tea was over I went out and lit the coloured candles on the Christmas tree, then Edward carried it in from where Merfyn had hidden it in the woodshed. Myfanwy was entranced. She'd never seen a Christmas tree before.

After tea we sat near the fire, eating nuts and talking or reading our new books. Then Edward took Baba on his knee and sang Welsh songs and some rousing army ones.

It was just before her bedtime that I watched the two of them, Baba on a chair by the window, looking out at the snow and Edward behind her looking out too. They were hoping to see deer.

'Shall we see any? Are they out there?' she asked. I remember that she wondered if they were cold and frightened, out in the dark, not like her, safe in the cosy sitting room, with the lamp lit and her father's hand on her shoulder. That was when I wept.

Eighteen

1917

The Frost family's move to Amherst created a stir in quiet Dana Street. Their battered Ford T Tourer drew up alongside the yellow clapboard house they had rented. Robert had become an authority on motor-cars and enjoyed driving and Elinor was taking yet another house move in her stride. To the four children motoring was still enough of a novelty to be fun, though Marjorie worried about the chickens in their coop tied on to the Ford's rear.

The house had enough land for their needs and even Elinor felt content to have neighbours again. Her next door neighbour, also married to a faculty member at Amherst, lent them all her spare blankets for their first night as their goods had failed to arrive. In time she became a good friend.

Robert's teaching was as revolutionary as his poems had been. He was to teach reading and writing poetry, and he would read aloud from Wordsworth, Elinor's copy of Emily Dickinson, George Herbert, in any or no order, to illustrate his favourite themes, especially the 'sound of sense'. Students read their own poems in class. They must revise and ponder and hand in their best work; then Robert was an encouraging teacher. His early drama class was not so successful and there were complaints about its indiscipline and lack of structure. Edward would have done better.

But when Robert read his own work most students and many of the staff listened and were entranced: he had a way of reading as though he were thinking what word to choose, pausing, taking up a word and placing it, inviting them into his thinking.

Someone said it was as if he were building a wall, raising the exactly right stone and choosing where to place it.

When the Farjeons' Christmas was over Eleanor heard from Edward. He had one final leave before he left for France. She must see him to say good-bye, but she knew that other friends would be going and she mustn't steal too much time from Helen's last days with Edward.

It was agreed that she should come on Monday evening and stay overnight. She walked through Loughton then up into the Forest and along the ride to Paul's Nursery. She saw some charming Arts and Crafts-style houses on the way and hoped the Thomases had found one for themselves; it was almost dark when she arrived but she could see that they had not. She could see that it was not really a home like their Steep house; there was something temporary and makeshift about it. There were no bookshelves and crates and boxes were still unpacked and jumbled together in the lobby. Without the Christmas decorations that were still up – it was Twelfth Night – it would have been terribly bleak.

Their evening passed in the old way, though. Helen made supper and the three children – not that Merfyn was a child anymore – showed her their presents. Edward sang to Baba as he dried her by the fire after her bath. When the children were in their rooms the three of them sat and talked.

'Frost hasn't written for a while, you know,' Edward said. 'He sent me a couple of photographs of their old farm. Of course they've moved now and he is teaching. He never was such a letter writer as we are, we three. Helen writes the best letter in the world – the only trouble is, every time you read it, it's a different letter.'

Helen laughed.

'I know, my terrible writing. But my thoughts always come in a rush and I have to get everything down, I hate stopping and thinking. If I do, I can't get started again.'

They talked about the edition of poems that Roger Ingpen was publishing. Roger was Walter de la Mare's brother-in -law, and the de la Mares were once near-neighbours and friends of the

Thomases.

'It's more than that, Edward,' Eleanor protested. 'They wouldn't publish anything on friendship's grounds, not in these times. Ingpen recognises your poems for what they are. I wonder when the proofs will be ready.'

'It seems to be moving rather slowly. I wonder if they've changed their minds.'

'Of course not.' Eleanor was to see the poems through the press for him while he was away.

'Well, when I get back home I'll send them a card in case they want to ask anything.'

'Back home? To camp, Edward?' Helen looked stricken. 'What are you saying?'

Edward said nothing in reply. He touched Helen's arm, then stood up.

'Well, I think it's time for bed.'

After Helen had gone upstairs to see to the bedrooms, Eleanor said goodnight. She went up, knowing that Edward had last things to do to the fire and to lock up. But when she was in her room she felt that she would break down utterly. That cool 'Goodnight' wasn't enough.

She heard him coming up the stairs and went out onto the landing. She must touch him at least. As he reached the top of the stairs she stepped forward and held up her face towards him for a kiss, saying in a shaking voice, 'Goodnight Edward.' He kissed her and said gravely, 'Goodnight Eleanor.' He looked at her and she knew that he understood. Back in her room she sobbed quietly into her pillow, then wiped her eyes and tried to sleep.

In the morning their parting was casual, as though daylight made nonsense of her ominous fears. They walked together to the outskirts of Loughton. He said he was not leaving for France for a few days and would quite possibly pass through London between camps.

'I might see you in London in three days.'

They shook hands, then parted, Edward back into the Forest, Eleanor towards the station, both turning back once to smile and wave. A last wave.

Edward spent the last days in a flurry of energy, making a good-sized log-pile with Merfyn's help, and sorting and polishing his kit. He made sure he had the knife, fork and spoon set that Helen bought for him, his pay-book, with its 'Last Will and Testament' form on the final page, his French phrase-book and his trench torch. When only two days of leave were left, the dread that filled Helen showed in his face too and they could scarcely look at each other. He began going through his manuscripts and old letters, arranging his papers and newspaper cuttings neatly on his desk, whistling while all the time his face was waxen pale and troubled. He spoke sharply.

'For goodness sake, Helen, make sure you're not careless with this key. All the important documents are here in this box – our marriage certificate, the children's birth certificates, my life insurance policy, in case you should need to find them. Keep all these drawers in the sitting room locked.' And she spoke sharply back to him, complaining about his failing to put up a shelf as he had promised.

On the last evening, after he'd read to the girls and carried Myfanwy up to bed, they were alone together. She slipped to the floor and sat between his knees and he read for a while from the Shakespeare sonnets she gave him, taking them from his breast pocket.

'You see, dearest, your Sonnets are already where they will always be.'

Then Helen wept and once she'd started all her fear and dread turned into terrible sobbing. He held her and stroked her hair as the weeping went on. But he knew himself well enough to know that he could not stand much more of such emotion.

'Stop crying, Helen; you know that it will make me cold,' he said. 'You have as much of my heart as I can find and no one but you has ever found my heart. No-one. But for you it has been a pretty poor thing after all.'

'No, no, no, your heart's love is my life. I'm nothing without your love.'

Her crying was over and she was calm. He was able to do that for her.

'I'll undress you here and carry you up to bed in my greatcoat,' he said. They made love and talked for half the night together until the cold light reflected from the snow showed on the bedroom wall.

He brought her a cup of tea and got back into bed. They held each other. 'Helen, Helen, Helen, remember that whatever happens all is well between us for ever and ever.'

Then hand in hand they went downstairs. Helen was still calm. After breakfast the children went outdoors, playing in the snow. They were to walk to the station to wave their father good-bye.

Helen stood at the gate watching him go, straining her weak eyes to see through a blank white mist.

Book Four

One

The paddle-steamer *Mona Queen*, requisitioned from her usual round of Isle of Man pleasure trips, took their unit from Portsmouth to Le Havre on a freezing January night. Her name reminded him of the Dryden play – the lost city of Atlantis where Mona was queen. It was the sort of thing he knew and his companions almost certainly did not. Was it of any use to him now, he wondered. No, but it was simply who he was.

His new tunic was making him uncomfortable, so stiff and tight-fitting when he always preferred things old and loose.

From Le Havre, they took train and lorry journeys across the snowy landscape to Beaurains, near Arras, only two miles from the German line, where in the ruins of the village the men would be billeted. That was one of his jobs, to find a barn or farmhouse intact enough to provide shelter for them. The men sat about while he negotiated with a farmer and they compiled the inventory of what remained in the house and barns.

He and the other officers found a modern house with only one shell-hole broken into it. They patched it up with sandbags, but still it was bitterly cold. What timber they could find among the ruins was never enough to keep a good fire. It was the worst and the longest enduring winter anyone could remember.

On the second day he went to the British front to look for likely observation positions. He gazed across the snow to the enemy line – no one to be seen, only wire and stark black posts. What would it be like to see his first German, his 'enemy'? There was no one, but shells rose almost continuously from the German line aimed at their own line, but mostly over-shooting.

Men of the Somersets and Cornwalls were gathered where a bend in the trench made a wider space, just waiting around, eating or smoking. They seemed glad to see him. He stood on the fire-step and by stealing quick glimpses over the parapet he was able to make panoramic sketches of the terrain. Afterwards he strode back to the Battery in the village, warm and content – he'd thoroughly enjoyed the day.

On the third day he went into Arras. The Mairie reminded him of a town hall he'd seen in Wales. One high building was blown half-open by shelling, a ruined armchair left displayed, but the town was still beautiful, with its pale shuttered mansions, courtyards and silvery plane trees.

A scrap of burnt paper fluttered past – but no, it was a bat shaken out from its place by the shelling. Arras had been full of bats and jackdaws; those town-house turrets and odd, complex chimneys were perfect for them. Now the blasted buildings, the ruins everywhere, would make new homes for them.

More work on the Observation Posts followed over the next days, fixing camouflage and digging funk-holes; he enjoyed it all. But he was too skilled at despatches; his competent sketches and maps were soon noticed and he was sent away to the brigade Headquarters in Arras as an adjutant. He was not pleased; he missed the Battery and his fellow officers and men. In the half-ruined mansion, their HQ, he found there was far too much time simply hanging about after a Group Commander. He felt his soul was not his own.

It was not even a safe posting, as it was even nearer to the German line and was constantly shelled. One of the sergeants was killed, his first experience of the death of a man he'd talked and eaten with. He was rather sorry to find that its effect was mostly to make him reflect on his own chances of survival, but perhaps that was inevitable.

The worst of it, he wrote later to Robert, was the way you readied yourself, time after time as you heard a shell approaching. You're ready for the worst, then nothing happens; it is almost a disappointment as well as a relief. And then it happens over and over again, a hundred times in a night.

How best to position your bed, away from the wall or against it? If there was a hit, was it best to have a wall fall on you or could you rely on it holding up the roof? There was no answer to such questions, or rather, he did not yet have enough experience to know which way these dangers came.

When he thought about his own death, he was clear that he would rather be dead than be grossly disabled by wounds, blind, or without the ability to walk. Would he be spared, would he go home, would he write again? He hoped so, but he held to the truth – that he just could not know.

As he worked on maps and plans, he learned more than a second lieutenant should about the offensive that was to begin on Easter Monday. He couldn't share this with his fellows in the Battery and this left him in lower spirits than before. Whenever he was free he walked the three miles to see his own officers and men; it was something like going home. They were not friends, less so than Paul and John had been, they were men spending time together because they must. Rubin, Horton, Thorburn – it was not that he was excluded from their friendship, he just felt that no one, himself included, was able to be himself – none of the officers, that is. They were all acting a part, pretending that they were the same as each other. No one talked of anything other than shop talk, or at times dirty men's talk like the troops. He joined in that, but he felt the futility and squalor of it. Yet the man who annoyed him most was the priggish man, Thorburn, who was upset by it.

Sometimes there was nothing to do at HQ, and these were the worst times. On one cold raw day all he did was walk to 244 Battery with the intention of getting a pair of socks and asking after letters. When he arrived everyone was busy, too busy to talk, with the usual tasks involved in trying to stay half-comfortable and being in readiness. He walked back heavily, hearing the wind howling in the empty rooms of the great house when he went in. He sat at the broken window, watching a dozen black crumpled sycamore leaves swirl round and round on the terrace.

Their occasional rustling whispers brought a memory to his mind: the very different lively chatter of aspens at the crossroads in Steep when a breeze blew, a breeze that often meant rain. Sunday, the village street utterly quiet, the public house closed and the smithy silent. Only the group of aspens had seemed alive on the earth at that moment, talking together, their lines suggesting an empty room, a room of ghosts. He'd had a strange sense of premonition that day: whether for the country ways of life he had known or for more than that he could not tell, but as he sat in that ruined landscape he thought of it.

Something made him think of Edna; he sensed that she was extremely unhappy. He wondered whether he ought to write to her. But it would do no good. A clean cut was surely the kindest.

Two

'Letters for you,' the Captain called, heaving the mail sack on to the trestle board. At first there had been no mail for three weeks. Probably the longest time in his life without letters, he'd thought ruefully.

Then they came regularly. Helen's letters most days, and the children's, and letters from Eleanor, his parents, Gordon Bottomley, Jack Haines; he wrote back endlessly to them. And he wrote to Frost, though those replies were too slow in coming.

With Robert's help, his first volume of poems was to be published in America. He wanted it to stand or fall on its own merits, so Edward Thomas was to be 'Edward Eastaway'. A disguise.

'Second Lieutenant PE Thomas': a kind of disguise too.

Robert wrote saying that he had a definite agreement with the American publisher for Edward's poems. He was annoyed, though, extremely annoyed, about the pseudonym; he knew what was best for Edward.

'*Dear Robert,*' he replied, '*You know the life is so strange that I am only half myself and the half that knows England and you is obediently asleep for a time. Do you believe me? It seems that I have sent it to sleep to make the life endurable – more than endurable – really enjoyable in a way.*'

What it is to be nearing forty and to know more or less what one is capable of and who one is, he wrote. Not to be too anxious about being up to things.

The Eastaway poems from the *Annual of New Poetry* were reviewed in the Times Literary Supplement and Jack Haines had sent him a copy. But he warned Edward to be aware that the only reviewers left at home were old men and maiden aunts – he must

269

not expect the sort of insights that he would have brought.

'He is a real poet, with the truth in him,' the review said. It claimed, though, that he was 'inhuman'; well, he didn't mind that, if it meant the reviewer saw detachment and irony in the poems. What annoyed him was that the reviewer said that he was *'blind to the last three years.'* The last three years! The one consolation for dying out here would be to confound that reviewer who thought he was too much absorbed by the natural world, as though the war made it irrelevant. His experience here was that the natural world and the war merged together with a terrible poignancy. However devastating the war, its effect would be transient, he was sure. On the hillsides scattered copses of larch and poplar survived, making a refuge for birds. It was the villages, the homes of man, that were destroyed; soft white stone, brick and thatch all tumbled in hopeless piles, with broken beams sticking out like fractured bones. He guessed they had once been beautiful.

He thought of his sonnet written a year before, February Afternoon, where ploughing still continued in spite of war. It was true even here: a few elderly men were still ploughing in the fields nearby, following the ancient boundaries. Man and the plough and the gulls and starlings that followed them had existed for a thousand years and would for another thousand, while wars were fought and an indifferent, stone-deaf, stone-blind God looked down on it all. He kept a notebook-cum-diary of course, making observations about the surprises of spring, this spring that manifested itself even under fire. The birds especially seemed determined to sing, to mate, to soar in the sky, in spite of it all. For him and for many of the men, the countrymen among them, they were signs of hope and reminders of home. So too was the emerging landscape, the rounded chalk hills with small clumps of trees on their tops. In the few as yet undisturbed places it was as if he could take a sudden turn into a secret path and find himself in Steep.

Eventually his HQ days ended and he went happily back to his Battery. The time there passed more profitably, but much more dangerously. His work in Forward Observation meant being in the front line, or even ahead of the line, watching where their own heavy artillery shells were falling and communicating back by field telephone should adjustments to the line of fire be needed. In between, he was busy with censoring the men's letters home, taking digging parties to replenish the trenches with fresh sand-bags, and with the constant 'housekeeping' to try to stay comfortable. His spirits had lifted and he knew he was almost enjoying the life.

Every evening he would read from Shakespeare's Sonnets, and from *Macbeth*. He read Robert's new volume, *Mountain Interval*, slowly, hardly more than a poem a day. Jack Haines had given him a copy at their last meeting. As he read he was transported back to the Leddington days. He remembered how Lesley had found a nest of fledglings left alive but exposed after the hayfield was mown and how she and Robert had tried to build a stook over them. Robert's moods and words came alive again on the page, especially with the final poem, The Sound of Trees. He felt close to Robert again. But he was slightly disappointed; the poems – what was it? He had a sense of all the poems coming from exactly the same man, not from a man who'd changed in any way, either in his thinking or in the forms that expressed his thoughts. But perhaps he'd missed something, and then he knew that some of the poems had been begun years earlier at the Derry farm.

He wrote to his brother Julian, *'I've suffered far more than this in other early springs.'* The physical discomforts are not so different from us cycling in icy rain, he reminded Julian.

They washed and shaved in a canvas wash-stand, warming the water on an open fire first. In a scrap of mirror he could see that his face was really gaunt. The Maconochie rations, tinned stew and bully beef, were not generous. Those, and tea and jam, were their meals. If it weren't for the food parcels that came quite regularly from Helen, Eleanor and his mother, he would go hungry.

Shells fell all around their billet, and he saw many dead and wounded. Death would come for him one day whether from appendicitis, old age or a bullet. Even so, he felt that he would enjoy this whole experience more if only he could be sure to survive it. He wanted to survive, to go on living having faced death. It would be a different life, he thought, and he in some ways a different man. To Robert he wrote that he could not think of being home again, but he dared not think of never being there again.

Three

'Can I have a volunteer for an all-night observation?' Colonel Lushington said at morning stand-down. Edward volunteered; he would spend twenty-four hours at the front with the infantry, seeing and hearing the moan of shells all night, with nowhere to lie down and no chance of sleep.

He decided to take his revolver and to leave his diary behind – just in case. At four in the afternoon he was to relieve another officer in the exposed front of the trenches. He trudged through the 'streets' of trenches, their ironic, wistful names painted on rough black boards – 'High Street', 'Pall Mall', 'Piccadilly'. Another board read 'Keep to the trench in daylight'. He hardly needed telling that. The duck-boards were sometimes under a sluice of grey water and sometimes they were absent altogether. He had to drag his feet out of the ooze of stiff deep mud. It took him an hour to reach the position.

The enemy shelling mostly went on over their heads and into Beaurains. The shells reminded him of flocks of starlings coming home to roost, twenty or thirty a minute. His job was to mark the position of the flashes of enemy guns throughout the night. Just once he heard a ghastly sound and felt the grisly sensation, a flap of air, as one shell landed nearby in his trench and a man screamed.

He hadn't come prepared for rain and once it started raining it went on and on. There was no shelter and of course no bed. It grew quieter, only a few men about. He stamped up and down the short stretch of trench either side of his post, wishing he'd brought some food with him. He tried to doze, leaning up against the mud wall of the trench. A young lad from another company came up to him.

'Would you like some tea, sir?'

'That would be very welcome. Thank you.' The tea was quite drinkable, even though there was always that slight taste, or smell rather, of oil from the cans they transported the water in. As he held the mug to warm his hands he thought of something he wrote years before, before he enlisted, when he'd no experience of war and could only imagine a soldier's life. An owl's call had made him think of a soldier or a poor man sleeping outdoors. It was an early poem that he had great affection for. He had affection for many of his poems, but as he recalled it word for word, he thought how true and right it was. He wouldn't change it at all.

But he thought that if he did survive, his poems might change. He would be done forever with the trappings of nineteenth century verse. He would still try to convey things that were fragmentary and unsayable. He would sometimes be sparer, more terse.

As morning came he climbed up on the fire step and looked out – the hill they called Telegraph Hill, where the Germans were, was quiet. He suddenly glimpsed two Germans and straightaway sniper fire burst from someone to his right.

Not until eight in the morning could he go back to the Battery, to the sweetness of food, fire and rest. He began to write up and sketch his observations in the grey dawn light. Once he'd returned to the broken house that was their billet, had another mug of tea in his hand and dry socks on his feet, he could sit quietly and write in his notebook about what he saw there too. His eyes were newly alert to the beauty of the bright snowdrops at the foot of the pear trees, of rooks' nests black against the sky. Then he fell asleep.

A tall factory chimney was still standing in Arras and he thought that if he could climb it he would be in an ideal position for observation. They had so few observation planes and what there were too often fell to earth in a mass of flames, as vulnerable as a heavy pheasant to the guns.

His companion saw him training his field-glasses on the chimney. 'You're not thinking of climbing that? Impossible.

Look, shells constantly fired all round it. If the Germans see you they'll know exactly what you have in mind and they'll blow the thing to smithereens.'

'Still, I'm going to try.'

He screwed himself up to make the dash over the hundred yards to the chimney. Shells whistled near as he ran but they were above his head. He ducked to get in through the low door at the chimney's foot and found himself suddenly in near-darkness; the only light was two hundred feet away at the top. Something about the chimney made the noise of the shells much worse. One after another exploded nearby and the chimney seemed to rock. I must be imagining that, he thought. But he couldn't be sure.

How could he climb? There were rusty iron rungs going up into the blackness of the tower above him. Some were sure to be loose. The worst of it was the inside walls tapered inwards so that he would be always hanging out a little. He went at it speedily, hands and feet moving fast up the rungs, until he was about twenty feet up. Then something snapped beneath his feet and he was hanging by his hands, his feet kicking wildly to find a rung.

It's no good, he thought, I can't do it. I'm going to funk it. It's the gamekeeper again. He hurried down and huddled beside the door until a lull came in the firing. Then he ran back to the dug-out, lingering near it, not wanting to talk to anyone.

It was the only thing he'd tried and failed to do.

But when he wrote to Robert a few days later he was able to make more sense of it. It was just another experience, he wrote, 'like the gamekeeper', but it was far less on his mind by then. The practical result of his failure was nil, he said; he found a better position at ground level where he could see more.

He didn't need to prove himself out here, to be concerned about his own courage. Something had changed. He remembered Colonel Shirley back at Hare Hall who'd discouraged them from risking their lives by acts of personal daring. What mattered was the everyday respect of the men. The fact was he knew what he was doing. Years of life in the open air at all seasons, his practicality and his liking for uncomplicated people, were all standing him in good stead. He simply had to be himself; it was only that practical, efficient and friendly self that was needed here.

Eleanor liked to send Edward treats. Once she sent a hamper from Fortnum and Mason. What he liked most were muscatels, almonds and preserved ginger. He wrote to thank her, telling her how he ate them in the spring sunshine at his Observation Post and how content he was. At least, he wrote, he could enjoy this life if he were sure he would survive. He admitted his trepidation as they prepared for a great battle, but she mustn't think that it was often fear he felt. Nor did he have any sense of foreboding.

'It is worse for you and Helen and Mother, I know.'

Eleanor would never forget those two words, *'for you'.*

Four

By April, after months of snow and rain, there are true signs of spring. Beautiful serene early mornings with larks and blackbirds singing before the shooting begins – it is hard to hear them later. So every morning he welcomes the brief quiet before stand-down, around dawn when there's no firing, feeling the morning chill on his skin as he washes, delighting in it.

The sun shines as he fills sandbags to reinforce the dugout for the battle to come, humming a Welsh tune quietly to himself. His height means he must stoop a little below the corrugated iron roof so he is always ready to emerge from the dug-out whenever he can.

His literary friends would be astonished at the change in him. Because he is so much older he can be fatherly to the men. As he censors their letters he grows to understand and to care for them. He grumbles about his boots chafing his ankles and about cold and wet – what soldier wouldn't? But he is cheerful, efficient and able and he enjoys knowing that.

On the 5th of April the turfs on the dug-out begin to show fresh growth of yarrow fronds like fine feathers and the mud begins to dry a little in the sun and wind. He is reading *Hamlet* – the play, he used to tell his friends with a wry smile, which Shakespeare wrote especially for him.

He meets two soldiers who are from Gloucestershire and is glad to hear again the names of the villages he and Robert once knew, Leddington and Dymock, Greenway Cross and Brooms Green.

On the 7th of April the shelling is continuous. The filth of war is everywhere – ruined churches, mortar, bottles, and broken glass. In the destroyed houses he sees damp beds, dirty papers, knives, crucifixes, statuettes all broken, smashed chairs. Yet owls still call in the gardens at dusk and larks, partridges, hedge sparrows and magpies flock around his Observation Post. He writes to Helen, ending, 'All and always yours...'

Easter day is warm and bright. It is the 8th of April, the eve of battle, like something from Shakespeare; the night before the major offensive to help the French drive back the Germans to the river Aisne. They are under constant attack now, so that the sunny day, one of the first that really means spring, is wasted as they have to retreat to their dank cellar.

Edward goes to the trenches for a practice barrage at three in the afternoon, dodging shells all the way. At his Post a shell falls only two yards away but it fails to explode. Then he and another officer are obliged to emerge and make their way to the dugout office to use the field telephone.

As Horton tries to get through on the phone Edward looks around. This is another sort of home. A canvas bed and wash-stand, a washing line with socks – always socks from the desperate attempt to have dry warm feet. Pictures of women and children pinned into the rabbit-netting that covers the sandbags. A whiskey bottle and a rum jar, a wind-up gramophone. Over it all, the acrid smell of cordite mingles with that smell, hard to define. The cold earth.

As he waits for Horton to make his despatch there is a hollow roar and a judder that shakes them both to the floor; a shell has exploded behind the dug-out. Part of a wall of sandbags collapses and shards of clay followed by a great cloud of powdery dust fall on them. He has a deep scratch on his neck. Just a scratch. The phone line is dead.

It's not their dug-out, nor their battalion's, but while they use it they are responsible for its viability. Untangling the rabbit-wire from where it lies among the treasured spilt possessions they pile back the sandbags, twenty high. With a long-handled French shovel they patch the wall and net it. Edward carefully dusts off the photographs and blows grit from the gramophone turntable. Horton retrieves the socks, reties the washing-line, and tips the rubble off the camp bed.

When the job's done they look around and laugh.

278

'There,' Horton says. 'Wouldn't our wives be surprised? Housekeeping – there's nothing to it.'

They are elated as they make their way back to Beaurains through the shelling. He notices, though, that now there is no sign of magpies or starlings and every tree is splintered and shattered. The gardens in the village are a churned mess of tiles and brick and everywhere is the chalky, white-grey mud, that terrible monochrome. No colour left in the world. Yet they are jumping about like children dodging fire-crackers and laughing. Once he grabs Horton and pulls him back from the course of a shell's trajectory.

He wonders suddenly, what *is* this cause they're fighting for? At such moments he finds it hard to remember. And when he remembers he is not so sure that he believes in it any more. It's as if they were fighting simply to save each other and to save their self-respect. Perhaps that is what it had become.

Back at the Battery they say he is indestructible.

'You'd have laughed to see us dodging shells,' he writes to Helen.

But he adds a postscript when he receives a letter from her: an outpouring of her loneliness and terror, different from her usual determinedly cheerful accounts of life at home. She ended: *'My darling, my own soul, I know that this pain will go and calm and even happiness come again. All that matters is that we love each other and that sooner or later we shall understand as we cannot now.'*

He answers as honestly as always.

'My dear, you must not ask me to say much. I know that you must say much because you feel much.' It is, he says, as if he is tunnelling underground and something sensible in his subconscious tells him not to think of the sun. He is so preoccupied with getting through the tunnel it is as if he'd forgotten there was sun at either end, before or after this business.

'If I could respond to you as you would like me to I could not go on with this job, in ignorance of whether it is to last weeks or months or years.'

He tries not to think too much about home. Why, he tells her, I don't even wonder if the drawers in the sitting room are kept locked. Helen will have to smile at that.

On the 9th of April he goes at dawn to the Beaurains Observation Post with a sergeant and another junior officer. He has mastered the field telephone and works quickly and calmly to communicate along the line, in readiness for the great barrage that's about to begin. Then he joins his team of six with their Howitzer gun nestled half into its dugout.

The Battalion is cheerful – they have a premonition that all will go well.

When the firing begins, it is as if a symphony were performed in hell. Like the Somme all over again but a hundred-fold, more weaponry than has ever been known on earth. The German trenches are destroyed, the Germans driven back. In villages fifteen miles behind the German lines every pane of glass is shattered.

Men from Edward's division come out of their trenches and are shouting, singing and dancing with relief. They think they have won the war. Edward comes out and leans on the dug-out doorpost watching them, slowly lighting his clay pipe. A retreating German fires a final shell.

Slowly the shouting and cheering stops.

His Captain writes to Helen:

'Your husband was very greatly loved in this battery, and his going has been a personal loss to each of us. He was rather older than most of the officers and we all looked up to him as the kind father of our happy family.

He was always the same, quietly cheerful, and ready to do any job that was going with the same steadfast unassuming spirit. I wish I could convey to you the picture of him, a picture we had all learned to love, of the old clay pipe, gum boots, oilskin coat, and steel helmet... We buried him in a little military cemetery a few hundred yards from the battery: the exact spot will be notified to you by the parson. As we stood by his grave the sun came and the guns round seemed to stop firing for a short time.'

A mouthful of soil.

He has Helen's letter with him when he dies. His heart stops, assaulted by air, that shell-burst flap of air he hates. It crushes his notebook into strange tiny creases and the photograph of Helen inside it is crushed too.

Five

Eleanor was summoned to be with Helen. She was to stay two weeks with her at High Beech, taking responsibility for the house, for meals, for the children. She slept in the same bed with Helen, lying where he had lain. Helen's grief, she felt, obliterated her own, and contained it somehow, although she felt as though she herself were dead. Her actions and the words she spoke seemed to come from an automaton.

When Helen's sister was able to come and be with her, Eleanor went home alone.

What did she have of him? Her memories. She thought of the day when he told her that his poems were a secret between them, and how he laughed when she reminded him that he believed he couldn't write a poem to save his life. It hadn't saved his life, but perhaps in a way it had.

And she had letters, a hundred letters, a handful of them from France. The one she treasured most showed her that he knew how much she loved him. Those words, 'It is worse for you and Helen and Mother, I know.'

If he would have wanted more from her than the constant loyal friendship she had given him, he had never shown it. Edward, she thought, made self-denial his creed. She loved him with all her heart, but he trusted her never to declare it. Only her brother and a few close friends knew what this death, among so many deaths, meant to her. She couldn't openly mourn him; she was not his widow, she had no place, no rights.

Only by staying close to Helen could she mourn a little as she needed to, but always it was restrained. Self-denial was Eleanor's creed too.

After a time she turned her thoughts towards the publication of

Edward's poems, with the dedication Edward wanted, *'To Robert Frost.'* But she wept at the thought of the white pages, the silence of poems that would never be written. One day she would gather his letters and make them the basis of the story of her love for him, dedicating it to Helen.

It was September and Helen still talked to him.

At first she would rage at him. 'Why did you go – you didn't have to go. Why have you done this to me? I didn't matter to you – all of us, me, the children – we didn't matter to you.' Then she felt ashamed. She knew why he believed he had to go – but why did he have to die?

The wretched little house was so full of him – his clothes, his books. His walking sticks, those old gardening boots holding the shape of his feet. Their bedroom, the old print of Tintern Abbey he kept all his life. The portrait of Shelley. Their bed. And what he said as he held her that last time: 'Remember Helen, whatever happens, everything is well between us for ever and ever.'

But it wasn't well. How could it be well? She was not interested in a life without him. She did not want to wake into yet another wretched day.

For the first few weeks the days and nights were all blurred together, sour, heavy days to be dragged through, nights when she fell into a dead sleep. Sometimes she would wake from a nightmare of Edward struggling in the earth, earth pressing down on his face.

She wanted to avoid everyone, to be left alone. But Eleanor had done what she knew Edward would have wanted; she managed Helen, taking her away to the cottage Eleanor shared with her brother. Away from the forest where they made love for the last time, where she watched him walk through the January snow to the station.

Then Helen had a strong sense that this time of grieving was something she must endure, some kind of test; then he would come home again and it would all be over. So she talked to him as though she were writing one of those hundreds of letters they'd exchanged in their life together. She told him news, how all his friends had visited and written, how much he was loved by them. And she gave him what news she had of the children. She could not manage them in those early days. They must find their own way, with their uncles and aunts, while she waited for it all to pass. But late spring gave her hope because she could feel him in it all. As she lay under an old apple tree heavy with blossom and bees he felt especially close to her, almost as though he were part of the tree.

Then she was back at High Beech. So little of him left; only the last of the logs he sawed to see them through the winter, and a few papers and books. Eleanor wanted to move them too, but he'll want them when he comes back, she thought – and then with the sensation of a great blow to her stomach she remembered again.

So her thoughts ran in the same groove. She was not 'getting over it', not at all. Five months passed and with it that protecting sense of it being a temporary agony. Now she knew the truth – that he had gone forever. It wouldn't pass – she was deceiving herself. It would go on always being true.

What was left for her to do? She could take care of his children again. But there was no new baby coming as they'd hoped so much. She couldn't help with what would have pleased him – seeing that his poems were published. His friends were organising that.

Time passed.

She thought, I'll try to do what Edward would do – to write. Perhaps I'll write about all our years together, my life with Edward, the way it was. But first I'll write about what this monstrous war did to us all. The war had gathered them up like a whirlwind. It had hardly troubled them at all at first, away and remote in those days in Gloucestershire, but then it had drawn Edward in, it seemed to her, until it took him entirely and he disappeared forever.

She pulled down the writing flap of his old bureau and sat for a while. Then she began:

'1914

So it had happened at last. War was declared.'

Robert opened the grey mailbox at the Amherst house they were renting – more invitations for him to read, and something from New York – from his publisher, of course.

A letter from England – he recognised it as coming from Helen. Reminded him, he owes Edward a letter, but he's been so busy. At least when he did find time to write, he thought, he could tell Edward that any day now his poems will appear in America.

He strolled back up the drive and called out, 'Ellie – letter from Helen.'

More interesting to her than his own activities, he knew that.

He went to his chair and opened the letter – it was long – God, the woman was so wordy. But he saw that she began a month before and there was a second instalment.

'Sounds like Edward's fine, only grumbling that he's not seeing enough action!' he tells Elinor. 'Damn, he *still* won't agree to use his own name on the Poems if they run to a second—'

He was reading on. There was a postscript.

'Oh no. No.' He thumped his hand down on the arm of his chair. 'No! He can't be.'

'What does she say?'

'Look for yourself. Look for yourself!'

'But today I have just received the news of Edward's death. He was killed on Easter Monday by a shell.'

Elinor, slight and frail, and Robert, so robust and full of his new success, dealt with the news in their own ways.

'Poor poor Edward! He was so loveable, we all loved him, you couldn't help loving him.' Elinor whispered. 'Poor Helen. And the children.'

'By God, *why* wouldn't he come to America? Why? Curse those Huns. And that damned gamekeeper – that's what was behind it all. He had to put himself in danger because of it.'

Elinor looked at him coldly. She murmured, 'I don't believe

285

that for a moment, Robert. I don't think it was that at all. He thought if a man was able-bodied he ought to go. You diminish his sacrifice by saying that.'

'I guess you're right. Oh, why hadn't I replied to his last! Why? Dammit Ellie I'm going to enlist. America's going in now. I'm going down to the parade ground in Amherst. They're drilling there and I can sign up. I can do something for him at least.'

'I don't believe you would dare,' she said. Robert stamped out of the door, and started for the parade ground. But he soon saw sense and came back. He sank down on the wooden kitchen chair, put his arms on the table cradling his head, and wept.

In the night, he came down to the kitchen and wrote to Helen.

'He is all yours. But you must allow me to cry my cry for him as if he were almost all mine too. I want to see him to tell him something. I want to tell him, what I think he liked to hear from me, that he was a poet. I had meant to talk endlessly with him still, either here in our mountains as we had said or, as I found my longing was more and more, there at Leddington where we first talked of war.'

The End

Acknowledgements

A book of this kind is utterly dependent on other books. My greatest debt is, of course, to Edward Thomas – to poems from the RG Thomas OUP edition of 1978, and prose works and letters in a variety of editions. I am very grateful to Rosemary Vellender of the Thomas estate for permission to quote at will from works and letters.

I drew much of the Helen Thomas family story directly from her *As it Was* and *World without End* republished in the 1988 edition as *Under Storm's Wing* by Carcanet. 'Her' first and final chapters are particularly close, in tribute. Again, thanks due to the Thomas estate. A new edition of *Under Storm's Wing* is available, published by Carcanet in 1997.

The third source was Eleanor Farjeon's 1958 memoir of her friendship, *Edward Thomas: The Last Four Years*, republished with commentaries by Patrick Kavanagh and Anne Harvey in 1997 by Alan Sutton Publishing. I am grateful to David Higham associates, of the Farjeon literary estate, for permission to pepper the novel with phrases and sentences from that work. I am particularly indebted to Anne Harvey, who clarified for me how crucial Eleanor was to both Edward and Helen Thomas.

Information about Edna Clarke-Hall came from Alison Thomas' work, *Portraits of Women: Gwen John and her forgotten contemporaries*, Wiley-Blackwell, 1996, and from the poems of Edna which she very kindly sent me. However I fully acknowledge that these episodes are very speculative and I apologise whole-heartedly if they have caused any offence.

For permission to use an unpublished letter from Edward Thomas to Edna Clarke-Hall, thanks are due to the Berg Collection, New York Public Library.

My main sources of external information about Edward

Thomas were the RG Thomas biography and notes to *Poems*; at the time of researching the novel Edna Longley's edition had yet to be published, though I drew ideas from her presentations, from *A language not to be betrayed*, and eventually from *The Annotated Collected Poems*, published by Bloodaxe Books, 2008.

For Robert and Elinor Frost I drew from two sources, Jeffrey Meyers' *Robert Frost: A biography*, Constable 1996, and *Robert Frost, a life* by Jay Parini, Heinemann, 1998. I was grateful to the Dymock Archive at the University of Cheltenham and Gloucester for a sight of the Frost family magazine, The Bouquet.

Excerpts from Robert Frost's letters are used by permission of the Estate of Robert Lee Frost and of Henry Holt and Company.

Linda Hart corrected several errors concerning Frost for which I am hugely grateful.

I was very much helped by the Thomas scholar Dr Guy Cuthbertson, now of Hope University, Liverpool and editor of the Edward Thomas Fellowship journal. He was really generous with his time for my questions and musings and gave me some interesting leads.

The late Dominic Hibberd's expertise gave me considerable help in person and in his and John Onions' superb anthology, *The Winter of The World*, Constable 2007, with understanding the changing phases of the First World War and its poetry.

I was greatly helped by Richard Emeny of the Edward Thomas Fellowship in all kinds of ways and other Fellowship members who helped with locations and settings.

StreetBooks

StreetBooks is a new Oxfordshire-based micro-publisher.

'My interest is in artisan publishing: which involves high quality, regional fiction, marketed locally in person and globally via the Internet. An analogy I like is that of the micro-brewery: a combination of tradition, passion and the opportunities offered by new technology.' Frank Egerton, editor, StreetBooks

http://www.streetbooks.co.uk

Lightning Source UK Ltd.
Milton Keynes UK
UKOW041500031212

203112UK00001B/4/P